Jenner couldn't help himself.

Before Mia could speak a word, Jenner leaned down and claimed her mouth in a long, slow kiss. There was an initial shock as their lips met, and Jenner felt dizzy, as though he'd unwittingly tapped into an electric current. He heard Mia's sharp intake of breath, knew she'd felt it, too. But she didn't pull away, either. And as his lips lingered on hers, shock quickly became a simmering heat that began to pulse in time with his heart. Jenner nuzzled her mouth, brushing his lips against hers, testing, tasting.

He didn't expect it when Mia simply melted into him, her mouth softening, opening beneath his as she gave in to whatever this strange pull was that existed between them. She sighed, a soft, simple exhalation. But Jenner felt the submission that had produced it, and that single sigh rocketed through his bloodstream.

Books by Kendra Leigh Castle:

Harlequin Nocturne

Renegade Angel #95
Vacation with a Vampire #139
  "Vivi and the Vampire"
The Wolf's Surrender #156

KENDRA LEIGH CASTLE

was born and raised in the far and frozen reaches of northern New York, where there was plenty of time to cultivate her love of reading thanks to the six-month-long winters. Sneaking off with selections from her mother's vast collection of romance novels came naturally and fairly early, and a lifelong love of the happily-ever-after was born. Her continuing love of heroes who sprout fangs, fur and/or wings, however, is something no one in her family has yet been able to explain.

After graduating from SUNY Oswego (where it also snowed a lot) with a teaching degree that she did actually plan on using at the time, Kendra ran off with a handsome young navy fighter pilot. She's still not exactly sure how, but they've managed to accumulate three children, two high-maintenance dogs and one enormous cat during their many moves. Her enduring love of all things both spooky and steamy means she's always got another paranormal romance in the works. Kendra currently resides in Maryland and also has a home on the web at www.kendraleighcastle.com. She loves to hear from her readers.

THE WOLF'S SURRENDER

KENDRA LEIGH CASTLE

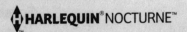

Recycling programs for this product may not exist in your area.

ISBN-13: 978-0-373-88566-4

THE WOLF'S SURRENDER

Copyright © 2013 by Kendra Sawicki

This edition published by arrangement with Harlequin Books S.A.

For questions and comments about the quality of this book, please contact us at CustomerService@Harlequin.com.

® and TM are trademarks of Harlequin Enterprises Limited or its corporate affiliates. Trademarks indicated with ® are registered in the United States Patent and Trademark Office, the Canadian Trade Marks Office and in other countries.

Printed in U.S.A.

www.Harlequin.com

Dear Reader,

For as much as I love writing about powerful, slightly mysterious supernatural men, I've got a soft spot for the sexy everyman who's comfortable in his own skin. So when Nick Jenner—a big, gorgeous werewolf mechanic who also happens to be in charge of the protection of his pack—arrived in my imagination, I couldn't resist.

Apart from the fur and fangs, Jenner reminds me a lot of the men in my life. He's earthy. He likes to hang out with other guys because, as much as he loves women, he often has no idea what to do with them. He's...well, he's a *guy*. That he is also an incredibly important member of his wolf pack is almost secondary. Jenner knows who he is and has things just the way he likes them. That is, until Mia D'Alessandro shows up and throws his entire well-ordered universe out of whack.

Jenner is just the sort of werewolf I'd like to curl up with, and I hope you'll feel the same as you watch him discover that sometimes, being pushed outside your comfort zone can be the best thing that ever happened to you.

Happy reading!

Kendra

For Brian

At the heart of all my heroes, there is you.

Prologue

Mia D'Alessandro ran into the darkness, knowing he followed, that he was toying with her before the kill. Shaking all over, blood oozing slowly from the jagged wounds on her shoulder and neck, she stumbled into the night's cold embrace.

He laughed, a breathy growl full of dark amusement that echoed hauntingly in her ears.

God, he's right behind me.

"Don't be afraid, baby. I'll make it good for you, I promise. Just wait until you see what I have planned for us...."

He was close, so close. But these woods were unfamiliar to her and, even with the moon riding high above, it was all she could do not to run headlong into one of the trees that lurked just out of sight, hulking menacingly in the deep shadows. A sound escaped her, a soft, pitiful moan of fear that she was barely aware of in her desperation to get away. And she couldn't hear him, couldn't hear anything but the crunch of her feet over dry twigs and hard earth and the ragged sounds of her own breathing.

But *he*...he made no sound at all.

It was unnatural for someone to be so quiet, so light of foot that there wasn't the tiniest hint of a footfall that reached her ears, she thought wildly, her terror now verging on hysteria. But then, there was nothing natural about the man who had only minutes ago sunk his teeth into her and torn her shirt wide open with his claws.

Claws. They were claws. And his teeth had been so sharp.

The stone, jutting about an inch out of the ground, seemed to appear out of nowhere to catch the toe of her shoe. Mia nearly lost it then, stumbling forward into the thick, oppressive blackness and only just catching herself. But the split second it took to right her balance had cost her, and she knew it. Any second now, she would feel his hand wrap around her arm, feel his claws sink into tender flesh that had already been scored and bitten.

Jeff Gaines, the wealthy entrepreneur.

The yellow-eyed monster.

She'd been giddy from the wine, the excitement, the pleasure of having attention lavished on her by the handsome man who'd swept her away for a romantic weekend. It had never occurred to Mia to refuse his offer of a moonlit walk. By the time she'd noticed the change in him, it had been too late. His hand had been over her mouth.

His teeth had been in her flesh.

"I don't know why you're running, Mia. I can see you. I can *smell* you. And I'm going to have you. You can't hide from the big bad wolf."

Somehow, she managed to find enough breath to scream. It felt as though she'd dragged it up from the very core of her being, a tortured, full-throated rail against what was being done to her, a demand that she be allowed to live. It echoed into the cold night sky, a final plea to an indifferent moon as Mia struggled forward, nearly sobbing with the effort. Time seemed to pause for a few precious breaths.

Then all hell broke loose.

Jeff's hand, hot and strange, clamped onto her wrist and dragged her forward as he gave a wild, triumphant growl that was utterly inhuman.

"Your blood is mine," he said, his voice thick, unrecognizable from the cultured tones of the man she'd come here with. "Did you really think you could hide it forever? I know what runs in your veins, witch."

The blood he spoke of went to ice in an instant. She'd been warned—she'd been so stupid—but she'd never imagined the threat drummed into her for so long could be *real.*

It was a lesson learned far too late.

Mia had only time enough to gasp before he bit her again, his teeth sinking again into the already-swollen

and bleeding flesh of her shoulder. Then, like the animal he had revealed himself to be, Jeff shook his head
like a beast with its prey, burying those teeth deep.

Mia heard another scream, distant. It was only when
the world began to fade to gray that she realized it had
come from her.

The blood ran fast now as her delicate skin tore. Mia
could feel her life's essence flowing from her, soaking
her clothes, running down her arm and chest. The world
began to tilt beneath her feet, and she felt herself leaning into Jeff's body, only because he was all she had to
cling to before going under.

She was afraid that if she let herself, she wouldn't
come up again.

He seemed to revel in her groggy embrace.

"We'll finish this now," Jeff growled, his voice reso-
nating with anticipation. He lowered her to the ground,
gently, as though she were only a sleepy child. *"Illuria
tira. Illuria m'ar hemana."* The words, foreign and yet
strangely familiar, resonated in the deepest part of her,
and she felt herself opening to the night. Power, dark
and forbidden, swirled through her. It was the other
half of her gift that Jeff called forth. The malignant
seed never allowed to grow, forced to shoot and bloom
all in one breathless instant…and it had been waiting.

No, Mia thought. And right on the heels of that, *yes.*

"Look at it glow," Jeff whispered reverently as he
drew back. Mia managed to open her eyes just enough
to see him looming over her, covered in what seemed
to be spatters of pure light. A hazy glow surrounded

both of them, and she knew at once, with numb horror, what it was.

Oh goddess...that's me. My life. She saw the flash of a blade as he lifted it above his head, and she closed her eyes against it, against what she knew was coming.

But the final blow never came.

Even in her half-conscious state, Mia managed to lift her head, sensing the subtle shift in the air, as though it had taken on an electrical charge. Somewhere in the distance, a howl rent the night in a mournful song. Then there was another. And another.

Jeff's body went rigid, and fury began to pump off of him in hot waves, intermingling with the madness that already burned like fever. Whatever was happening, he didn't like it.

Hope bloomed, small but fierce, deep in Mia's chest.

"Hang on to me," he snapped. "I don't care whose territory this is. You're *mine.*"

Then she was lifted, carried through the rushing blackness, dimly aware of short, sharp barks and snarls in the world that existed beyond her closed eyelids, rapidly increasing in volume.

The sounds of pursuit were everywhere around them now. *Search-and-rescue dogs?* Could she be so lucky? But something about the sounds surrounding them, without a single human voice shouting commands, told her these were no dogs. Pictures flashed through her mind from the book she'd stolen from her grandmother's library, the one she was never to read. Sketches of men wearing the skins of animals, *becoming* the animals...

beautiful men and women, full of light, dancing wildly beneath the moon…dark creatures with shining eyes that were always watching…

Werewolves, she thought, her mind struggling to stay in the moment. *More of them, a pack of them. To save me…or to finish what Jeff started.* It seemed impossible. But then, she of all people should know better. Whoever was pursuing them, whatever their intent, Mia knew without a doubt that taking even the smallest chance at rescue was far, far better than dealing with what was going to happen to her should she not struggle. Her will to live, rearing its head with surprising force even as her strength ebbed, gave Mia the drive to try, one last time, to stop this madness.

She caught just a glimpse of Jeff when her eyes snapped open, his eyes glowing a burning gold, lips peeled back over glistening fangs as though he were a creature straight out of Hell. Then she threw back her head and screamed one last time, thrashing in his arms so suddenly and violently that he stumbled.

She thrashed again, and he couldn't hold her. Mia slammed into the hard earth, barely feeling the jolt of it, forcing limbs that seemed to have gone liquid to move and propel her backward. But nothing seemed to work right, and her frantic motions seemed far too slow. Nightmare slow.

Jeff whirled on her, his lips peeled back over teeth that were far too sharp.

Oh my God, he is *a monster….*

She stared right into his blazing-yellow eyes when she cried out this time, giving it all she had left.

"Help! Help me, I'm here! He's going to kill me!"

"You're not going to get away from me that easy, Mia," he breathed. "I marked you. The ritual is already begun. You belong to me."

But she knew it was at least half a lie, because the glow from her life blood was already dimming where it covered him. She knew so little, so much less than she should. But she knew when Jeff's chance was slipping away. And from his expression, so did he.

"There he is!"

A man's voice, deep and strong, bellowed nearby. The ground, cold and solid beneath her, was oddly comforting. She would rather the earth held her than the monster.

Jeff's face contorted with raw fury before he vanished with a single inhuman roar, his figure already lengthening and changing as he rushed past her into the yawning darkness beyond. And then there were other voices, surrounding her as the world began to swim again. *Humans, after all.* Relief coursed through her. But it died, a short, brutal death as she looked up into eyes that glowed as bright as the moon. And no amount of willpower could convince her that she was imagining it. Not anymore.

"Just hang on," someone said. "We've got you now."

I hope that's a good thing, she thought faintly. *I really do.*

Then, blissfully, reality finally went dark.

Chapter 1

If there was one thing you could count on, it was that things always got weird right before a full moon. Still, Jenner held out hope, month after month, that there would come a night when his fellow creatures of the night would collectively behave themselves.

Tonight was not that night.

You're gonna want to get over here, Jenner. We've got a biter.

"Hell." Nick Jenner gave a low growl and shoved away from the pool table, where he'd been about to make the shot that would relieve a couple of his pack mates of twenty bucks. Dex's voice had sounded loud and clear in his head, and there was no mistaking the urgency in the message. Being able to communicate telepathically with the other members of his pack came in handy, and it sure beat walkie-talkies, but there was also no hiding from it when you didn't want to be bothered. Especially when you were your pack's Lunari, second only to the Alpha in both power and responsibility, and said Alpha was giving you a dirty look from across the room.

Bane was linked in to the conversation, of course. He always was. Jenner gave him a sharp nod.

I'm on it.

Bane nodded back, then returned his attention to the pretty blonde who probably had no idea she was being hit on by a werewolf, much less one who headed up one of the larger packs in this part of the country.

No way would he ever want to be an Alpha, Jenner thought as he headed out the door. He couldn't stand to have all those voices yammering away in his head all the time. He liked Bane, though he was an ornery bastard…hell, probably because of it…but running herd on all the Blackpaw in the area was a deeply unappealing thought. For one thing, it meant having to talk to people. A lot of people. And often.

Being what basically amounted to captain of the guard could be a pain, but Jenner would take the hunt-and-chase any day over all of that *talking*. His opinion was often asked for, and given, in private, but he much preferred being the silent half of the pack's leadership in public. Diplomacy had never been his strong suit. Fighting, on the other hand…well, it turned out he had quite a knack for that. And being a werewolf meant having some interesting things to fight on a regular basis, if you wanted your pack to continue to exist.

His father, pampered and entitled, would be horrified if he knew the full truth of it. Actually, he was horrified enough at the little he did know about his oldest son's life. The thought made Jenner smile.

On my way, he thought, giving it the little mental push he'd learned quickly after his own life-changing bite years before. Instantly, he felt a flash of Dex's relief, and sighed irritably. If Dex was twisted up about it, it couldn't be good.

Goddamn biters. It had been quite a while since the last one, which was good considering all the other crap he had to deal with out in the woods. There had been a lot more activity lately, a bad sign, though the shadows had started up and then quieted down just as everyone got really jumpy many times before. But Jenner knew his luck couldn't hold forever. He just hoped that the woods were clear of any other annoyances tonight. Last night's hunt should have cleared those blood-sucking shadows out for a day or two, at least.

Jenner paused just outside the door of Rowdy's, the small, ramshackle bar that was a pack favorite on weekends. He inhaled deeply, his sensitive nose painting him a mental picture of everything going on in the area. The air, faintly damp and with a snap of chill that was typical for a late September night in Northern Pennsylvania, was full of the scents that had become familiar, even comforting, since he'd come here ten years before.

Maple and pine, earth and early fall air. Human and wolf, each with their own distinct musk.

And best of all, not a hint of brimstone.

Ferry's Hollow had come to smell like home. Jenner had no problem doing what needed to be done to keep that home safe.

He pushed another thought at Dex. *What's the status on the biter? Roaming stray from another pack, do you think?*

Dex's response was rapid-fire. *Biter's missing. We're looking for him now. He wasn't a Silverback, that's for sure,* Dex continued, referring to the nearest pack over a hundred miles to the North. *Didn't like the smell of him. Or the look, once we got that close. Hate to say it, but I'm thinking feral.*

Jenner frowned, loping quickly down the street toward the place where the open land dissolved into forest. The Hollow was nestled deep in the woods, surrounded on all sides by it. The humans who lived alongside the werewolves here, by and large in blissful ignorance of all things supernatural, had no idea that the town's being a veritable island in the forest was by design.

What about the bitten?

There was a pause. Then: *We've got her. She lost a lot of blood, but she's already starting to heal. She was only out for a couple of minutes, seems pretty with it since she came to. Other than that, she's in shock and confused. About what you'd expect. Pretty little thing.*

Jenner snorted to himself. It didn't matter to him if

this woman was the second coming of Angelina Jolie. Nothing good ever came from a feral bite.

Are they linked, then? he thought, and Dex's immediate blast of anger was an answer in itself.

He didn't seal the deal, lucky for her. And when we find him, I'm going to rip his throat out myself. The moon is too close to full to be pulling this crap. We need her connection to him while it lasts, but you know damn well somebody's going to have to make her part of the pack before long. We've got less than a week, Jenner. Not much time. For her, either...

Dex's voice trailed off in Jenner's mind, but it didn't matter. Jenner already knew what he meant. It could take some time to smoke out a clever feral who'd decided to take to the woods, which covered hundreds of square miles. But the unwitting victim was going to have to be brought into the pack before the moon rose full. Otherwise, they'd have *two* ferals on their hands.

The tenuous connection forged between biter and bitten was always a good way, sometimes the only way, to find a jerk like this. But the clock was ticking. Once his victim started to turn, that temporary mental link to her attacker would vanish right along with her sanity. Unless this feral got his paws on her again, of course, to make things between them permanent. But that wasn't going to happen. Not on Blackpaw territory. And not on his watch.

How strong's her bond to him? he asked, hoping for the quick resolution that there was no way, in his experience, he was going to get.

Hoping you can find that out. She's been a little skit-tish with me. Weird thing is, she hasn't asked for a doctor, cops, nothing. It's almost like she knows...but I guess it could be the shock.

Has she said anything to make you think that? Jenner asked, beginning to frown. If this woman knew who and what they were, it meant the feral had a big mouth. That made it even more imperative to find the asshole. Loose lips could do in a wolf pack just as easily as a gang of well-armed were-hunters. Dex's reply was small comfort.

No. That's the thing. She's not saying anything, just watching with those big eyes. I dunno, Jenner, this isn't my thing! I've never had to deal with one of these be-fore!

It was a sad day when he got asked to play media-tor, Jenner thought.

I hear you. Headed in.

A loose biter, and a potential feral. And it was only ten. Jenner gritted his teeth and headed into the trees.

Mia D'Alessandro sat with her back against the rough bark of a tree, pressing a wadded-up ball of fab-ric that had once been a shirt against the open wounds between her shoulder and her neck. An odd sense of calm had settled over her, one that she was sure, in the detached way she seemed to be thinking right now, was a pretty good indicator of shock. After all, how else could she be sitting here, calmly and quietly, when half her shirt was shredded and covered in her own blood?

At least there was no pain. Not anymore. And the bleeding, oddly enough, seemed to have stopped…but maybe that was just wishful thinking on her part.

At least my blood isn't glowing anymore, she thought, but shut that down quickly. These men didn't seem to have any idea what she was, so as far as she was concerned, she would be playing the normal, traumatized human woman until they let her go. If they let her go. She knew so little about these things, these other creatures.

Silently, and for the millionth time, she cursed the woman who had raised her so indifferently, family or no. Her life had been about hiding, about suppressing the truth until she had hardly believed it herself. And then Ada had simply been gone.

Five men milled around her in the moonlit clearing, eerily silent, though the meaningful looks they were giving one another made her wonder exactly what she was missing. One of the men had been kind enough to give her his shirt to stanch the blood, at least. He was the one who kept checking on her. The one who had reassured her, in a tone that brooked no argument, that she wasn't in any danger of dying.

It was hard not to believe him, even though she knew she would need medical care, stitches, at the very least. Maybe the wounds had felt worse than they really were? It was all she could figure. These men didn't look the type to just watch her bleed out. At least she didn't feel like she was going to pass out anymore, though Mia wasn't sure whether that was a good thing. Then again, this whole thing was so surreal; she wasn't entirely convinced she was truly conscious anyway.

"Here comes Jenner," someone said. Mia looked up. And then he was just…*there*.

He seemed to melt right out of the trees, appearing with a swift silence that was even more unnerving because of his size. He was big, well over six feet tall, with broad shoulders and the sort of powerful, muscular build that she associated with professional quarterbacks. He didn't say a word, only shared another one of those odd looks, what she thought of as a "speaking look," with Dex. Then he turned his gaze on her.

"I'm Jenner," he said, in a deep, melodious voice that seemed to fill the night. "I'm here to help. How are you holding up?"

Honey-gold eyes blazed out of a dark and handsome face that might have been chiseled from stone. His hair was short, spiky in a way that made her think it was naturally like that, and so dark she wasn't sure whether it was brown or black, setting off strong features that bore not a trace of softness. With one look, Mia felt a punch of heat in her belly. Appalled at herself, she pushed the feeling away, instead concentrating on getting to her feet to answer him. She'd be damned if she spent one more second as the damsel in distress tonight.

Of course, her effort might have been more effective if she hadn't nearly fallen over again. Dizziness swept over her, but just as her knees started to buckle Mia felt a pair of strong arms lift her with surprising gentleness. A wonderful smell enveloped her, woodsy and masculine.

Epic fail on being an empowered woman, she thought, knowing immediately who had caught her. Heat rose to her cheeks so that they burned. The world stopped spinning around her pretty quickly, but she really didn't want to look.

She also knew she didn't really have a choice.

Sure enough, she found herself pinned by a sharp golden gaze the instant she opened her eyes. Mia took a little solace that this Jenner looked about as uncertain of what to make of her as she was of him. They stared at one another for a long, drawn-out moment, and Mia again felt that strange warmth beginning to flood her. She was suddenly very aware of his large hands on her, the steady rise and fall of the chest she rested against as he cradled her. She could even feel the beat of his heart.

It was, hands down, the oddest sensation she had ever experienced, which in her case was really saying something. It felt as though invisible threads were even now winding around them, binding them together in a way she couldn't quite fathom. And she had no interest in breaking those new and fragile bonds, preferring instead to forget everything but the intriguing lines of the face bent over her own. She felt drugged, almost, but pleasantly so. His lashes, she noted with some pleasure, were inky black and incredibly long. Such beautiful eyes.

Mia's hand, which had been fisted against his chest, loosened, and she spread her fingers against the place where his heart beat steadily, thudding reassuringly against her palm. Her head filled with music, the way it always did when her blood called out, and was answered. Jenner's song was wild and sweet, and for one breathless instant, Mia could hear her own singular melody twining with his, perfectly matched, creating something new and amazing. Her skin broke out in gooseflesh at its beauty…but it was short-lived. She heard Jenner's startled intake of breath, watched the quick bob of his Adam's apple at his throat. He looked quickly away, and as neatly as if it had been severed with a knife, the immediacy of their connection was broken. The song stopped short in the midst of a crescendo, locked back away.

Those invisible bonds, however, remained, comforting her even though she didn't know this man from Adam. For the moment, he was all she had.

Mia found herself quickly set down, though Jenner's hands lingered to support her. This time, despite an initial wobble, her footing was steady. Inside, she was anything but. A shiver rippled through her at the loss of Jenner's heat, and the snap of a twig somewhere near her made her jerk. Every head turned sharply in the direction of the sound, at least reassuring her that she hadn't imagined it. Without a word, two of the men dashed off into the trees with a speed and grace that surprised her. Quickly, fear bubbled back to the surface.

Jeff was still out there. Maybe he'd come back to finish what he'd started. Maybe—

"Don't worry about them. They're just being cautious," Jenner said, pulling her back to the moment. He had obviously seen her watch the two men go. She looked at him, his eyes giving off a soft glow. Did he even realize it? she wondered. He seemed so calm. No sense of urgency. All things considered, Mia thought she would have preferred someone who acted at least a *little* like the crazed werewolf running around in the woods biting people might be a problem.

"Sorry. I'm not used to being bitten by my dates, and then left to die. I guess it's made me a little jumpy," Mia said, finding her voice raspy from the bloodcurdling scream she'd sounded earlier. One dark brow winged up, and Mia wondered if he was surprised she wasn't just falling apart.

Probably she should fake it. But she didn't know how. Tears had been outlawed for too long to ever really come naturally to her.

"Point taken," he said, his voice a resonant growl that scraped in an interesting sort of way against her ragged nerve endings. His eyes dropped to where she'd been wounded. "You seem to be healing up well, at least."

Mia just looked at him, aghast. Healing? No, not yet, not by a long shot. Magic was her gift, but she could bleed with the best of them. Hadn't she proven that?

"You've got to be joking," she choked out. "I've been *attacked*! His name is Jeff Gaines, and he tried to *kill* me! What about all of this is holding you people up? I need the police, I need a doctor, and I need to get out…of…these…*oh my God*." She happened to look at her ruined shoulder during her tirade, and what she saw shouldn't have been, *couldn't* have been possible. Beneath the bloody fabric, torn and bleeding skin had already knit together, leaving small scabs in most places. A few spots, she noted incredulously, had already healed completely.

The pain, it seemed, was gone for a reason.

And suddenly, falling apart seemed a much more doable option than it had only seconds ago.

Mia's mouth opened while she stared at Jenner, who was gazing steadily back at her. He looked like this was the most natural thing in the world. She tried to make words come out, but none came to her. Her heart began to pound, and all of her instincts were screaming at her to run.

"She's going to freak out," a voice muttered somewhere behind her. "They always freak out."

"She is *not* going to freak out," Jenner replied, but his eyes never left her, and his voice was low, as though he was speaking only to her. "You're going to be fine. And you're not going to lose it. Not if you want him to pay for what he did."

"But," Mia said softly, trying desperately to keep it together. This couldn't be. This wasn't supposed to happen. "But…"

"I can make him pay," Jenner said, and something about the way he said it, the words themselves, steadied Mia in a way probably nothing else could have in that moment. "You have to trust me. What this Jeffrey did isn't allowed among our kind any more than it is among yours. Less, in fact."

"Your *kind*," Mia repeated in a whisper. "What is that?" Deep inside, she knew. But she still needed to hear the words. It had been so long since that day in her grandmother's study, poring over fantastical pictures that sometimes moved and danced beneath her fingertips. Revelations to her young eyes that had been cut brutally short in the wake of the older woman's fury at being disobeyed.

At some point, she had stopped believing that these creatures were real, and started believing what she'd always been told. That she was alone in her strangeness.

"*This* is where she freaks out," Mia heard someone else murmur softly, and it so incensed her that anger finally overrode fear. There was nothing she hated more than being underestimated, condescended to. She snapped her head around to glare at each of the other men in turn, until they shifted uncomfortably and looked at the ground.

"I am *not* going to freak out," she said through gritted teeth before looking again at Jenner. Amusement flashed across his face, as striking as a bolt of lightning in a dark sky.

"I can see that," he said.

"Then tell me what's going on!" It came out as far more of a shout than she'd intended, but it was hard to regret it when she still had no information, and now a wound that seemed to be healing itself at incredible speed through some medical miracle.

Jenner studied her for a moment longer, as though sizing her up, and then nodded.

"Okay. You were bitten by a werewolf we think is a feral drifter. Unless you give us a hand, he stays loose, and you wind up just like him." He tipped his head, studying her. "How's that for starters?"

It was true, then. These were all werewolves. Jeff, somehow, was a werewolf who'd managed to pass for as normal as could be and slipped easily past her defenses. Mia's heart leaped in a mixture of joy and fear. She wasn't the only human cursed with a little something *more*. These creatures were as real as she. She wanted to open her mouth and spill out everything, everything she knew about her own strange gifts. Maybe they would know what she truly was. Maybe they could help her.

Or maybe they would use her the same way Jeff had wanted to. She couldn't trust anyone. Not yet. And especially not when her problems had just been added to. Mia knew nothing about werewolves outside of movies and TV, and most of that was probably garbage. Being bitten by whatever a feral drifter was, however, didn't sound good.

So many questions, and all that came out was a stammer.

"I...I need to know..." Mia looked at him, noted the raised eyebrow, and felt the eyes on her back, waiting, she had no doubt, for that freak-out they were all so sure was coming. All but him. Jenner watched her steadily, calmly, with twin pools of honey gold. Forest eyes, she thought, focusing on the sanity, the steadiness in them.

Wolf eyes.

Mia felt something inside, a lot inside, actually, that

did indeed want to just let loose and completely freak out. Instead, she took a deep breath, squared her shoulders, and put her chin up. She was far stronger than they thought. This Jenner wanted to help her. She needed to concentrate on that. He knew what Jeffrey was, where Mia was sure that normal cops would chalk up her description of his transformation to hysteria, or worse. And if they didn't believe her, Mia realized, Jeff would never be caught. He would find her. He had promised...

"He's going to come back for me," Mia said, wrapping her arms around herself in an effort to ward off the chill that seemed to be seeping into her very bones. "He said he would. To...to finish."

"He picked the wrong place to bring you, then," Jenner said. "We're not going to let that happen."

She looked around at solemn, serious faces and eyes that glinted with more than just the reflection of the moonlight. And knew she had no choice but to accept their help...and all that might come with it.

"So...I guess this means you're all werewolves, too," she said slowly, keeping her tone carefully neutral. Too much calm would raise suspicion. Hysteria would probably get her nowhere but a psych ward.

"We are." Jenner nodded, and she didn't think she was imagining the relief that flickered across his face. Mia took a twisted sort of pride in that. She slid a defiant look at the stocky blonde who'd been so sure she was going to lose it. He smirked back as Jenner introduced them.

"I'm Nick Jenner. Everyone calls me Jenner, though,

so you might as well. That's Dex Clark, Jake Pascal, and Ian James." She watched as each of the men nodded their heads in turn, flashing reassuring smiles at her.

"Tommy and Kev Payne were the ones who took off a few minutes ago."

Mia frowned, feeling a sick twist of fear at the reminder of the two men vanishing into the woods. "Do you think they're okay? If it was Jeff—"

"It wasn't," Jenner said quickly. "I would know. They're just taking care of a…pest…we have out here from time to time. Nothing to worry about. You can trust me on that," he said, and there was something in the way he said it that left Mia no doubt she could believe him, at least on this. And as for the pest he'd mentioned, she was pretty sure she'd rather stay in the dark on that. The werewolves and, of course, Jeff had been enough of a revelation for one night.

"We're all Blackpaw pack," Jenner continued, "and you're right in the middle of our territory. Not a problem for a human. Big problem for a drifter, especially a feral like this…Gaines, did you say?"

Mia nodded. "Jeff Gaines."

He tilted his head just a little, putting her in mind of a predator listening for its prey.

"Hmm. Boyfriend?"

Mia felt her shoulders begin to hunch defensively. Yes, she wanted to say. I'm one of those women who ends up dating a psychopath. Apparently, I'm blind. Instead, she kept it simple.

"Not anymore."

That prompted a small, sexy smile that left Mia feeling a little breathless. Werewolves in movies were almost never this gorgeous. Of course, werewolves in movies weren't real, either. All she could think of was the way she'd felt when Jenner had touched her. Not a great idea…but better, she supposed, than focusing on what Jeff Gaines had almost managed to do to her. And what it seemed he *had* done to her.

"Fair enough," Jenner said, and turned to the others. "Ian, why don't you go back to the Hollow, have Buddy run the name just in case. It's probably not his real one, but you never know. Maybe we'll get lucky."

"You got it," said one of the men, sandy-haired and with bright green eyes that lit on Mia with keen interest and a surprising amount of compassion. "Don't worry, miss. You'll get used to us. Well, except maybe Jenner." He grinned at the name Jenner called him under his breath, then added more somberly, "We'll make sure this guy gets his."

He dashed into the trees at a speed that was far beyond anything Mia had ever seen, then vanished. She assumed he hadn't just gone ahead and turned into a wolf out of deference to her, though at this point, Mia thought, he might as well have just gone for it. She turned her attention back to Jenner.

"Buddy's the sheriff in Ferry's Hollow. He's one of us," Jenner said.

"Convenient," Mia said.

"It comes in handy sometimes." Jenner looked at her closely. "Look, you seem to be healing well, but you're paler than I'd like. That bite's going to take you down hard at some point. That's just the way of it. No getting around it, but you'll feel a thousand times better once you've slept. I'll take you back to town so you can rest. The others will start hunting for Gaines, and call out the others who can help. Not much else we can do without you, and I don't want to risk it until tomorrow, at the earliest. The details can wait until then."

He offered his hand, and Mia looked at it, how large and strong it was, feeling more than ever like she was having an out-of-body experience. She was suddenly very, very tired, and her memories of the evening had begun to press insistently against the cocoon of her shock, threatening to take her places she didn't want to go. Rest might be the best thing, Mia decided. But before doing so, she had one question left to ask.

"This bite," she began, lifting her gaze from Jenner's still-extended hand to meet his eyes. She saw the subtle change in his expression, and knew the answer before she even asked it. The truth stunned her. Didn't she have enough to grapple with? Still, she needed to hear the words.

"You said if I didn't help you I'd wind up just like him. A…a feral, whatever that is. Does that mean I'm… I'm going to be a…"

"It's not so bad," Jenner said softly. "Saved my life, anyway. But that's enough for tonight. There's plenty that will wait for morning. You're going to be fine, miss. That I can promise you."

She felt no real horror. Not when she'd been living with her own secrets for this long. What was one more? But she also knew that this foggy indifference would evaporate by morning, when the cold light of day would probably see things looking awfully different to her. For now, it was enough to know. She'd deal with it…but later.

Mia looked back down at his hand. Given the choices she had, there was really only one option. Tentatively, she placed her hand into Jenner's, struck by how small her own was in comparison. And then struck again by the hot snap of connection where their skin touched. It still seemed wrong, to feel such a thing on a night like this, but Mia had no strength left to fight it. His fingers closed gently around her own, and again she felt those threads between the two of them, tightening and pulling them closer.

"I'm Mia," she said. "Mia D'Alessandro."

"Mia," Jenner said, and no one had ever said her name that way before, as though it was being tasted, savored.

"Welcome to the Hollow."

Chapter 2

Dex hadn't been kidding, Jenner thought ruefully. She was a pretty little thing.

And if he kept noticing, it wasn't going to do either one of them any good. He had a feral to catch, and Mia had a lot to adjust to in a short amount of time. He was going to make sure the latter was someone else's problem, though. He had enough on his plate. Still, the way her hand had felt against his chest was going to haunt him. He hadn't touched a woman in a long time. Too long, since it hadn't taken much for him to start imagining that Mia's fingertips had some kind of magic in them. It wasn't just the attraction, either, which was going to be tough to ignore. He could have sworn, just for an instant, he'd heard music...

Shaking off the strange feeling, Jenner steered Mia

toward his beat-up old pickup. One of his pack mates had left it for him on the side of the road heading back into town at his request. Walking home wasn't going to be an option tonight.

And neither was carrying Mia, for entirely different reasons.

The others had peeled off one by one, eager to join the hunt for the night. Jenner couldn't blame them. Hell, it was what he would be doing if the woman wasn't the key to finding the feral. The thrill of the chase was one of the things he loved about his position in the pack. The Lunari always led the hunt, and often took the kill. As it was, he was stuck playing both babysitter and guard, at least for tonight. Until he knew more, Jenner wasn't comfortable passing off the job to someone else. Wasn't likely Mia's erstwhile boyfriend would try and come back for her, despite her fears, but you never knew with that type. So he'd let her crash at his place, then tomorrow get her set up with one of the mated couples who had some space to spare.

He glanced over at her, at the long waves of chocolate brown hair that glinted in the dim light, the strong, classical profile that could have been printed on a Roman coin, and thought: *Early tomorrow...the sooner the better.* She wasn't Angelina Jolie.

She was far more beautiful than that.

Mia, thankfully, seemed oblivious to the scrutiny. Her eyes were pointed determinedly forward, as though it were taking everything she had to get where she was going. Likely it was, he knew. Her strength would return in spades, but it wouldn't be tonight. Still, she hadn't complained, which he hated, or cried, which he hated even more. It spoke well of her character. Hopefully she'd make a good addition to the pack, once she accepted the way things were.

She was very lucky some of the pack had been out for a run. A few more minutes alone with her attacker and she would have been linked to a feral, cut off from anyone who could help her make a normal transition and possibly, probably, damaged beyond repair.

The thought of it, of that faceless psycho forcing himself on her, filled Jenner with a slow burning rage. He clenched his teeth. Yeah…he wished he was still out in the woods tonight.

"What's wrong?"

Jenner turned his head and was instantly caught by a pair of large almond-shaped eyes, hazel with fascinating little flecks of green. Her arms were crossed over her chest, wrapping the jacket he'd given her to cover the tattered remnants of her shirt tightly around her, like armor. It surprised him how easily she had picked up on his tension. He'd always been very good at keeping his thoughts and feelings to himself—it was part of what made him effective at his job, and a tough werewolf to crack besides. But then, Mia was different. He'd sensed it from the first.

Whether that was good or bad remained to be seen. His instincts told him there was more to her story. But it was going to have to wait.

"Do I look like something's wrong?" He tried to

ask it lightly, and knew it had come out sounding surly anyway. She didn't seem fazed by it, but at this point, it didn't surprise him. Whatever else she was, Mia was a woman with some spine…though she might have been better off being a little more intimidated by him.

Well, *he* might have been better off, anyway.

"You look like you want to kill someone," Mia said, weary eyes regarding him in the darkness. "But as long as it's not me, I guess it's fine. Carry on."

Her sense of humor caught him by surprise, charming him. He didn't want to be charmed. He set his jaw, determined to keep this as impersonal as possible.

"I was just thinking about next steps," Jenner replied. And that was true enough. "This is my truck, here. Hop in." He led her around, opened the passenger side door for her. Mia hesitated as she peered into the dim interior of the truck, which Jenner was relieved to find was pretty clean except for an empty soda can in the cup holder.

"I'm sorry, but…where are we going, again?" she asked, stifling a yawn mid-sentence. Her gaze was cloudy when she looked at him. Jenner didn't expect her head to really clear until sometime tomorrow—the feral's saliva had only been working on her for about an hour, and he'd seen with his own eyes that the initial effects of a werewolf bite could cause all manner of strange symptoms. In Mia's case, it seemed like it was going to take her down into the inevitable deep sleep sooner rather than later.

That was likely better for them both.

"I'm going to take you someplace where you can get some rest for the night, remember? You've been through a lot. Some sleep will do you good."

He kept his voice casual, reasonable, and that, coupled with Mia's fatigue, was enough to get her in the truck with little more than a resigned sigh.

"I'm not going to wake up with fur, am I?" she asked when he'd gotten in, found the keys beneath the seat, and turned on the engine. Jenner chuckled at the expression on her face despite himself.

"No fur. Not even a headache. Trust me, when you make your first change you won't sleep through it."

"Oh, *yay.*"

He snorted at the way she wrinkled her nose and closed her eyes. Pretty—yeah, she certainly was, and stubborn to boot if he'd been reading her right. The smile faded quickly when he thought of the choice Mia would have to make in the coming days.

There were only two ways to link into a pack. Being born to at least one parent of the blood…or a joining of a much more intimate nature. It was why there were such strict rules, why packs rarely saw newcomers who weren't already part of a love match. The bite was only part of the equation. The bond, the connection with the pack mind, would only be complete after she'd joined with a Blackpaw in a physical sense, at least once.

He didn't want to be the one to tell her. No doubt she'd be furious, and with good reason. But the alternative was one he didn't think she'd find acceptable, to turn feral, to lose all sense of right and wrong, all humanity. Jenner was already sure she'd have her pick of the young, single males in the pack.

All but him. The only joining he would ever be a part of was the one he'd already gone through. That couldn't have turned out a whole lot worse.

Jenner frowned. He didn't want to think about Tess tonight.

"Oh, crap," Mia muttered beside him.

"To which part of the night so far?" he asked.

"My stuff. I mean, I have stuff. At the hotel." She shoved the heels of her palms against her eyes and growled her irritation. The noise had Jenner's senses kicking into overdrive before he could think to try and block them, and in an instant he found himself breathing in air scented with light citrus, some sort of vanilla body wash, and beneath even that, clean, feminine skin. He could hear every breath. Every heartbeat.

Then it was his turn to feel like growling.

"You staying at the inn? Down the road in Greenview?" he asked instead, irritated all over again when he realized she'd had a room with the biter at a fancy, scenic, known-for-its-romance hotel, had no doubt planned on sharing a bed with the psycho…hell, maybe they were engaged, how did he know? And more important, why did he care?

"The Sylvan Inn, yes," Mia said, taking her hands away from her face and blowing out a breath. "God, why can't I *think*?"

"It'll get better."

Jenner could feel her eyes on him, trying to bore

holes in his skin, but he kept his own on the road. He needed to get it together. Hadn't he told himself a million times to keep life simple, to avoid complications? Because he had the distinct feeling that Mia D'Alessandro could be one huge complication if he let her be.

"Better when?"

"Tomorrow, probably."

"Probably?" She managed to sound both sleepy and outraged at the same time. Jenner bit back a smirk. She was fighting the sleep hard…she should have gone down by now, but that stubborn streak he'd suspected seemed to be preventing it.

He couldn't help but egg her on a little.

"Yeah. Tomorrow or the day after."

Her tone was acid. "Wow. You're a font of information, Nick."

"It's Jenner," he said quickly, not liking the way it felt to hear his given name roll off her tongue that way. It was too familiar, reminded him too strongly of his old life, and his journey into this one. "Everyone calls me Jenner."

"Jenner," she repeated. "Like that big rat in the kids' movie. *Secret of NIMH*."

"Rat?" Jenner looked over at Mia, and immediately understood what the problem was. She was no longer just fighting sleep. Sleep was actively fighting her, and the two appeared to be locked in an epic battle for supremacy. It seemed pretty obvious sleep was gaining the upper hand.

Not a surprise, since after a werewolf bite it was less like sleep and more like falling down a black hole for a whole bunch of hours.

"Bad rat," Mia said. "Got stabbed. Was a happy ending." She yawned.

Jenner grimaced. "Stabbed. Great. You're making my night, Mia. Thanks." What kind of literary asshole named an evil rat Jenner, anyway?

"I like Nick better," she said, slurring her words. "Iss nice." She yawned. "Nick the werewolf. Awoo." Another chuckle.

This time, she sounded so young and exhausted that he didn't have the heart to correct her. And he guessed he had to give her points for the little wolf howl she did at the end before falling silent. He drove on in silence, making the turn onto the heavily wooded road on the outskirts of the Hollow where he lived. It occurred to him all at once that he'd never brought a woman out here. Whenever he'd scratched that particular itch, a thing he did only infrequently because of complications he wanted to avoid, he'd done it elsewhere.

Well, it wasn't like he was bringing her home to go to bed with, Jenner thought with a frown. And it wasn't like she was staying long. And if she made him feel a little itchy that way, well…he could deal with it.

Mia sighed in the seat beside him, a breathy exhalation of pleasure that had his mind immediately racing for the gutter. He was pretty sure that after he got her carried into the house and tucked into bed, his mind was going to stay in that gutter for the night and roll around for a while.

He could handle it, Jenner thought, his jaw tightening. He could handle most anything.

But really, did their first feral victim in ages have to be quite so appealing?

The soft gasp beside him made him jump a little as he pulled into the long drive. The lights he'd left on glimmered through the trees ahead.

"What is it?" he asked. "Mia? You okay?"

"We forgot my stuff," she slurred, her voice soft and getting softer with every word. "Di…did I tell you I was staying at…at the…"

"I'll have someone get your things," Jenner said, relieved. "No problem." Bite complications were rare, but always a worry. This, though, was just Mia's last stand against unconsciousness. He smiled a little. It was hard not to appreciate her effort, futile though it was. She'd lasted far longer than most. He pulled the truck up in front of the garage, put it in park, and killed the engine.

"We're here, Mia. Time to go to bed."

"Um. Mmm. It was…inna room…blue room…" She trailed off, and when Jenner looked over at her she was sound asleep, mouth slightly open, head tipped back. His smile faded as he looked at her, finally letting his eyes wander over her sleeping form. Small, slim-waisted but with curves in all the right places. Naturally, since he was a sucker for an hourglass figure. And that face… she really did look like a Roman goddess. Not Venus, though. More like Diana. Goddess of the hunt…and of the moon.

Pretty little thing, Jenner thought grimly, remembering Dex's words. Hell with that. Mia was beautiful.

And if he didn't want his life screwed up all over again, he was going to have to be very, very careful.

"Just for tonight," he told her, though her only response was the deep breathing common to those soundly asleep. Jenner just shook his head, then got out of the truck and headed around to the other side to get his passed-out charge. The only sounds in the night were the crunch of gravel beneath his feet, the distant call of an owl. And, as he gathered Mia into his arms, the uneven beat of his own stupid heart.

Mia awoke, mouth watering, to the tantalizing scents of coffee and bacon. She could hear the sizzle and pop of the bacon in the frying pan, could almost taste the decadently rich coffee on her tongue.

Kona, she thought dreamily, drifting in the peaceful place between waking and sleep. *Who bought the Kona? It's my favorite…*

Reality intruded far too quickly, and all at once. Mia's eyes fluttered open as memories of the night before returned with a vengeance, each horrible image cascading into the next. Her heart quickened, the impulse to throw off the covers and run somewhere, anywhere, almost overpowering.

Almost.

Mia closed her eyes again and forced herself to think,

to remember the rest. The rescuers in the woods. The ride in the truck with Nick Jenner, foggy though that last bit was. Jeff was gone, Mia told herself firmly. She was safe. She was being protected now.

A pair of big, golden eyes surfaced in her memory, and a husky growl of a voice. *I can make him pay. You have to trust me.*

In the company of werewolves. What a comfort. Especially since, along with her myriad of other problems, she was now on her way to becoming one. Or something like one. What exactly *did* you get when you crossed a werewolf with her sort of blood? Somehow, she didn't think that would be a great conversation starter here.

With a strangled groan, Mia opened her eyes, sat up, and slowly pushed the covers back, blinking rapidly as she realized her contacts were dried out and stuck to her eyes.

Crap. An attempted run of her fingers through her hair indicated that it, too, was showing the effects of a rough night. Snarl city. She exhaled loudly and swung her legs over the edge of the bed, dangling them above the floor for a few moments as she got her bearings. Gooseflesh prickled over her exposed skin. Mia looked resignedly down at her bra, a lacy black number that seemed ridiculously out of place this morning. Her tattered, bloodied shirt had been removed, a gesture that left her torn between gratefulness and embarrassment. At least her jeans were still on, slightly dirt-stained though they were. Her feet were bare.

The thought of big, handsome Nick Jenner removing

her socks and shoes and tucking her into bed made her flush…and wish she'd been just a little bit awake for it. Quickly, she pushed the thought from her mind. She had more pressing things to worry about now. And after last night, another man who could sprout fangs was the last thing she needed. She took full responsibility for Jeff. She should have known better. She'd always gone for the damaged ones, the ones who might just need her enough not to push her away if they ever discovered what she was. Mia was old enough to know that secrecy didn't have to mean shame, but the feeling that she was somehow *wrong* had lingered…and her choice of men had borne that out over the years.

But even by her standards, Jeff had been needy. Charming, yes, but unmistakably broken in some way she couldn't begin to touch.

The thought of him brought a mix of emotions to the surface: fury, betrayal, even shame that she hadn't seen him for the predator he was. And underlying it all, sadness. Maybe one of these days she'd learn that fixing emotionally wounded men—or trying—wasn't going to fix her own problems.

At least he'd tried to kill her before she could sleep with him. Small favors. And now she was here with Jenner, who didn't seem like the kind of guy who needed anyone, least of all her. Not her type.

Yeah, she'd just keep telling herself that…

Mia slid off the edge of the simple iron bed and wiggled her toes into the plush area rug that covered much of the wood floor of the small bedroom. Her eyes wandered a room lit by muted daylight, which was filtering in through a window hung with sheer curtains in a shade of deep cream. A single, low dresser sat opposite her against the wall, an old-fashioned basin and pitcher resting on top of it. A small nightstand sat beside the bed, and the little clock on it put the hour at a little past 9:00 a.m. The walls of warm, honey-colored wood left no doubt she was in a log home, and on them someone (Jenner, she assumed) had hung a couple of photographs, gorgeous shots that had been blown up, matted and framed. They showed a forest, probably this forest, in full autumnal glory.

As she looked around, Mia's eyes lit on the weekend travel bag placed neatly on the floor beside the dresser. Her bag. Tears pricked her eyes as reality began to fully penetrate the protective cocoon she'd been wrapped in since last night. This was really happening.

She'd done exactly what had always been expected of her: the worst.

"You've the dark blood in you," Grandmother Ada's voice whispered in her mind, the rasp so familiar, so real that Mia shivered. *"I knew it the instant you were born. Tainted. I warned your mother what your father was, but she wouldn't listen, and look where it got them. My family's light snuffed out, your parents' lives lost, and only you to show for it. A little girl who'll draw the shadows like flies to honey. They'll break you, Mia, once I'm gone. And then you'll break everything."*

Mia closed her eyes against the tears and forced that awful voice back into the dark corner of her mind where it belonged. She was determined not to lose it now. If she was going to be dealing with a pack of werewolves today, at least she could do it without looking like an extra from *Night of the Living Dead.* At least Jeff was something the werewolves seemed to know how to hunt. The shadows in her grandmother's warnings, always feared but never seen, were her problem. She'd just make sure to get out of here before they became anyone else's.

"I've managed so far," Mia told herself in a bare whisper. "I can handle this. After last night, I can handle anything. No matter how weak anyone thinks I am."

And as she dug into her weekend bag, she almost believed it.

Chapter 3

Ten minutes later, Mia padded quietly down a short hallway, drawn by the delicious smells that had flooded her senses the instant she'd left the bedroom. Rich coffee, toasting bread, potatoes and eggs and bacon…it was easy to push her nerves into the background when she was positive she'd never smelled anything so heavenly. And she felt much better since she'd changed into a fresh pair of jeans and a simple, fitted V-neck sweater. Her hair had been de-knotted, and she'd been glad to find the gorgeous bathroom across from her room so she could brush her teeth. Tired of her itchy, dried-out eyes, she'd opted to soak the contacts and had instead put on the geeky-chic glasses she favored for work. Thick woolen socks warmed her feet.

It was, Mia figured, no time to try to be glamorous,

not that she'd really packed for that sort of charade. She'd stupidly thought that Jeff had appreciated her being basically casual and earthy, the sort of girl who liked to run barefoot in fields and catch fireflies on lazy summer nights before dancing wildly under the moon.

She really should have known better.

Troubled by the way her thoughts kept circling around Jeff, Mia tried to concentrate on the mouthwatering smells wafting through the air and followed her nose into a room that opened clear to the peaked ceiling. As soon as she stepped into it, she forgot her nerves entirely.

Before her was a wall of enormous windows, turning nearly the entire thing to glass. And just beyond, seeming to be a part of the room itself, was a forest ablaze with color. Crimson and gold, vibrant orange to deepest rust—the colors flooded her vision until they were all she could see. Though her job and her fears had long kept her bound to the anonymous city, Mia was possessed of a sudden, wild urge to dash into the waiting arms of the trees and just…run.

Wow, she thought. Except she must have said it out loud, because the next thing she heard was his voice, deep, resonant, and just as gruff as she remembered, though now colored with a hint of amusement.

"Thanks," he said. "I'm partial to the woods, myself. Thought breakfast might get you up. Coffee?"

Mia turned her head toward the sound, seeing the portion of the great room that had been turned into a kitchen. She saw gleaming marble in deep earth tones, glass-front cabinets, a scatter of containers and appliances that indicated the kitchen wasn't just for show… and in the middle of all of it was Nick Jenner. Still bigger than life. Still simmering with the kind of latent sensuality that left her nerves raw and quivering.

Damn it, he was even better-looking than she remembered. And he'd asked her something. Which she couldn't seem to remember for the life of her.

You wanted a way to get your mind off of Jeff, she reminded herself. Of course, she hadn't wanted her brain to shut down completely, either.

"Hi," Mia said, and immediately wanted to cringe. Whatever he'd asked her, *hi* wasn't an answer.

Jenner lifted one eyebrow before turning to fiddle with something he had going on the stovetop. "Hi yourself. You feeling all right? Last time I checked the wound it was healing up well, but it could take a while for you to get your thoughts all the way back together."

He'd checked on her. Of course he had. Still, she was absurdly touched. People simply didn't take care of her…that was *her* job. Mia breathed in deeply, forced herself to concentrate on forming a coherent answer. He was right…she did still feel a little scattered. But she couldn't afford to stay that way for any length of time. She had a lot of questions that desperately needed answering. And goddess forbid she slip up and say something.

"No, I'm fine," she replied, and tried for a friendly smile. "Still a little foggy, but I think some coffee might help with that."

Which was what he'd asked in the first place, Mia realized. What a great impression she was making. She walked to stand at the edge of the kitchen, all while Jenner watched her with his intense eyes, more like a wolf's than a man's. He didn't return her smile, but he didn't look irritated by her presence, either.

"Well, I've got plenty of coffee," he finally said in his deep rumble of a voice. "Probably too much food, too, but I didn't know what you'd like, so…" He trailed off with a nonchalant shrug that Mia found ridiculously attractive. "Cleaned out the pantry. Made a little of everything."

"Oh, I like everything," Mia rushed out. "Eating everything, I mean. Er, but not all at once." She wanted to die, Mia decided. Just lay right down on the floor and give it up. Her foot was already glued into her mouth. Maybe she could just choke on that.

A slow, lazy smile curved up both corners of Jenner's mouth and deepened the appealing little lines at the corners of his eyes. The bundle of nerves all knotted up in Mia's lower belly seemed to tighten all at once.

"Good," he said, his amusement clear in his voice. "Try to eat a little more of everything all at once *this* morning, though. You're going to need the energy."

"Yes, I guess I will," Mia said, glad that he didn't seem to think she was as ridiculous as she felt right now. She felt as skittish as a deer scenting a predator on the wind. It was both unfamiliar and unnerving. But there was something she needed to get out of the way before anything else was said this morning. She took a deep breath and plunged in.

"Look, I want to say thank you," Mia said. "For helping me. Your friends saved my life. And you took care of me. If there's any way I can repay you…"

Jenner's eyes seemed to brighten as she trailed off, their strange honey-gold lighting with some inner fire for just an instant as he eyed her in a way that made heat spread from the tips of her toes to the top of her head. But before Mia could do more than register it, he had turned back to the eggs and was poking them with his spatula.

"No need," he said, his voice slightly huskier than before. "Wolves like this Gaines are scum. Dex and the others were happy to run him off. Just like we'll be happy to make sure he never hurts you or anyone else again." He paused, flicked a glance at her before shoveling some eggs onto a plate, then beginning to butter a slice of toast roughly enough that it looked slightly mangled when he put it back down.

Disappointment flooded her. "Oh. So they didn't catch him last night," she said.

Jenner shook his head. "No, not yet. But we will. Which reminds me, Bane's going to want to talk to you as soon as you're up to it." He sounded apologetic, Mia noted with a prickle of unease.

"Who's Bane?" she asked.

"Jayson Bane. He's Alpha of the pack. Don't let him intimidate you when you meet him, though. He can be a hardass, but he's a good man. I sure as hell wouldn't want his job, but he does it well."

"Oh," Mia said, slightly taken aback. Considering Jenner's size, the aura of power and confidence he projected, it hadn't occurred to her that there would be other men in charge of him. "I thought maybe *you* were, you know…the leader," Mia confessed before she could stop herself.

Jenner lifted his brows, and he chuckled, a warm rumble. He looked genuinely surprised, but not in an unpleasant way.

"Me? No. I'm not what you'd call Alpha material. You could say I'm sort of his second-in-command, I guess, though that's not exactly right, either. We're more like…two halves of a whole. He handles the stuff that requires talking."

She watched him curiously, fascinated by the casual, predatory grace in every small move he made.

"And you do the stuff that requires…"

His grin was fast, wolfish, and moon-bright. "Not talking. Come on and sit down, Mia. Not all of us bite."

Jenner loaded the rest of the plate with bacon and hash browns, grabbed a fork out of a drawer, and set the plate down on the island, which looked as though it doubled as an eating space. Mia hesitated only a second before approaching. She settled herself on the leather-padded seat of a stool, trying not to feel unnerved by Jenner's watchful gaze.

"Wait a sec. Napkin," he said with a frown, and brought her a hastily torn off paper towel. Her fingers brushed his when she took it, and Mia shivered, pulling it quickly away. Even that slight contact left her with the ghost of that beautiful melody she'd heard singing through his veins last night. It was only one of her gifts, but it had never come to her so effortlessly, nor had any man ever responded to her abilities so openly, even if Jenner seemed unaware of how receptive he was. She could only imagine the heaven of joining with him, skin to skin...

"Thanks," she said, trying for a smile as her heart fluttered wildly. What was wrong with her? Yesterday at this time, she'd been happily imagining a romantic weekend with Jeff. But Jenner's mere presence seemed to eclipse every thought of Jeff, good and bad.

"No problem." He drew back almost as quickly as she had. Did he feel it, too, she wondered, this weird chemistry between them? She decided it was a stupid question almost as soon as she'd come up with it. Jenner was a big, sexy, supernaturally powerful man. And she was just...Mia. Not that she was unhappy with *being* just Mia most of the time. But it was not something that seemed to have set the male hearts of the world aflame just yet.

Because it was easier than forcing her mind to formulate coherent sentences, Mia shoveled up a forkful of the hash browns and dug in. Her taste buds sang their praises so immediately and loudly that she was pretty sure her eyes rolled back into her head in pure pleasure. Apparently, she'd been hungry.

"Umm. Mmm," she heard herself say.

When she opened her eyes again, Jenner had paused in the middle of sitting down next to her with his own loaded plate and was looking at her with that intense, heated expression again. Almost as though he was thinking about taking a bite out of *her*. But as quickly as she could blink, it was gone, leaving her to wonder if she'd imagined it.

It spoke to her addled state, Mia supposed, that she kind of hoped not.

"Tastes okay?" he asked.

Mia swallowed. "Yes, thank you."

Jenner slid onto the stool beside her without saying another word. Not much of a talker, that much was obvious. And it seemed like whatever questions she wanted answered, she'd probably have to ask them herself. While she pondered what to say next, she ate another bite of food. It was so good she quickly had another, and it took some time before Mia realized that she and Jenner had been eating for several minutes in complete silence. She glanced at him, certain she'd be confronted with at least an odd look, some sign that her lack of conversation was off-putting. But to her surprise, Jenner seemed perfectly comfortable in the quiet, eating and lost in his own thoughts.

It was easy to imagine him doing much the same thing every day of his life. A cozy thought, one that gave Mia a warm feeling she knew she had no business having over this man. But…it was so unusual, to be with a person who felt no need to inject words into a moment that was fine without them. Jeff had chattered ceaselessly, sometimes nervously…mostly about himself, Mia realized.

And he was as different from the man she was sitting next to as night was from day.

She looked back down at her plate, which she discovered was nearly empty. Jenner, it seemed, was noticing the same thing. He leaned over just a little to look, and now Mia could smell him again, a musky blend of forest and wood smoke. She had a mad urge to stuff her face in his neck and breathe it in.

"I guess that agreed with you," he said.

"I…yeah, it did. Thanks," Mia replied.

He eyed her plate, amusement glittering in his eyes. "I don't know where you put all that, but there's more where that came from if you want it."

"No," she said with a laugh. "Any more and I'll explode." She put her fork down and watched Jenner return to his breakfast. Mia took a sip of coffee, thought a moment, then plunged in.

"So," she said, not missing the way his shoulders stiffened ever so slightly, as though he knew what was coming. "How long do I have before I turn into a werewolf? And when can I go home?"

Jenner had known she was going to ask the questions.

He just wished she'd waited until someone else had shown up to answer them.

He looked at Mia, her expression open and earnest as she watched him through a pair of glasses that shouldn't have been nearly as sexy as they were on her. All that thick, dark hair was tucked behind her ears, and she looked like a young, bookish innocent.

Young, she most certainly was. Bookish, maybe. Innocent…well, he hoped Mia wasn't as innocent as she looked, because otherwise her life was going to be very unpleasant until she got used to the way things worked with a wolf pack.

And she was still staring at him with those pretty eyes of hers, waiting for an answer.

"Well, you see," he started, and then stopped again. Damn it, explanations weren't his deal. Running off intruders and taking care of the filthy menaces that oozed around the edges of their territory was. He wasn't valued around here for his communication skills…and he was now getting a very potent reminder of why not.

A crease appeared between Mia's eyes, the beginnings of a frown. "I *am* going home soon, right? I've got work."

"Work. Yeah." God, he sounded dumb. What would a woman like Mia do for a living? he wondered. His curiosity about her—strange for a man who was picky about who he spent his attention on—prevented him from giving her an answer that was vague enough not to upset her.

Or any answer at all, for that matter.

"Okaaay," Mia said, drawing out the word. "We have now established that we both understand that I work. Nick—"

"It's Jenner," he said reflexively, and knew at once how defensive he'd sounded. Well, great. That would do a lot to help his cause. He snuck a glance at the clock on the microwave and wished it were sometime in the afternoon instead of morning. Then Bane could deal with all of this. He'd expected, hell, *hoped* for a groggy Mia to feed and send back to bed. Instead he was getting grilled over breakfast.

Mia blinked at the sharpness of his tone, but to her credit, it didn't seem to put her off much. "Jenner. Right, sorry. Look, I don't know what you thought, but I'm not exactly living a life of leisure back in Philly. I need to get out of here as soon as possible, today if I can. I know you said you needed my help, and I'll be happy to tell your…your Alpha, or whoever…everything I know about Jeff. But that shouldn't take more than an hour or so, tops. I haven't known him long." She looked away. "I really think we should call the police. I don't want him coming after me. I *can't* have him coming after me. If he does, he'll kill me. But I can't stay here."

Her blunt assessment, and the resigned way she delivered it, surprised him. Suspicion, always his first reaction, made the hairs at his neck prickle. He tamped it down as best he could, knowing it was unfair. Or maybe he was just hoping it was.

He still couldn't shake the feeling that he was missing something important here.

"I don't think he was trying to kill you, Mia," Jenner said slowly, unsure of how close he should get right now to the truth of werewolf bonding. She looked back at him sharply, and in that moment, despite her previous uncertainty with him, he could see the steel spine lurking beneath the surface.

"Yes he was," she said flatly. "I saw the knife. He was about to finish it when your men arrived."

"Jesus." Jenner stared at her, astounded she could be so calm about this. "Why didn't you say something last night?"

"I didn't know the knife made a difference," Mia replied, shifting a little. "I thought it was pretty obvious he was trying to kill me. What, did you think he just wanted to…to make a new werewolf girlfriend or something?"

Jenner resisted the urge to get up, get away from that too-perceptive stare of hers. "We thought he wanted to turn you and keep you, which is bad enough," he said, skirting the issue as best he could. "Why would he want to kill you?"

He knew it was a stupid question the second it was out of his mouth, and Mia's withering look said as much.

"Because he's crazy. He thinks—" She hesitated, then shook her head. "It doesn't matter what he thinks. He's insane. I'm glad to know you and your pack are hunting for him, but I really think it would be best to involve the police, too, just to keep the bases covered. They don't need to know what he is."

Jenner's instincts sharpened. He could hear the uneven beating of her heart, could smell the fear beginning to taint that seductive citrus scent of hers. His feeling that there was more going on here had been dead-on. He could see it in the stiffening of Mia's shoulders, hear it in that unfinished sentence. But the look on her face, and the weariness still hovering over her features, made him stop. She'd tell him, or tell someone. She was going to have to.

Given what she'd been through, he'd wait to push her on it.

But not long.

"You're forgetting, our sheriff is on it. Anybody asks, you've already been to the police. Buddy will get the word out, but this is going to work its way through both channels, Mia. Isn't that better?"

She sighed and shook her head. "I suppose. I wish I'd never met him. Or at least that I hadn't been so *stupid* when I did."

He shouldn't have felt relieved, but Jenner couldn't help himself. All of his questions about her relationship with the feral were now answered. Mia hadn't been engaged, or in love, or anything much at all with this Gaines. He could read it all over her face. And giving a damn about it, Jenner knew, was bound to put him in a foul mood when he had a chance to mull it over.

"It wasn't stupid," Jenner said, unsure why he was compelled to soothe her. Maybe she had been stupid about it, but he doubted it. "Sometimes we just get… unlucky."

He knew more than a thing or two about that, and he could see that she got it right away.

Mia curved one corner of her mouth up in a small, self-deprecating half smile.

"Yeah," she said. "You can say that again. Though

fangs and fur kind of pushes the situation somewhere past just unlucky."

Jenner chuckled. It seemed like he was going to end up liking Mia D'Alessandro, whether or not it was in his best interest. Her own smile faded away far too quickly, replaced by grim resignation.

"So about the going home?" she asked. "Like I said, I'll talk to whoever I need to, but this was only supposed to be a weekend getaway. Just tell me what I should be expecting."

"What you should be expecting," Jenner repeated. He'd never met anyone who treated becoming a werewolf like catching a cold. He shook his head, amazed. "You're a strange one, Mia."

He could see right away he'd said the wrong thing.

"I'm not strange, I'm trying to be practical," Mia replied, bristling. "Whatever's coming, I can handle it. I can even come back at the full moon or whatever if it would help. But before anything happens, I need information."

Jenner couldn't do anything but stare at her. It was obvious Mia needed a few basic things explained to her, and he had no interest in being the one to do the explaining.

Damn you for sticking me with this, Bane, Jenner thought, taking care to keep it to himself. And though he hated to invade the Alpha's thoughts almost as much as he hated having his own picked up, Jenner pushed out a request with as much force as he could muster.

Bane, could you get over here? Mia...that is, the bit-

ten from last night…she's asking a lot of questions, and I don't think I'm really the guy to be answering them…

The response was quick, and though terse, laced with a little amusement at his expense that Jenner didn't miss.

You're one of us. Why not you? I'll be over later, Jenner. Didn't expect her to be up and lucid so early. Little busy right this second.

Jenner set his jaw and fought back a groan.

The blonde from the bar?

You got it. Smugness, Jenner decided, came through telepathy just fine.

"You can't keep me here against my will," Mia said. "I don't care what you turn into, or what's supposed to happen to me on the full moon, I'm not staying here indefinitely. I want Jeff caught, but as long as someone explains how it all works to me, I'll handle my own… stuff. At *home.*"

The voice Jenner had found rich and warm just a few minutes ago had moved further into just plain "heated" territory. Innocent or not, he decided, this one had plenty of fire in her. Mia was obviously no pushover, nor a simpleton, which meant she'd probably do just fine here. Once she accepted the way things were.

He guessed an upside of being the bearer of bad news, though, was that Mia would probably want nothing to do with him after this. That would make things a hell of a lot easier on him. At least, he thought as he watched Mia cross her arms over her chest and glare at him with enough heat to set the house ablaze, it ought to. If he could somehow manage to ignore her presence in the Hollow altogether.

Which was unlikely at best.

Chapter 4

"Mia," Jenner finally began, not really sure what he was going to say but aware he had to say something before the woman decided to punch him, "you must have seen a werewolf movie or two. I'm not saying they're accurate, but they did hit a couple important points. You realize you're going to turn into a wolf at *least* once a month from now on, right?"

That reminder took a little of the heat from her eyes, Jenner noted, and replaced it with worry. It was a step in the right direction.

"Well, yes…I was only thinking once a month, but… yes," Mia said. "But, I mean, there's got to be werewolves in Philly, right? I figured if there were a group or club or something, you know…they could help me sort it all out. Get used to it. What do you mean by *at least* once a month?"

The only thing that kept him from laughing was knowing it would hurt her feelings. He kept his voice carefully emotionless. "We'll get to that. Are you talking about some kind of werewolf support group?"

"Why not?" she asked, and sure enough, a defensive note had crept into her voice. "It wouldn't be any weirder than everything that's happened to me so far. You're telling me there are no werewolves in Philadelphia?"

Jenner shrugged, a gesture that seemed to irritate her.

"Does that mean no, or that you don't know, or that you're just not going to answer me?" Mia asked.

"It means I don't know any, and even if there are, they're not the kind of wolves who would be in some kind of club that would help you. There's no known pack in that city, so any werewolves you'd find there would be outliers."

"Outliers?"

"Yeah, you know…" He lifted his hands as though he could grasp the words he wanted out of the air. Had he wondered whether Mia was intelligent? This conversation was like being cross-examined by a particularly bloodthirsty lawyer.

"Werewolves congregate in packs," he said. "It's natural. We're linked to one another. Telepathically."

To his surprise, this bit of information seemed more of a revelation to Mia than a shock.

"Oh," she murmured. "That explains why there were a lot more funny looks than actual talking last night."

"It does," Jenner said, relieved not to be challenged on something. "Pack mates can all speak that way, even over great distance. It's a little weird at first, but you get used to it. And without it, the change, and learning to live with all of the other effects of being what we are, can be way too much for one person. The pack, *this* pack, is the support group you're looking for, Mia. The group helps curb the basest instincts all of us deal with from time to time. Living away from the pack is unnatural. I'm not saying it doesn't happen sometimes... but mostly, in an area without a pack, you're going to find ferals."

"Like Jeff," Mia said. Jenner watched the way her eyes dropped, the way she wound her hands together and began toying restlessly with her fingers. The sight hit him with a flood of guilt. However much he didn't want to be the one introducing Mia to the facts of her new life, he needed to remember what it was like to be on the other side of things. It had been ten years for him, years that felt like a lifetime away from the man he had been. And Mia had the added burden of not having asked for this. Whatever she might be holding back from him, right now she needed some sympathy, not suspicion. He knew a lot about evil. Mia wasn't it.

He needed to remember that.

Jenner shoved his plate aside and leaned in close to her, wanting to catch her gaze. It was a mistake, he knew immediately. The scent of her, sweet and carrying the hint of orange blossoms, swamped his senses. His heartbeat accelerated, blood beginning to pump more quickly through his veins. The animal within him stirred, stretched.

Hungered.

"It's going to be okay," he said softly. The need to comfort Mia surprised him with its strength. She looked back at him, eyes wide and full of misery.

"I don't see how," she said. "I really don't. Not unless there's a way out of this that you haven't mentioned."

"Well," he drawled, hoping to erase some of the pain from her lovely face, "there is the one ritual with antelope blood and goat heads."

Damned if she didn't suddenly look hopeful. "Really?"

He shook his head. "Uh, no, Mia. You're stuck being a werewolf. But like I told you last night, it's not so bad. You'll probably like it, once you get used to it."

She closed her eyes and gave her head a tight little shake, as though she could will all of this away.

"No, I won't. I have enough to deal with. And whether you like it or not, whether your Alpha likes it or not, I'm going to be one of those outliers. I have no interest in quitting my job, moving to the middle of nowhere, and starting all over *again*."

"Again?"

She opened her eyes, but couldn't quite meet his.

Of course she has secrets, Jenner thought, hating the bitter, cynical feel of them. *You're a magnet for women like this. Get suckered this time and it's on you.*

"My upbringing…wasn't the greatest. So I got away. I want to put down roots, not keep pulling them up."

There wasn't even the slightest hint of deception in her words, and Jenner immediately felt like an ass. Maybe she wasn't the one with the issue, here.

Wouldn't be the first time.

Flustered, Jenner tried to shift gears. "Don't write it off when you haven't even really begun changing, Mia. It isn't easy to live away from the pack. And I bet we could find you a job here," Jenner said. "What do you do?"

Her voice was flat. "I do web-based PR for a software company, and I do freelance web design on the side."

Jenner thought of the Hollow's one internet provider and single video game store and fought back a grimace. "Okay, maybe not the software company thing. But you can design websites from here as easy as in Philly. Just because it's quiet in the Hollow doesn't make it the middle of nowhere."

Mia's look said volumes about what she thought of that.

"Just because you love it here doesn't make it *not* the middle of nowhere. This isn't my home, and it isn't going to be."

"It's a lot better than some soulless city," Jenner shot back. "And if you weren't being so busy trying to plan your getaway, you'd think about the fact that all the men who saved you last night were out running, as wolves, just for the fun of it. There's room for that here, for what we need and what you're *going* to need—whether or not you like it."

His voice had risen without him meaning for it to in his defense of his home, his way of life. Jenner realized it too late, catching the flash of Mia's eyes just before she stood up, shoved in her stool with an angry little kick, and stood glaring at him with her hands settled on her hips.

"Maybe I like my soulless city," she snapped. "And if you weren't so busy being defensive about your little wolf commune out here, you might remember the fact that I have gone from being relatively normal to being a paranormal creature with a psycho after her in the space of one night. You've just told me I have to plug into this pack deal, however that's done, or go nuts. That I'm going to suddenly have an overwhelming desire to move away from my life and relocate here. I am, and this is an understatement, I promise, *a little overwhelmed*."

She turned away, started to go. "Forget it. I'll talk to Bane, but then I'm out of here. I'll figure this out on my own."

Jenner stood, sensing the fear beneath her burst of anger, regretting having caused it. Regretting whatever had put that desolation in her voice, like she was used to handling everything alone. He told himself he felt the way he did because he had the good of the pack in mind.

It was easier than admitting the truth, and he was just fine with that.

"Mia," he said, though his voice came out more growly than soothing.

"Don't," she said, stiffening. But she stopped.

"Just hang on. Don't go off like that," Jenner said. He didn't know why, but he couldn't let her just storm off in her current state. Not only was it a miserable start, but he didn't want her hurt. And he didn't want to be the one who had hurt her. There'd been enough of that for Mia last night, whatever she was or wasn't hiding about herself. It was probably none of his business.

Even if that strange prickle at the back of his neck insisted that it was.

Mia turned to look back at him. When she spoke, he could hear the quaver in her voice, could see the sheen of moisture in her eyes. That was all it took to make him feel like a big, blundering ass. Things were finally beginning to hit home, he could see. He was immediately caught between guilt and a sudden, desperate urge to flee.

"Don't tell me how great this all is, Jenner," she said. "I'll…I'll come to terms with things in my own way, but try to remember I'm not getting a choice here. Story of my life." Then, to his horror, she burst into tears.

He watched helplessly as glistening droplets began to roll down Mia's cheeks from beneath her glasses. She pressed her hands to her face and tried, very unsuccessfully, to choke back a sob.

"Oh, damn it," she said, looking just as horrified as he felt. "I was fine. I wasn't going to do this. I don't *do* this!"

"Um," Jenner said, at a complete loss. Women didn't cry in front of him. And to his knowledge, he didn't make women cry. Probably because he tried to be around them as little as possible.

Mia waved her hand at him. "Crap. Ignore me. No, you can't ignore me, I guess. I'll just…I'm sorry, I guess you'll have to excuse me…"

She started to turn away again, and what Jenner did then shocked him likely even more than it shocked Mia. Before he could think, he'd closed the distance between them in two long steps.

"Hey," he said softly, seeing her shoulders begin to shake. "Hey, don't do that."

Then his arms were reaching out, wrapping around her small form and pulling her against him. By the time he might have stopped himself, he would have looked like a complete fool…all he could feel was Mia's pain. His senses were full of it, of the scent of her tears, the sight of her reddened cheeks, the sound of each shuddering breath. And some instinct Jenner had never even known he had was set off almost instantly, demanding that he stroke and soothe. His first coherent thought was that despite their size difference, Mia fit perfectly in his arms. His second was that she was going to push him away, outraged at his presumption.

But Mia only stiffened for a moment. Jenner drew in his breath and held it as she went rigid, feeling without any good reason that her reaction was very important. Then, slowly, Mia relaxed into him, almost melting into him as she resumed crying quietly, with the occasional hitching breath.

Jenner stood in his kitchen, holding Mia in his arms while she wept, and wondered what the hell he was doing.

"Sorry," Mia said against the new wet patch on his chest. She sounded mortified. "I'm sorry. I'm just… this is all…"

"No," he replied, surprised at how calm his voice sounded when holding Mia was setting off chain reactions in his nerve endings that were rapidly going to start causing some problems. "There's nothing to be sorry about. It's a lot to take in, especially when you weren't looking for it. It's why we take ferals so seriously. Fortunately, we don't see them that often out here."

Mia gave a watery hiccup. "Why did one have to find *me*?"

It was a good question. One that he'd have to look into, he knew. But Mia's voice was muffled, her body warm and inviting in his arms, and Jenner found himself swamped by a wave of protectiveness. She pulled back, just a little, and looked up at him with a sort of raw earnestness that he found completely disarming. He knew she was going to say something. But all he could see was her big, innocent eyes, glittering in her lovely, angular face, and the soft, plump invitation of her lips as they parted to speak.

Jenner couldn't help himself.

Before Mia could speak a word, Jenner leaned down

and claimed her mouth in a long, slow kiss. There was an initial shock as their lips met, and Jenner felt dizzy, as though he'd unwittingly tapped into an electric current. He heard Mia's sharp intake of breath, knew she'd felt it, too. But she didn't pull away, either. And as his lips lingered on hers, shock quickly became a simmering heat that began to pulse in time with his heart. Jenner nuzzled her mouth, brushing his lips against hers, testing, tasting.

He didn't expect it when Mia simply melted into him, her mouth softening, opening beneath his as she gave in to whatever this strange pull was that existed between them. She sighed, a soft, simple exhalation. But Jenner felt the submission that had produced it, and that single sigh rocketed through his bloodstream like a rare and potent drug.

Jenner growled low in his throat as he pulled Mia closer against him, tasting her more thoroughly as his tongue swept inside her mouth. God, she was sweet… so sweet. He deepened the kiss, and Mia arched into him with a sound that was almost a purr. Her fingers laced behind his neck, and he grew rougher, more demanding as the beast within recognized she was more than willing. One hand slid up into the dark silk of her hair, while the other skimmed down the length of her, exploring curves that felt even better than they looked.

Mia's body fit perfectly against his, better still when he cupped her backside and pulled her hard against him, letting her feel just how badly he wanted her. His blood surged in his veins, and he thought he heard the faintest fragment of some wild and sweet melody before he crushed his mouth against hers again. Jenner groaned when Mia responded in kind, shocked at how quickly he'd gone from interest to raw need. He wanted to take her clothes off with his teeth. He wanted to bend her over the counter and—

Recognizing that he was about to snap his tether despite the sexual haze, Jenner managed to tear his mouth away from Mia's and disentangle himself in a matter of seconds. It was all he had, Jenner knew, before he did something they would both regret. His hands shook as he stumbled backward, a rare misstep for him in more ways than one.

It had never been like that. Not ever.

It couldn't mean anything good.

Mia swayed on her feet as she watched him fumble away from her, her eyes unfocused and gleaming with the sort of lust that made the wolf inside him sing. Lucky for him, the human part was in control right now.

Barely.

"I've…got stuff to do," Jenner bit out, backing away as quickly as he could without running. "You should… rest. I'll be in the garage."

He left before she could collect her thoughts enough to tell him what an ass he was. Hell, it wasn't like he didn't already know.

Jenner turned quickly and walked away from Mia as fast as he could manage without breaking into a run. Still, once out of her sight, Jenner fled the house as though the hounds of hell were at his heels. He could feel her eyes on his back all the way to the door, and hoped that by the time she figured out what to say to him, he'd be too far away to bother.

Jenner gritted his teeth as he slammed out of the house, anger at himself beginning to roil and churn in his stomach. In his thirty-four years of life, he had never lost control with a woman. Not even with Tess, if he were honest with himself. Back then he'd been rootless, looking for something he couldn't find, and he'd wanted what she had to give. But Mia…hell, he could lose himself in her. That kiss had been like drowning in moonlight.

Only when he was safely ensconced in the relative sanctuary of his detached garage, which he'd converted into a cavernous workspace specifically for his personal projects, did Jenner begin to feel centered again. It didn't stop his craving for her, or the ache that meant he was denying his body the thing it most wanted, but this was a place he could make himself calm down.

Crawling under the hood of the old Chevelle was like crawling into a dark, quiet cave that smelled reassuringly of motor oil. This was real, solid, he told himself as he began to work. He knew what he was doing with cars.

The exact opposite of how he felt about Mia D'Alessandro right this second.

He wasn't a stupid man, though Jenner had realized long ago that his size and relative silence caused enough people to underestimate him in the brains department. He'd used that to his advantage on more than one occasion. But this searing awareness of Mia was utterly beyond his experience, and it made him feel like a fool. He wasn't quite sure what to do about it. Hopefully, it would burn itself out naturally.

Soon.

For now, though, he'd retreated to his favorite hiding place. Here, it was just him and several tons of American muscle car…and the ghost of Mia's kiss, lingering on his lips long after the taste of her should have gone, provoking questions Jenner had never intended to ask himself…and was still determined not to answer.

Chapter 5

By the time there was a quick, sharp knock at the door, Mia had decided that Jenner had not in fact just gone outside, but that he had possibly relocated to another county altogether. It had been a couple of hours since the kiss that had come close to knocking her socks (and every other article of clothing she was wearing) completely off, and she was still having a hard time thinking of much but the fact that her lips had managed to send one very large werewolf into horrified flight. From his own house. For *hours*.

If that wasn't a sign that she needed to get the hell out of here as quickly as possible, she didn't know what was.

Mia headed for the front door, still trying to decide whether she was angry at Jenner, disgusted with herself, or both. She was leaning toward both as she caught sight of a couple of big, masculine forms through the Craftsman-style sidelights flanking the heavy wooden door.

Her nerves kicked back up immediately. She was pretty sure this would be Bane (and what a name that was), the Alpha of the Blackpaw pack.

And she was very sure that of all the times to meet him, this was far from the best where her state of mind was concerned. Still, better to get this over with.

Mia took a deep breath, straightened her shoulders, and opened the door. Exhaling, however, was temporarily forgotten while she took in the sight of the two men looking back at her. Neither of them had been in the woods last night—that she was sure of. Even in shock, she wouldn't have forgotten faces like these.

The one on the left was, in a word, adorable. He was about average height, with sandy blond hair that was tousled and spiky. Big shoulders, big blue eyes, and dimples when he smiled, which he did the moment he saw her. She found herself returning it before she really knew what she was doing. Her own smile faded quickly, however, when she turned her attention to the blonde's companion. This one looked to have been created from sin itself. If the villain in a movie were a werewolf, Mia decided, he would be their idea of perfect casting.

He was tall and lean, with a rangy, wiry build that still managed to give the impression of incredible strength. His dusky skin looked gold-dusted in the shadow of the doorway. Angular features set off a pair of thickly lashed, almond-shaped eyes that watched her unblinkingly, glowing deep amber. His black hair was shaggy and attractively mussed. A flash of gold caught Mia's eye, and she noted the small gold hoop in the stranger's ear.

He looked like a gypsy, Mia decided. Beautiful and dangerous. And not exactly friendly. The polar opposite of the classic Boy Next Door he was with.

"Can I help you?" she asked, feeling a little foolish. But what was she supposed to say? Inwardly, she cursed Jenner. No matter how little she knew him, he was going to get an earful whenever he decided to slink out of his hidey hole. If he hadn't enjoyed kissing her, fine. But that was no reason to take off for hours. Especially when that kiss hadn't been her idea in the first place.

The dark-haired man gave her a small smile, the faintest lift of the corners of his mouth. She got the unnerving feeling he was busy sizing her up. What he saw, she had no idea. She probably didn't *want* to know, Mia decided. No doubt these were more werewolves, and werewolf material was one thing she was almost positive she was not. Not that it made much of a difference now. Then he spoke.

"Mia. I'm Jayson Bane."

His voice was rough and sexy, like fingernails on velvet. Mia gave an inward sigh as she moved to take Bane's proffered hand with her own. It had been too much to hope for that the friendly looking blond would be the Alpha.

"Nice to meet you. Jenner said you'd be coming to talk to me," she said, shaking his hand. It was rough, and warm…and she felt nothing like the bright spark of connection that she felt whenever she touched Jenner. Obviously, her weird thing with Jenner was an individual problem.

Like she needed one more.

Now Bane really smiled, a brilliant flash of white. Mia might not have felt pulled to him the way she was to Jenner, but it was hard not to appreciate that he was utterly gorgeous…and that the smile just took it to an entirely different level.

"I guess Jenner talked to you, then," he said. "Good. I wasn't sure. You may have noticed he's not what you'd call…chatty."

Her laugh was genuine, and was soon joined by Bane's low chuckle. With the sound came a burst of relief. Maybe he wouldn't turn out to be quite so intimidating after all. That is, once she got used to looking at him.

"Yeah," she said, "I noticed. But he did make me breakfast."

Bane raised his eyebrows. "He talked *and* he cooked? Are you sure we're both talking about Nick Jenner?"

Mia managed a smile, but she immediately wished she hadn't said anything. She didn't know enough about Jenner to say how he was or wasn't…all she knew was that he seemed to have a lot simmering beneath the surface. Her cheeks heated as she remembered the taste she'd had of *that*. It would be better, she knew, to put it out of her mind. Jenner certainly seemed to want to.

Thankfully, whatever else Bane thought about Jenner's behavior with her, he kept it to himself.

"Mind if we come in?" Bane asked. "Jenner knows we're here. He should be in shortly."

It was that pack telepathy thing, Mia supposed. At least Jenner hadn't fled the country. Feeling awkward because it wasn't her house, but unsure what else to do, she stepped aside and motioned Bane and his companion forward.

"Sure." She noticed that Bane didn't bother to introduce her to the blond, which she found both strange and rude. But the other man didn't seem to mind. He let Bane go in first, and then stopped beside Mia to take her hand in his, blue eyes twinkling with what looked like good-natured mischief.

It was impossible not to be charmed.

"Not that anyone cares, but I'm Kenyon. Kenyon Chase."

"Mia D'Alessandro. And no one cares who you are because…"

He leaned in as though he was about to share a secret. She inhaled the scent of his cologne, something warm and spicy. It was oddly comforting.

"Because my father had the poor taste not to be born a Blackpaw, and my mother had the even poorer taste required to marry him." At her startled expression, his grin widened. "Don't worry. She still loves him, inferior genes and all. But I don't think her family has ever really gotten over it. My mother was a Blackpaw by birth."

"Which makes you…" Mia prompted.

"Not a Blackpaw," Kenyon replied. "Don't worry. Bane will explain everything. Just know that I'm here to help." And with that, he gave her hand a friendly squeeze, winked, and released it before following Bane into the house. Mia watched him go, fairly sure that on top of having been kissed senseless by one werewolf already today, she'd just been flirted with by another.

Her life, which she had often regarded as pathetically boring in spite of her odd gifts, had gotten really weird really fast.

Mia leaned for a moment against the doorjamb, trying to settle her sudden attack of nerves enough to go back in and…what, entertain a couple of werewolves? That wasn't her job. Bane would have questions, she'd answer them, and then she'd need to find a way to rent a car or…something. It felt like running away, though, something she'd sworn she would quit doing. And thinking of going home with Jeff still out there was just…

She blew out a breath, flustered, and tried to distract herself with her first real look at the land where Jenner made his home. It was more easily done than she'd expected, since the view from the porch was, quite simply, lovely. She saw a well-tended expanse of yard, still a rich green, rolling away beyond a front porch that was occupied by a couple of inviting-looking rocking chairs. A long gravel drive veered off around the side of the house, and in the opposite direction headed toward the road through a thick screen of bright October trees. It seemed they were surrounded by forest here. The solitude would have gotten to her if she'd lived here alone, but she was beginning to understand that Jenner enjoyed keeping his own company. For her, she would need someone to share a place like this with. But if she had someone, Mia thought, her chest tightening at the wild beauty surrounding her, she couldn't imagine anywhere more perfect. If she had someone…

As though she'd summoned him with just a thought, he was there. Mia's heart tripped into double time as Jenner rounded the corner. It was stupid, she told herself as his big, muscular form loped into view, his scuffed boots crunching on the gravel. It had only been a kiss. One random, ill-advised, mind-blowing kiss. She should be able to set it aside, at least for now. There were more important things.

Or so her mind insisted. The sight of Jenner had her body protesting that nothing could possibly be more important than getting her hands on him again as soon as possible.

She made the mistake of catching his eye as he headed up onto the porch, and Mia watched his step falter ever so slightly. She felt a surge of triumph that was purely female. He might have run from her, but there was no way she was going to let him ignore her. And from the flash of heat she saw in those unusual golden eyes of his, ignoring her wasn't what was on his mind. But Mia could tell he wasn't happy about it, and that was the part she didn't understand. If either of them had a right to be upset about what had happened in the kitchen, it was her.

Unfortunately, she just couldn't bring herself to feel that way.

Jenner clomped up onto the porch, the set of his jaw tight. He looked so grim it would have been funny, Mia thought, if the look had been about anyone else. It was hard to believe this was the same man who'd held her earlier while she'd cried. It still shocked her that she'd been able to let go like that with him. She never cried. Why would she? There had never been anyone to soothe away the tears. But his touch, such a contrast to his fierce looks, had been so gentle, so easy to fall into…

He gave a short nod, a quick jerk of his head that she interpreted as a greeting.

"Bane inside?"

His brusque manner stung. *That's what you get*, she told herself, *for letting everything* but *your head guide you. Again.*

"Mmmhmm," Mia said out loud, her lips pressed into a thin line. "He and Kenyon are waiting for us."

Jenner frowned, stopping short. "Bane and *who*?"

Mia arched a brow. "Kenyon? Blond, blue-eyed werewolf guy? Kenyon…" She searched her memory for it, finally remembering. "Chase. Kenyon Chase. You don't know him?"

Even knowing what he was, it surprised Mia to see Jenner go very still, tip his head back to scent the air, and finally, curl his upper lip over teeth that suddenly looked unusually sharp. It excited her in some deep, primal way that was as worrying as it was strangely arousing.

"Silverback," Jenner growled. He looked like he wanted to bite someone. Mia took a step back, nerves beginning to dance in the pit of her belly. She had no interest in watching two male werewolves tear into each other over territory, or whatever Jenner's problem suddenly was. He didn't seem to notice her reaction, however. On his way past her, he caught her hand in his to pull her along with him. The sudden, unexpected contact sent a bright shock of warm recognition through her system. She tried very hard not to like it, and failed miserably.

"Come on," he grumbled. "If Bane brought a Silverback with him, he'd better have a damned good reason."

Mia let herself be pulled, temporarily powerless to do otherwise…though there was a part of her that enjoyed the way his roughened palm so fully enclosed her hand.

Bane and Kenyon had settled themselves on the squat, overstuffed couch, and watched Mia and Jenner come in. Bane's eyes flicked quickly to her hand entwined with Jenner's, then away. He looked troubled, though Mia couldn't think of a reason why that would be.

Suddenly nervous, Mia pulled her hand free and headed for one of the plush, faded chairs that sat across from the couch. Jenner went for the other, though not before commenting on the soda Bane was popping open.

"Make yourself at home," he said.

Bane smirked. "Always do. If you'd quit stocking

your fridge so well, we'd quit coming over and *un*-stocking it."

Jenner snorted. "And here I thought it was my sparkling personality that brought you back. Or maybe just my new TV." He settled himself into the other chair, and Mia wondered how he could now seem so at ease. Despite the casual demeanor of the men, the tension in the room was thick. She thought longingly of her apartment, which was quiet and werewolf-free, and fussed with the ends of her hair.

"You know I'm going to ask what this is about," Jenner said, jerking his head toward Kenyon. It wasn't exactly a friendly introduction, but Kenyon seemed unfazed. He simply waited, as Jenner did, for Bane's answer. If there had been any doubt in Mia's mind that Bane was as powerful as Jenner among the Blackpaw, those were dispelled right then. Just because the power sat easily on Bane didn't mean it wasn't there…and she could see now that it was, in spades.

Bane took a pull from his soda, then set it on the rough-hewn coffee table in front of him. When he spoke, he surprised Mia by addressing her.

"Should be pretty obvious. I need to know everything you know about Jeff Gaines, Mia. How you met, who he is—or pretended to be. Why he might want to hurt you."

She went cold, but there was no hint of malice in Bane's expression. This was what she'd been waiting for, turning over what to say in her mind since last night. Maybe it would be a relief to have it done.

"I—"

"The Silverback don't need to be involved in this," Jenner interrupted. "Whatever she's got to say doesn't concern them. You could have mentioned you were bringing company."

Bane's eyes narrowed as he turned his attention to Jenner, who didn't look the least bit fazed.

"The Silverback have a right to be involved," Bane said. "Looks like the feral may have been one of theirs." When Jenner started to reply, Bane held up a hand in silent warning.

"After, Jenner. Let Mia talk. Then Chase can explain."

Jenner went very still, and Mia noted the way his expression went carefully blank. There was an order to things here, and she'd just been reminded of it. So had Jenner, whether he liked it or not. And whatever he was to the pack, he wasn't Alpha. Still, he took his time complying. Mia watched him stretch his legs out in front of him as he leaned back in the chair, appearing to mull this over. Finally, he looked at Mia.

"Go ahead."

As gruff as he was, there was something about the tone of his voice that bolstered her. She took a deep breath, then began.

"I met Jeff about a month ago."

Bane tilted his head, an action she'd seen from Jenner when he was interested in something.

"Work?" he asked. Mia shook her head.

"No. Bookstore. It was just one of those things. I was

thumbing through the new Stephen King, and he struck up a conversation. He was a fan, too, so we started talking…"

"Go figure," Jenner muttered. Mia ignored him, though she supposed it *was* fitting. Just as she knew she had to sound very naive. The chances that their meeting had just been "one of those things" were slim to none. She knew that now. How long had Jeff been stalking her, waiting to make a move? How had he known about her at all?

"It really isn't very interesting," Mia continued. "We exchanged numbers. Went out a few times. He said he came from money but was trying to make his own. He has a financial consulting firm. At least…that's what he said. I believed him. He was comfortable throwing money around, but he…seemed to have some issues with it too."

"Issues?" Bane murmured.

Mia nodded, suddenly embarrassed. Her cheeks flushed despite her best efforts to stop it. "He depended on the family money, but he talked a lot about wanting to prove himself. About not being thought good enough to take over the company one day. There had been problems between him and his father before he died, and Jeff wanted to build something great on his own. He wanted…" She trailed off and sighed, remembering those conversations. Jeff had been more than determined. He'd been angry. She'd chalked it up to being raised indifferently and with far too much, but she knew now that at least some of the problem had been within Jeff himself.

"He wanted lots of things. He could be charming. He could also be moody."

Jenner was looking at her strangely. "You liked that? Charming and moody?"

Mia shrugged while Jenner ignored Bane's glare. "Everyone has baggage. I liked him. Obviously, I didn't really know him. This weekend would have been the most time we'd spent together at once. Maybe I would have noticed more was wrong if it had worked out that way, but he saved me the trouble." She looked away, remembering. "He surprised me with this. I thought the whole whirlwind getaway thing was kind of romantic. That'll teach me."

"No," Kenyon said, drawing her attention back to his earnest expression. "This was just him, Mia. *Is* him. He was just the same before he left the Silverback, and trust me, he fooled more than just you."

"What makes you so sure this guy was a Silverback?" Jenner asked, and Mia let out the breath she didn't even know she'd been holding. They had what they needed, or most of it. It didn't matter why Jeff had targeted her, as long as he was caught.

Then she would be safe…and so would everyone else.

But the guilt that began to gnaw at her spoiled whatever relief she might have felt quickly enough. She'd seen no evidence that these Blackpaw wanted anything more than to catch a violent feral and protect her. Despite all her grandmother's warnings about never getting too close to anyone, about how no one would ever want her for anything other than her magic, she felt as though she was the dangerous one here.

Kenyon's lips curved into the barest hint of a smile as he watched Jenner. "Your sheriff got in touch last night after the attack. Since our territory is the closest to yours, it made sense to check. And in this case, I'm pretty sure we have a match, at least based on the description we were given."

Jenner's voice didn't betray a hint of what he was thinking. "That's a pretty rough secondhand description you would have gotten, since Mia didn't even talk to Buddy—that's Sheriff Stokes—last night. She was with me."

Maybe she was imagining it, but the way he said those words gave Mia a dark little thrill. He'd sounded almost possessive. And from the way Kenyon's blue eyes narrowed, he'd heard it too.

"I understand that. But if this is who I'm thinking, he's going to be hard to catch."

"If? I thought you said you were sure."

"I'm not going to tell you I'm positive until I've got my teeth in his throat, but I'm about as sure as I can be otherwise."

Bane inserted himself into the conversation then, and Mia was glad of it. She didn't like the way Jenner and Kenyon were looking at one another. There was an unspoken challenge hanging in the air, and she swore she could feel an excess of testosterone in the atmosphere all of a sudden. She didn't know what this was about, but she figured it had a lot to do with Kenyon encroaching on Jenner's territory.

She felt strangely included in that at the moment.

"Kenyon has recently been chosen as Tomas's future successor, Jenner," Bane said, a warning in his voice. "It's appropriate that he learn to deal with situations like this."

"I suppose," Jenner grumbled. "*If* this is their guy. But even if it is, this is our territory. We don't need the Silverback to catch this dirtbag." His gaze sharpened and pinned Bane to the spot. "Would have been nice if you'd given me a heads up, too. I'm the Lunari, remember? You're the one who insisted I take this position. You ought to know the protocol."

"I barely had any warning, so you got none," Bane replied with a shrug. "Anyway, I figured you had enough on your hands without having to get pissed off about this in advance. Little did I know you were hiding under the hood of that damn car. Again."

Something about the way Bane said it struck Mia as funny despite everything, and she couldn't quite hide her amused snort. Bane's quick sidelong glance, prickly and disgruntled, did nothing to dampen her sudden amusement. And in a way, it was nice to know that it didn't take much to send him to his preferred hidey hole. That it wasn't just her.

And right about now, she was grateful *something* could make her chuckle.

"If he *was* one of ours," Kenyon said pointedly, turning the subject back to the matter at hand, "you'll want our help catching him, especially if it's who we suspect. And if it is, then the Silverback have more than one interest to protect…it's our right." He paused, a small muscle in his jaw twitching as he looked straight at Jenner. "Unless you feel like going against the Pack Laws."

Mia watched the way Jenner's eyes went to gold flames at that statement, the way Bane was watching the two men with a look on his face that clearly said he wasn't going to tolerate much more posturing. Her amusement faded as quickly as it had appeared. She didn't have a clue what they were talking about, but she was fairly sure they were now only seconds away from someone throwing a fist into someone else's face. With that in mind, she decided she ought to speak up. Kenyon's assertion that he knew Jeff had piqued her interest. And she wasn't going to get to hear any more about it if he and Jenner decided to sprout fur and have it out right there in the great room.

"I'm assuming you brought a picture?" Mia asked Kenyon, and as she'd hoped, both pairs of hot, glowing eyes fixed on her. The sudden and intense focus on her made her feel slightly lightheaded. It was hard not to appreciate the bizarre position she found herself in. It had never occurred to her that she would ever be one of those women who was actively sought after by the opposite sex.

Apparently, all she'd needed to do was be bitten by a werewolf.

It was a hell of a way for her luck to change.

Kenyon's voice sounded slightly strangled. "Ah, yeah. I brought it with me." From an inside pocket of the wool peacoat he hadn't yet taken off, Kenyon produced a photo and handed it to Mia. He let his fingers brush against hers when he handed it off. His eyes, very blue, caught hers and tried to hold her gaze, but it didn't take much for her to look away.

The sensation of Kenyon's skin against hers was pleasant, but still, nothing like what she'd felt when Jenner had touched her. She could have tried to let her magic call to him if she'd wanted, to let her blood sing and see how his responded, but Mia had no interest in the uncomfortable aftermath that might provoke. All she got was the faintest impression of a sweet Highland tune before she drew her hand away. She glanced at Jenner quickly, catching his gaze for only the barest of seconds before he turned his attention elsewhere. Instantly, heat raced over her skin, making her flush.

With Jenner, her problem went far beyond touch. And she was way too interested. He could be a fascinating distraction if she let him, Mia knew. Fascinating, and ultimately painful. She didn't know enough, have enough experience, to even think about playing with a man like him.

With an inward sigh, Mia looked down at the picture to examine it. Instantly, she was floored. It was a candid shot at what looked like a summer barbecue, with a trio of laughing people in the foreground. There was a grinning, dark-haired man holding a spatula. A pretty woman with curly dark blond hair. And there, with his arms wrapped around the woman, looking as though he was having the time of his life, was Jeff.

Mia hadn't anticipated the reaction she would have to seeing his face again. Her heart kicked into an uneven staccato, and a clammy chill slithered over her skin. Her fingers shook as she shoved the picture back at Kenyon, wanting it away from her. Jeff's voice echoed in her head.

Come back here, you stupid bitch...you can't run from me forever!

"Here. I don't need to look at it anymore." She knew her voice sounded clipped, strained. And to his credit, Kenyon took the photo back quickly, without any more playful brushes of his hand. He looked more concerned than anything.

"Are you all right, Mia?" he asked, his voice echoing strangely in her head. The room seemed to shift beneath her feet, and she felt herself wobble. She couldn't seem to get enough air.

Then Jenner was right in front of her, filling up her vision. It was a relief...Mia felt like she was sliding down into a black hole. Her vision started to waver. All she could think of were yellow eyes staring wildly at her in the darkness, of the sensation of a mouthful of teeth sinking into her skin.

"Of course she's not all right," Jenner said, his voice sounding to her as though he were shouting at her from very far away. "Mia? Hell, Bane, she's going to pass out..."

She felt his hands on her, but then the floor dropped out from beneath her, and she was floating, floating in darkness.

Chapter 6

She was still very much aware of herself, and of the sensation of movement, but she was body-less, weightless. Mia felt like she was flying in the dark, headed somewhere very quickly. The sound of masculine voices drew her, growing louder as she sped toward them. It wasn't long before she was surrounded by those voices, men arguing over the best way to go about…something.

Need to go back and get the girl…

Full moon on Tuesday, going to be a problem if it doesn't happen soon…

Don't care if I have to kill twenty wolves to get to her, I will…

Then she was surrounded by another voice, one she knew all too well.

Mia. I can feel you. I'm coming back to get you,

sweetheart. Nothing will keep me from you. I know where you are. The shadows are waiting. You're the key...the key...the key...

A pair of red eyes opened in the darkness, not Jeff's, but something far older, and infinitely more dangerous. When they fixed on her, she felt as though she'd been plunged into ice water.

"No!" She cried out as her body bowed upward, slamming back into reality with incredible force. It reminded her of the times she'd awakened from dreams when she'd felt like she was falling, except that this time was far more frightening, and she actually hit bottom.

Though her eyes had opened, it took Mia a few seconds to process what she was seeing. She was on her back on the floor, three very pale faces hovering over her. Something was gripping her hand so tightly that it was cutting off the circulation. And she was freezing.

Mia flexed her own hand gently, and Jenner's grip relaxed, though not much. She began to shiver as warmth slowly returned.

"What happened?" he demanded. "Jesus, Mia, you're like ice!"

Mia blinked, trying to organize her scattered thoughts and impressions into something coherent. Finally, she said, "I guess seeing him triggered...something. I heard Jeff. In my head." She looked into Jenner's eyes, and the anger she saw there steadied her. He had promised to keep her safe. In the midst of all the madness, she believed he would at least try his best to honor his word.

"More than one voice, though Jeff's was the strongest. They were talking about looking for me, getting me before the full moon. And then there were red eyes..." She trailed off, shaking her head. "That was when I got cold."

"Gaines had red eyes?" Kenyon asked, obviously confused.

"Son of a bitch," Jenner said flatly. He turned an accusing look on Kenyon. "What kind of a picture did you show her?"

Kenyon glowered back. "This isn't my fault. Her link to him is obviously strong. He's out there thinking about her, she saw his face, and that's all it took."

Feeling slightly woozy, Mia sat up. As though he had only just realized he'd been hanging on to it, Jenner quickly withdrew his hand. Still, he stayed on one knee beside her, close enough that Mia could feel the warmth radiating from him. It was welcome...right now, she felt as though she would never be warm again.

"What is it? What just happened to me?" she asked.

It was Kenyon who answered her, getting to his feet and sparing Jenner a single, scathing glance before focusing back on her with eyes that warmed instantly with worry and compassion.

"A werewolf bite is a powerful thing, Mia. It links people together, just as the initiation ritual links the bitten to a pack. Usually both things happen at the same time, since we take pains to ensure those who join us are willing and understand the process. But Jeff Gaines only got halfway. You're linked to him mentally, just

as wolf packs are able to communicate telepathically…
and through him, to others he's bitten. But if he doesn't
finish what he started by the full moon, that bond will
be broken."

"I want it broken now," Mia said with a shudder.
"And whatever you mean about finishing what he
started, I think you're all still assuming he wants to
keep me alive. *He doesn't.* He just wants to be the one
who kills me."

"He won't," Jenner said flatly. "No matter what happens, and whether you're right or not, you'll be part of
a pack by the full moon."

"That's when I'm supposed to, um, turn into a werewolf, right?" she asked, trying not to grimace at how
odd the words felt rolling off of her tongue. "I understand why I have to join a pack, but not how. Is there
some kind of ceremony?"

Mia looked at the three men surrounding her, saw the
light blush on Kenyon's cheeks and the way he suddenly
refused to meet her eyes. Jenner still looked angry. And
Bane…well, Bane's handsome face was tinged with regret. That bothered her more than anything. Apparently,
what she'd already been through hadn't been enough.
There was more.

"What aren't you telling me?" Mia asked, keeping
her voice even, though she wanted to shout. She looked
at each man in turn. "What do I have to do to get him
out of my head?"

Bane cleared his throat. She hadn't thought he was
capable of looking embarrassed until now.

"Linking in, making a bond to another wolf or wolves permanent, isn't just symbolic. It's…ah…physical. The bite is just part of it."

It was hard to miss the gist, especially when Bane dropped his eyes. Mia's stomach did a slow roll, and she felt all the blood drain from her face. Still, she kept focused on Bane. She couldn't look at the other two without suffering mortification so intense that she worried it would cause her to simply melt through the floor. "Are you saying," she asked, her voice sounding hoarse and strange to her own ears, "that by the full moon I'm going to have to…to have to…"

Oh, God, she couldn't even say it. It was the smallest of blessings that Bane didn't make her. All he did was nod.

"I'm sorry, Mia. I know you didn't ask for this. But that doesn't change things. There's no other way. It's not—it doesn't have to mean anything. It's not marriage."

"No, it's just a mandatory one-night stand," Mia replied, knowing her face was glowing some shade of volcanic red right now and barely caring. It was so ridiculous, in an awful sort of way. Having her pick of hot werewolves for one night sounded great in fantasyland. In reality, this was more than a little gross.

"Don't think of it that way," Bane replied. "Please. No one will force himself on you, Mia. Someone *must* initiate you by the full moon…but that choice is yours. Before that, though, we'd like to try and use your connection to Gaines to find him. We know that his connection to you will draw him here eventually, but it would be better for everyone if we could find him first."

Mia nodded slowly, wearily. The thought of Jeff coming here, of him finding her and dragging her off, was nothing short of terrifying. It was the only thing that made the thought of having to sleep with a relative stranger manageable.

Jenner's gruff rumble of a voice drew her attention away from her troubled thoughts, and she immediately flushed when their eyes met. If she had to choose, right this second, there would be no contest...

"I don't like that you heard other voices. Ferals usually run alone. Smacks of throwing together a pack, which is forbidden." His eyes darkened. "You can't think of any reason why he's hunting you in particular, Mia? He's going to an awful lot of trouble just to catch and kill you."

Mia simply shook her head, feeling miserable. What was she supposed to say? She doubted these wolves even knew about the shadows drawn to blood like hers. *She* didn't even know if they were real. All she had to go on were a bunch of old warnings and stories...and the fact that one crazy feral werewolf had decided it was all true.

Trusting strangers went against everything she knew. Hiding her secret was too deeply ingrained. As was the belief, impossible to shake, that if these men knew the truth, they'd throw her out so quickly her head would spin.

Tainted, her grandmother's voice whispered.

Jenner's expression was full of doubt, but he was silent as he watched her. She could feel his gaze on her, warm as the sun, could smell the wonderful earthy scent he carried with him. They centered her in a way that nothing else ever had. It was wonderful…and worrying. Her intense awareness of Jenner was beginning to make her realize just how alone she'd been…and how little she wanted to return to being that way. But letting her guard down, letting herself crave his company, would leave her with nothing good. He'd pushed her away once already.

Jenner didn't need her, Mia thought. And it was just as well.

"He was one of yours. Why did you cut him loose?" Jenner snapped out the question at Kenyon, who frowned and looked away.

"He was going by Jeff Markham then." Kenyon sighed and ran a hand absently through his hair. "He made a play for Alpha. Fought dirty, too, but Tomas shut him down."

Bane looked sharply at Kenyon. "The penalty to challenge and lose is death."

Kenyon hissed out a sigh, and Mia couldn't tell where his exasperation was directed.

"The ultimate choice falls to the Alpha, and Tomas chose mercy. Not that exile is such a mercy. Jeff's link to the pack was severed. Tomas made it clear that if he ever saw his face again, he *would* kill him." Kenyon shook his head. "Exiles aren't the same as regular ferals. Much saner, just alone, which I guess can do things to you. But he hasn't been gone from us long. The madness must have been there to begin with. You're right, we should have just ended it. But it wasn't my decision."

"Those laws are there for a reason," Jenner growled. "And now you've unleashed *this* on us. A feral with a makeshift pack loose on our territory, and an innocent woman being hunted to ground." He slid an unreadable look at Mia. "He must think—"

Kenyon bared his teeth and growled, cutting him off. "It doesn't matter what he thinks. He's insane. The Silverback will take responsibility. And we'll protect our own. She'll be safe."

Jenner's lips curled. "Mia is *not* the Silverback's responsibility."

"Enough!" Bane's sharp command made Mia jump. But his tone seemed to be enough, barely, to keep Jenner and Kenyon from ripping into one another. The Alpha's eyes flashed as he looked between them.

"I think we've found out as much as we can from Mia right now, so you two can postpone your pissing match for when I don't have to watch it." He looked at Mia, gentling visibly. "I'd like to try to guide you in connecting with Gaines again, to see if we can find out where he is."

She didn't want to say yes. But she also knew that if she wanted him caught, there was little choice.

"When?" she asked.

"The sooner we can get him the better. Tonight."

Mia nodded, though the thought left her cold. Still, the sooner the better. She now had no doubt he would come for her if she didn't do something, and on her own there was no way she could fight him. He knew his own abilities. She was nowhere near comfortable with her own. At least, in working with the Blackpaw to find Jeff, she wouldn't just be the damsel in distress on the sidelines.

He needed to be caught. She needed to stay sane and alive. Right now, that was all that mattered.

Feeling strangely better now that her situation had been laid out so plainly, Mia accepted Bane's hand and got to her feet, then watched him issue his orders with the brutal efficiency of a general. Jenner hovered close by, even more intimidating than Bane because of his silence and the steely glint in his eyes. He had called himself a Lunari. She wondered what that was, though she had a feeling knowing might make his presence more unnerving than it already was.

"Go ahead and call Tomas," Bane said to Kenyon. "Tell him what we know."

Kenyon gave a quick nod. "He should be here himself before long. We'll need to discuss Mia's protection. She should be under constant watch."

Jenner shifted and crossed his arms over his chest, fixing Kenyon with a piercing stare. "She is now. Are you questioning my ability to ensure her safety?"

The Silverback hesitated. "No, of course not," he allowed. "I just wondered where you intend to keep her—"

"*Keep* me?" Mia interrupted, looking between the two angry werewolves. "Okay, one, I'm standing right

here, so you might want to take that into consideration
when you're talking about me. Two, nobody is *keeping* me anywhere. Believe it or not, I can handle myself pretty well when I'm not alone in the woods with a
guy who hasn't mentioned he can grow fur and fangs.
I appreciate the offer of protection, but if it's going to
turn into some kind of weird house arrest thing, then
I'll find somewhere to stay that's less—"

"Intense?" Bane asked, a hint of a smile playing at
the corners of his mouth.

"Exactly," Mia agreed. Bane's grin, handsome
though it was, did exactly nothing for her frayed nerves.

"Good luck finding that around here," he said. "And
I'm afraid that these two are your best bets. You don't
know all the things Gaines might pull. We do. A wolf
will need to be with you here, Mia, whether you like
it or not."

"She stays with me," Jenner said flatly. Mia looked
sharply at him. His words surprised her. But more than
that, his expression, which was nothing short of deadly,
filled her with a strange combination of nerves and pleasure. Despite the fact that he'd already shown himself
to be surly, difficult, and rude, a part of her was glad
he seemed determined to keep up his role of protector.

She felt safe with him. And right now, with everything in her life shifting beneath her feet, that counted
for a lot.

Kenyon opened his mouth to say something, but
Bane cut him off neatly before he began. "She'll be
protected," Bane said, eyes fixed on Kenyon. "The de-

tails will be worked out today. But this is our pack, our people's territory. Careful how much you question a Lunari, Kenyon. He's hunted far more frightening things than you."

Kenyon didn't look happy about it, but he didn't argue. Instead, he stepped forward to take Mia's hand and, to her surprise, give a small bow. "It was nice meeting you, Mia. Anything you need, I'm at your service. I won't be far."

She smiled at him, charmed, despite what sounded a lot like a low growl from Jenner's direction. Kenyon seemed genuinely sweet, Mia decided as she watched dimples wink in his cheeks, and there was no question he was handsome. Unfortunately, he was nowhere near as interesting to her as the werewolf who glared daggers at him all the way out the door.

An awkward silence descended over the room as the door shut behind Kenyon.

"Asshole," muttered Jenner. Mia widened her eyes at him.

"What is *wrong* with you?" she said. "He seemed nice enough."

When neither Jenner nor Bane bothered to answer her, she decided it was time to remove herself from the raging testosterone still filling the room, lingering in the air like invisible fog…or a foul odor.

"Okay," she said. "I'm going to go sit on the porch and get some air. If I scream, I'd appreciate it if one of you came out to check on me. Thanks."

Shaking her head over the idiocy of men, which supernatural powers apparently did nothing to cure, Mia headed out the door.

Chapter 7

"You and I need to talk," Bane said as soon as the door closed behind Mia.

"So talk," Jenner said. He was already regretting his assertion that Mia was staying with him. Hadn't he worked this all out in his head when he'd been in the garage? Except that had been before that cocky little Silverback walked in and started making eyes at her. When that had happened, the rational, planning ahead part of Jenner's brain seemed to have shut down completely.

And now here he was, about to suffer a dressing down from one very pissed off Alpha. Jenner knew the look on Bane's face, all too well. He ought to feel good about the warning he knew was coming, should be glad that there was now no chance at all of Mia becoming his.

Of course, that would be a lot easier if he wasn't still envisioning punching the smile off of Kenyon Chase's face.

"I think Mia asked the right question, actually. Except she was too nice about the way she phrased it, so I'll give it a try. What crawled up your ass and died, Jenner?" Bane began to pace the room restlessly, more comfortable in motion than he was still.

Jenner, just the opposite, settled back into a chair and watched Bane make the circuit around the couch, in front of the windows, around the other chair, and back again.

"Nothing's wrong, except that next time I'd like a little warning before you bring the crown prince of the Silverback into my house."

Bane shot a glare at him. "Crown prince my ass."

"Please," Jenner grunted. "Young, pretty and cocky. He's got hereditary werewolf written all over him, and you know as well as I do that with the Silverback, that equals power."

Bane stopped and shoved a hand through his unruly hair, looking as though he was praying to the ceiling for guidance. "Not everyone works the way we do, Jenner. Kenyon is going to be the Alpha one day. He seems like a reasonable, thoughtful man."

"I bet he spends an hour in the bathroom every morning doing his hair."

Bane's lips quirked. "Maybe. But I would rather not start a war with him, and potentially his whole pack, just because you decide you don't want him touching your stuff. Which, by the way, Mia D'Alessandro is *not*."

"Didn't say she was," Jenner muttered as Bane resumed pacing.

"You didn't have to say it," Bane replied. "I think the growling did that for you."

Uncomfortable as he recalled that particular (and satisfying) moment of weakness, Jenner lifted a hand to rub at the tense cords of muscle that joined his neck and shoulder and sighed. What was he supposed to say? "Okay," he finally allowed, "I growled. Look, you saw the way he looked at her right when he walked in here. Mia had a hell of a night, she's finding out that she can't go back to her life the way it was before, and she's got a psycho after her who's planning to either rape or kill her. The last thing she needs is some smarmy Alpha-in-waiting trying to put the moves on her." *Or some jackass non-Alpha with impulse control problems,* he thought, then pushed it quickly from his mind. That wasn't going to happen again.

For both their sakes now, it couldn't.

Bane was looking at him, his dark eyes shrewd. "That's a noble thought, Jenner. And I think you mean it on some level. But I also know you. Loyal as you are, you don't put yourself out for just anyone." He looked out the window at the fiery trees, pensive. "You know the rules. Gaines was one of the Silverback. They cut him loose, and he bit Mia. If they want to force the issue about where she belongs, they very well can."

"We found her," Jenner pointed out. "Our men saved her. That should make her one of us."

Bane shook his head. "I know you don't want to hear it, but Kenyon Chase wants her. It's pretty obvious."

Anger, and some other, even darker emotion, reared its ugly head. The hairs on the back of Jenner's neck prickled to attention. "This isn't the Dark Ages, Bane, and those are some old rules you're talking about invoking. Mia's stronger than she looks. She got through last night and she hasn't come close to breaking yet. You think she's going to take it if the Silverback tell her she's got to take one of them, no choice?"

Bane's gaze was piercing. "You know very well there are ways around that. If I tell our men to back off, let Kenyon court her or whatever he's got in mind, she'll never think twice about the possibility that she had anything less than free choice."

Jenner curled his lip and turned his head, hating this conversation. "Don't you think she's been manipulated enough?"

A pause, then a heavy sigh. "Look, Jenner," Bane said. "I get that this is a sore spot with you. You're entitled. But you've got to separate this from what happened with you and Tess. It's been years."

Jenner's head snapped around. It was all he could do not to bare his teeth, an action that would have been a grave mistake. Bane was a fair man, but he didn't tolerate disrespect.

"This has nothing to do with Tess," he managed to grit out.

"Sure it does. She was one of the most manipulative women I've ever known. I hate to think what would have happened if you hadn't finally seen through her, Jenner."

Jenner exhaled loudly. He hated talking about it, even though it had been years. Sometimes he thought he should have known so he could have stopped her sooner. Other times he wondered if he might have been able to save her instead of—

"No, quit it. I can see the pity party starting, and you should be way past that. The Shadowkin hunt us, we hunt them. If a wolf heads to their side, it means either their death, or all of ours. You did the right thing." Bane's tone brooked no argument, and Jenner knew he was right on some level. Most levels, even.

"Yeah, I try to look at it that way," Jenner said with a small shrug, an attempt to cover how strongly he felt about it. "Would be easier if I didn't think there was still some part of her in there that wanted to stop and do the right thing, even at the end."

"It would have been a small part, because she never did. She caused the deaths of some good wolves, Jenner. Don't do them the disservice of forgetting."

"You know I wouldn't," Jenner replied flatly, his temper prickling again. "Now if you're finished lecturing me about old news, again, I'm sure you can think of someone more interesting to bother. You want to let Chase paw at a feral victim because of some archaic notion of property rights? Go for it…on your own watch. While I'm keeping track of her, it isn't going to happen."

Bane's eyes flashed, and Jenner knew the man well enough to realize that the long, slow exhalation that followed was an attempt to refrain from shouting. Jenner had to fight back a smirk, despite his anger. It took a lot to get Bane to this point, but he'd always been pretty good at it.

"Would it kill you to follow the rules on this, Jenner? Mia's not attached to any of us. What does it matter which pack she ends up in? Letting Kenyon at least try to get in her good graces doesn't do any harm. If she rejects him, so be it. But stepping back will keep the peace. Besides, I can't think of any Blackpaw who's seriously in the market for a mate right now. I'm sure as hell not." He paused, lifting one black eyebrow. "Or maybe you are."

"Of course I'm not," Jenner muttered. "I like my life the way it is." And he did. So why was this so important to him? Why was the thought of her with someone else so unconscionable? Imagining Mia alone with Chase had his nails lengthening, sharpening, and digging into the arms of his chair.

Bane prowled over to perch on one of the arms of the couch. His gaze was piercing, and saw far too much. "You seem awfully invested in this woman."

Jenner felt his shoulders trying to hunch defensively, and fought it. "No."

"You've known her for one night," Bane continued, speaking as though he hadn't heard Jenner's denial, "and you're arguing to keep her for the pack, not to mention getting in a high-ranking Silverback's face when he takes an interest in her. That looks like you've taken quite an interest to me. If you want to challenge for her..."

"I *don't*," Jenner growled, and now his shoulders did hunch. "Not liking the idea of setting her up to feel a certain way doesn't mean *I* want her. Jesus. You know me better than that, Bane."

"Uh-huh." Bane watched him curiously, as though Jenner had suddenly become a part of a particularly riveting circus sideshow. "Thought I did, anyway. But this breakfast-serving, warm and fuzzy side of you is something new."

"Bite me."

Bane snorted. "You know, normally I'd enjoy giving you a rough time about this. But you keep acting like a possessive mate around Mia, you *are* going to have a fight on your hands. Kenyon will challenge you for her outright."

Jenner glowered, hating Bane's habit of cutting straight to the heart of an issue with a minimum of finesse. "That would be a mistake. I'd beat his ass."

"Of course you would. You're the frigging Blackpaw Lunari. But you beating his ass would create some... diplomatic issues." Bane's eyes were not unsympathetic, but Jenner knew that sentiment had no place in this. Jenner was almost certain that Bane would back him if having Mia were that important to him, despite the strain it might create for a time between packs. But Jenner had no intention of creating a situation there.

If Mia took a shine to Kenyon Chase's particular lack of charm, that was.

Which meant that right now, he had no answers for Bane. No good ones, anyway.

"She trusts me," Jenner finally said. "I'd prefer to be worthy of it."

A slight smile touched Bane's lips, not mocking, but genuine. "You are, Jenner," he said. "I wouldn't like you half as much as I do if you didn't have a raging justice complex. No one's going to make Mia do anything she doesn't want to do, or steer her in a direction that would cause her further harm."

"But you still want to steer her."

Bane chuckled. "Sure. But it remains to be seen if she's steerable. Hopefully she isn't anything like you."

The two men grinned at one another, and Jenner felt a few of the knots he'd tied himself into relax and unwind. They were all right again. It was important to him. More important, Jenner reminded himself, than the unknown feelings of a woman who was little more than a stranger. And he needed to remember that the next time he thought about beating up the Silverback's Alpha-in-waiting.

"Okay. She stays here, then. Not like you were going to listen to me if I said otherwise anyway, but I'll defer," Bane said.

Jenner managed a half smile.

"For what it's worth, I won't try and scratch any itches I might have with Mia. Apart from the pretty package, she's not my type. I won't have anyone harassing her, but if she decides to give Chase a shot, she can have him. Just don't expect me to play nice with him, and we're good."

Bane looked relieved.

Jenner got to his feet, taking great care to keep his thoughts shielded behind a wall of casual, superficial amusement. He could feel Bane in his head. Once, it might have offended him. Now, he understood it as just a necessary caution taken by an Alpha who didn't want trouble outside of what he was normally saddled with. So Jenner blocked him out, though not without considerable effort. After a moment, the probing sensation vanished.

"All right, then. I'm guessing the Silverback contingent will show up before long," Bane said. "The numbers will help us cover more ground tonight after…well, after. Maybe next time Mia can give us a better picture of where Gaines is hiding. Though I'm not sure anymore that it'll be much help. A feral who's been exiled from a pack is different than one who went through the change alone." His lips thinned as he looked away. "He's going to be a lot better at hiding."

"We'll catch him," Jenner said, feeling the truth in it. The Blackpaw didn't lose. *He* didn't lose. As he thought it, the memory of Mia's pale, shell-shocked face arose in his mind. The bastard who'd hurt her wasn't going to get away with it. He'd make sure of that. Still, one thing Mia had said continued to trouble him.

"Bane," he said. "What Mia saw today…the red eyes, and the cold…it reminds me a hell of a lot of before."

How many times had he heard Tess talking in her sleep about the cold, and some terrible, unseen gaze? The bewildered shame of it rushed back to him, as fresh as though his emotions from that awful day had been preserved in amber in his memory. He should have known…but he had been only a hunter then, not Lunari, and unaware of the full extent of what the Shadowkin could do to corrupt a person. Jeff Gaines being insane didn't mean he didn't know what he was doing. He'd targeted Mia for a reason—whether or not he was right about her almost didn't matter. She was in danger either way. Except…

Bane pressed his lips together and nodded. "Yes. And no. The vision might be the same, Jenner, but the woman in the middle is very different."

"She knows more than she's saying," Jenner said quietly, glancing toward the door.

"Probably. But she also doesn't know us. Not yet. Give her time before you pass judgment."

Jenner gave a curt nod, but quietly, he wasn't sure they *had* time. What if the Shadowkin had already gotten to her, gotten inside…he would have to do his job. Again.

A chill like ice washed over his skin as he imagined his hands around a woman's throat, her eyes full of unearthly fire. Tess's eyes. Mia's eyes.

God, he hoped not. He didn't ever want to have to do that again. But it was one more good reason to keep his emotions all the way out of this thing with Mia. He would do his duty. Nothing more, nothing less.

He would never open himself up to pain like that again.

"You remember the signs, Jenner, better than anyone," Bane said, surprising Jenner with the weight of his hand on his shoulder. "You'll know."

Jenner nodded, grim.

"I'll know."

Chapter 8

Mia rode shotgun in the pickup on the way to dinner, trying to study Jenner without looking like she was doing it. She was looking for some sign, some faint and barely detectable sign, that he realized he had a living, breathing human in the truck with him. Unfortunately, Jenner was inscrutable, driving with his eyes straight ahead, both hands on the wheel. He was as silent as a ghost.

He'd been that way all afternoon, and it was slowly driving Mia out of her mind.

He'd surprised her with the news that she'd be staying with him for the time being. Surprised and, truth be told, a little dismayed. She needed to be clear-headed about what was happening. Being around Jenner was not exactly conducive to that state of mind.

"Where are we going again?" she asked absently, more to break the oppressive and continuing silence than out of true curiosity. She didn't really mind finding out when they got there, mainly because she was too hungry to be picky.

There was a barely intelligible grunt given as a response. At least he'd wanted to get out of the house, even though the decision had only been made after he'd stood in his nearly bare pantry for a good ten minutes trying to figure out an expedient way to feed her. Mia was glad that some things about single men seemed to be universal, and that the tendency to only have beer and junk food on hand was one of them. Hopefully, getting out in town would ease this unpleasant tightness in her chest.

Or at least, she could find more things to distract herself from it. With one more glance at Jenner's stony profile, his eyes fixed on the road ahead of them, Mia sighed and turned her attention to another problem on what was shaping up to be a long list of them. Tomorrow, Sunday, she was going to have to start unraveling the threads of this mess, beginning with giving herself cover for staying here for at least the week. It didn't seem like Jenner and his buddies would accept anything less, and she was still too short on knowledge about this werewolf thing to comfortably skip town. Unfortunately, it looked like her banked vacation days were going to take a serious hit.

The thought made her sick to her stomach, which gave her an idea.

"Stomach flu," she muttered.

"What?" Jenner looked sharply at her.

She looked over at him, at the sudden concern stamped onto his bold, handsome features, with a sort of rueful amusement. Nothing like the mention of vomit-inducing germs to get a guy's attention. Especially when the guy in question was taking you to dinner.

Those sparks her temper had been shooting off started to catch.

"Oh," Mia said, careful to keep her tone impassive. "Are we speaking again? I was trying to figure out a plausible excuse for being out of work all this coming week. Because otherwise, I'm going to get fired."

He turned his eyes back to the road, but not before she saw a hint of guilt in his expression. It wasn't nearly as satisfying as she'd hoped. But at least her comment had broken through Jenner's silent brooding. She wished she wanted to do more than snarl at him now that it had, but an afternoon of being made to feel like a perpetrator instead of a victim had taken its toll. And to make matters worse, Jenner didn't appear to understand her frustration.

"We did talk about the job thing, Mia," he said without looking at her, sounding as though he was lecturing a difficult child. "You're not going to want to stay alone in the city after...all of this. And what do you mean, are we speaking again? I didn't think we'd stopped."

Mia slowly tucked a lock of hair behind her ear, inhaling deeply. The anger reared its head before she could talk herself out of it, before she could silence it.

The speed with which her mood went from irritable to furious would have shocked her, if she'd been able to do more than cruise on the dark fire that flooded her system at Jenner's words. Everything she'd been put through since last night, the betrayal, the violence, and then the havoc Jenner's very existence seemed to play with her emotions, coalesced into a singular fury and directed itself at the nearest available target.

She struggled to get out the words in something less than a shout.

"What I mean," she said, her voice quavering only slightly with the effort, "is that ever since you kissed me earlier and then took off, you've barely said two words to me. Since I didn't throw myself at you, and since I'm assuming you helped decide to keep me at your house until this mess is worked out, it would be great if you could stop treating me like I've got the *plague*."

There was a moment of silence that stretched out painfully. Finally, Jenner managed one word.

"Oh."

That single word burned right through her. Especially because Jenner didn't seem inclined to immediately add to it. It wasn't like her to let her emotions get the better of her. But there was something more, something unfamiliar fanning her feelings like a prairie fire in a high wind.

"Oh?" Mia snapped. "That's it? You kiss me senseless, take off, pretend it never happened, and when I call you on it all you can say is *oh?*"

Jenner slid a sidelong glance at her, a slight frown marring his brow.

"I'm trying to figure out what to say about it that isn't going to make me sound like an ass. I didn't realize it had pissed you off so badly."

"You didn't realize…"

Mia repeated those words in astonishment, trying to calm herself down a little. But…he hadn't known? Did he think she just wouldn't *care?* Her skin tingled, her pulse quickened. And still, the emotional tsunami inside her continued to build. All she could do was ride the building wave.

The world suddenly seemed too bright, every tiny detail standing out in sharp relief. Sensory input, far too much of it, crashed into her system. All she had to cling to was the anger. When she finally managed to reply to him, her teeth felt strange in her mouth. Sharp.

Somehow, she still had the strength to suppress the urge to bite. Barely.

"You don't know what to say about it? How about either, Mia, I'm interested in you and would like to do that again sometime, or Mia, it was a big mistake and we should probably forget about it. There. Two ready-made options. Pick one. Just stop ignoring me as though I've done something *wrong!*"

Her voice had thickened and changed somehow, her words coming out in a roughened, growly version of her normal voice. Jenner gave her another look, and Mia noted that a lot of the color seemed to have left Jenner's face.

"Mia, you're going to want to take a few deep breaths. It's okay."

Now she did bare her teeth at him. "No! It's not okay! Don't you think I have enough to deal with without you playing with me? The kiss, the theatrics with Kenyon, pretending to be concerned…what, you figure you can string me along just enough so that I'll let you take me to bed on behalf of the pack? I'm good enough for a quick screw, but too pathetic to get really interested in, right?"

Even as the words poured from her mouth, some still-sane part of her recoiled in horror from what she was saying, from the fact that she was giving voice to her deepest insecurities and darkest suspicions even though she knew they were probably unfounded and almost certainly unfair to both of them. But she felt like she was catching fire inside and out. All she had was fear and fury, and Mia was helpless in the face of them.

Through a reddish haze, she could see that Jenner looked appalled. "Mia, calm down, seriously, you're going to—"

"Don't tell me that!" Mia snarled. "I don't even know you!" The heat beneath her skin had spread all over her body and was becoming unbearable. There was a terrible itching. Her canines lengthened to become dagger sharp, and she had a wild urge to snap at Jenner. She growled, straining against the seatbelt. Rational thought vanished, and for just an instant she forgot there was such a creature as Mia.

There was only beast.

Her head fell back as she fought back to some semblance of human thought, but her grasp was slipping already. She wanted to run, to claw...to *howl*. Her heart galloped in her chest. Jenner's scent filled her senses, and she could hear another thundering rhythm, catching up to and then matching her own. It was his heart, Mia thought, stunned in the small part of her mind that hadn't been consumed by this inner storm. She could hear his heart...how was that possible? The sound of it was a drumbeat in her head. And she wanted...she wanted...

Jenner's voice was more urgent now, and full of concern she didn't want to hear. The fury came from nowhere, was everywhere. How dare he be concerned about her? How *dare* he? If he cared, he would put his hands on her...take her...join with her...

Or you could just drink his blood, suggested a new, sinister voice that whispered through her mind. *Open his throat, open all their throats, turn the forest red with wolf blood and open the doors to me, to us, open them wide...*

"Mia—"

A sharp bolt of pain sliced right through the center of her, blinding white in its intensity. Mia threw her head back, her cry that of a wounded animal. She arched sharply in the seat, stiffening as though she had an electric current running through her body. Finally, the rational part of her mind managed to get a word in, strained though it was. For a moment, fear had the upper hand, allowing her to speak.

"Help…it hurts…" she gasped.

"Damn it. Hang on."

She barely registered it when he pulled the truck over to the side of the road, slammed the shifter into Park, and then ripped off his seatbelt. Another wave of pain crashed through her, and she only dimly felt Jenner drag her into his arms.

At the contact, so intimate as Jenner wrapped himself around her, the storm within her fell instantly silent. It was the strangest thing: one second, she'd been a human hurricane. The next, she had gone limp and shaking against Jenner, her body slicked with cold sweat. Wrung out and wanting nothing more than the comfort of the warm buzz their physical connection created within her, Mia clung to him. Unthinking, Mia nuzzled into Jenner, wanting nothing more than to get as close as she could. She was shivering uncontrollably, her heart fluttering like a panicked bird inside her chest.

"Shhh," Jenner soothed her, and she felt his hand rubbing gentle circles into her back. "Just breathe, Mia. Just breathe."

"Trying," she gasped out. Her teeth began to chatter as heat became bone-chilling cold. Her head was still full of the sound of her own thundering heart. But beneath it, she could still hear the sound of Jenner's, slowing, calming. Mia focused on it, willing her own heartbeat to match it. The response was quick, both a surprise and a relief, as its frightened and erratic rhythm slowed and steadied. Then there was only one sound, one soothing drumbeat, neither heart distinguishable from the other. For the moment, the strangeness of it was secondary to Mia's relief at being able to speak and think like normal again.

Then, it was just her, curled into the lap of an utterly inappropriate man. But the memory of that sinister voice, not Jeff's but someone or something *other* in her mind, kept her there even when she knew she should let him go.

"Wh-what was that? What happened to me?" she asked.

His voice rumbled against her ear through his chest. "I'd say you were pretty pissed at me."

She would have laughed, but she didn't seem to have any laughter in her. "I've g-got a t-t-temper, Jenner," she said, shaking. "But not like that. Tell me the truth. What just happened?"

The soothing circles he was making on her back continued, lulling Mia. His voice was contemplative, without a hint of the fear that had all but consumed her. That helped, even if his words didn't.

"Getting angry tends to wake up a person's wolf side," he said. "I should have warned you. If you're not expecting it, and don't know how to control it, you can throw yourself into a shapeshift without meaning to. If nothing else, now you probably understand a little why it's so important to have the support of your pack when all of that instinct and power wells up, trying to get out."

Then she did hear concern creep into his voice, and it went a long way toward healing whatever residual bad feelings were left over from her raging at him.

"You damn near just turned into a wolf in my truck. And if you had, I wouldn't have been able to reach you. No one would. If you change, with no pack, even if it's before the full moon, it'll break you. That's it."

"Oh, God."

"It's not going to happen. Now that you know what's at stake, I know you won't let it. It's all right."

She didn't really feel like it was. Not at all. But Jenner's faith in her, however unwarranted it might be, soothed her.

"I'm so sorry," Mia said. "I really was upset, but that was kind of...beyond."

"You're telling me. I've never made a woman so angry she turned into a wild animal."

Mia shivered and kept her head tucked against Jenner's chest, more out of mortification now even though Jenner had sounded slightly amused. The waves of cold that wracked her body were ebbing, replaced by nothing but a liquid warmth that seemed to flow like water from Jenner into her. It felt wonderful, even if nothing else about the situation did.

"There's a first time for everything," she said, and was slightly mollified to hear the deep rumble of Jenner's laughter. "It hurt," she said more softly. That was something she hadn't understood. Hadn't counted on. His voice softened.

"Only the first time. Your body hasn't done it before. After that, it's much, much better. Gets to be as natural as breathing. Trust me."

Her anger seemed to have burned up in whatever her

now-treacherous body had just tried to do to her. The shadows of her hurt, however, remained.

"I'd like to trust you," she said. "But you're not exactly making it easy."

He was quiet for a time, continuing to rub her back. She knew she should stop him, but couldn't quite make herself. With her immediate terror gone, she could feel the life pulsing in his veins, could already begin to hear the singular song that was Jenner's in her mind. She wanted to spread her hands against his bare skin, to let the dark song of her blood mingle with his, the way she'd always imagined she might be able to with a man. Even her grandmother's most dire warnings had never stopped her from dreaming of it. The magic would bind them, body and soul…and he would know what she was. Or at least, he would know she was much more than a newly minted werewolf.

It would probably send him running as far and fast as he could, Mia knew. So she kept her hands curled loosely into themselves.

Finally, Jenner said, "You can trust me, Mia. I won't hurt you. And I didn't say anything about what happened this morning because I guess I didn't know what to say about it. Not that you'd know it, but I'm not normally one to take advantage like that."

"You weren't taking advantage," she admitted. "I wanted it, too."

She felt him tense against her, and knew she'd somehow said the wrong thing. It was amazing, how quickly all that lovely warmth could become a sick feeling in the pit of her stomach. She heard his sigh, and knew their moment was over.

"I think you'd better get situated again," Jenner said, gently easing her away from him. "There are a couple of things I need to tell you, and this isn't the best way to do it."

Mia went, though every inch of her body seemed to protest at being taken away from him. She climbed back into the passenger side, buckled herself in, and took a quick look at where they were parked. Jenner had pulled to the side of the road in a pretty, residential neighborhood, where well-kept saltbox houses lined the streets. A pretty blonde woman jogged by the truck, giving it a curious look. When she saw Jenner, there was a bright smile of recognition, and she gave a wave as she passed them. Jenner raised a hand in greeting as well, and Mia wondered how much gossip they'd just managed to create. After all, no one here knew her. Yet, at least.

Mia took a deep breath, trying to prepare herself for what she knew would be an unpleasant discussion. "Okay," she finally said. "What do you need to tell me?"

He frowned at the steering wheel, collecting his thoughts, she supposed. Her initial impression of Jenner, of a deep pool that was only calm on the surface, hadn't left her. Mia couldn't help but wonder about what went on beneath the quiet, watchful façade.

Finally, he spoke.

"No matter how you feel about this morning, I take responsibility for it. Because the fact is, I should know better. I'm not...there's no possibility of anything happening between you and me. I'm sorry, Mia. I know I gave you the wrong idea. That's on me."

Mia watched him and tried not to be hurt, though the words twisted in her gut like a knife. It was for the best, she told herself. So much easier to protect her secrets when there was no one very interested in prying. Still, to be rejected the one time she'd allowed herself to let go, even a little, was a wound far deeper than she'd expected it might be.

"Okay. Fair enough. And I guess I appreciate your honestly," Mia said carefully. "But, I mean, what is it? Was the kiss that bad?" She was a little afraid of the answer…but she wanted to know.

Jenner gave a short, sharp bark of laughter that had no humor in it at all. "No," he said. "No, believe me, that is *not* the problem." From the heat in the quick look he gave her, Mia was inclined to believe him. It made her feel slightly better, though she was as confused as ever.

"Then what? Girlfriend? Wife?" she guessed, barely choking out the last word. Jenner seemed to find the idea of it just as awful as she did, though she wasn't actually sure that was a good thing overall.

"Uh, no. None of the above. And that's the thing, Mia. I plan on keeping it that way. My position in the pack is powerful, and pretty damned dangerous. I hunt things that humans don't know exist, things that would destroy everything my pack has built and then some. It's not the kind of job that lends itself to a stable home life, so I like to keep things simple." When he turned his head to look at her again, his golden eyes were guarded, inscrutable. "More than that, I've tried the relationship thing. I don't want to get into it, because it's long ago over and done. But you'll have to trust me when I say I'm not cut out for that kind of thing. Some wolves never take a lifemate. I'll be one of them."

Mia saw the grim resolve stamped clearly on his handsome face, and felt a shiver of fear. She no longer wondered what a Lunari did. On some level, maybe she'd known all along. The connection between them was so strong, Mia couldn't muster much surprise that there would be this sort of tie as well. It should have been a comfort, that fate had brought her to a man who hunted the things that would seek to harm her. But her gifts made her vulnerable, attractive to the darkness that lurked at the periphery of the human world. And Jeff's bite had opened a crack through which those things had begun to whisper, somehow.

Jenner would understand about shadows after all. Just as he would understand that she was a perfect vehicle for them to destroy everything he cared about.

Mia would have shaken her fists at the heavens, if she'd thought it would do any good. As it was, all she could do was try to accept things as they were. Wretched and impossible, as usual. She sighed softly as she buckled herself back into her seat, watching Jenner put the truck back in gear and pull back onto the road. Connection or no, this wasn't going to work. Jenner wasn't interested—or not interested enough to cross the boundaries he'd set for himself long before she got here.

It was better to know, she told herself. It was almost always better to know.

Even if it didn't feel that way right now.

"I'm going to assume this means you're not going to be involved with my initiation," Mia said, surprised to hear the words falling from her own lips. It wasn't like her to be so blunt. But then, recent events had left her without a lot of room to dance around things. Everything right now was important.

As she'd expected, Jenner shook his head.

"It wouldn't be a good idea. For either of us. Don't worry, though," he said gently. "It might be awkward, but the situation could be a lot worse. There's a Silverback contingent that's coming in to help us catch Gaines. You won't lack for candidates, and trust me, any man you choose will be honored."

The strangeness of Jenner trying to make her feel better about the situation was momentarily outweighed by her surprise.

"I thought I would be joining the Blackpaw."

Jenner kept his eyes on the road. "Well. Since Gaines was a Silverback, they'd technically be responsible for you. But you were here when it happened, and nobody's going to push it. It's completely your decision."

Very sensible. Inexplicably infuriating. Mia couldn't think of anything to say to it, so she chose silent brooding instead. *Her* decision? That was a joke. She had fallen victim to one of the oldest rules in the book, best articulated by the Stones: "You can't always get what you want."

The solution, of course, was to stop wanting him. But that was unlikely to happen if she didn't start thinking of him as a potential friend instead of a potential lover, and if she didn't find some other werewolf to focus her attention on.

Mia watched, only half paying attention, as they turned onto the Hollow's old-fashioned square. She let the prettiness of it distract her from wallowing, admiring the way even new buildings had been styled to match the old, wondering what sorts of fun little dustcatchers she might find to buy behind the gleaming windows of the little shops. Even in the truck with the windows up, she could pick up the mouthwatering scents drifting from the few mom-and-pop restaurants littering the square. She hadn't been imagining how strong breakfast had smelled this morning, she realized. Her nose really was substantially more sensitive. Her stomach growled its agreement.

Idly, she wondered if werewolf females gained something akin to the Freshman Fifteen. God, she hoped not.

Jenner pulled into an open space in front of a squat brick expanse of the square. Directly in front of them was a scatter of wrought iron tables, and beyond those, a restaurant over which was mounted a brightly painted sign that read Jana's Cupboard. Mia could see that the place was bustling.

"Here we are," Jenner said. He reached to turn off the ignition, but his hand stilled just before he closed his fingers around the key. He looked at Mia, and she could see he was struggling with something he wanted to say to her. She waited, and finally, he got it out.

"Look. We haven't exactly gotten off on the right foot, you and me."

Oh, hell. He was going to apologize. If there had been any wind left in her sails, this would have taken care of it. She'd suspected it as soon as he'd caught her in his arms last night, and now, despite everything else, she knew: Nick Jenner had a heart. Probably a fairly big one. And now he was going to unwittingly torture her with this revelation, since that heart was forever off limits to her. That it was also off limits to everyone else was beside the point.

Desperate to keep him from revealing anything else endearing about himself, Mia put her hand in front of her, gesturing him to stop.

"Don't worry about it," she said, hoping she sounded convincing. "We're good. Consider this a fresh start. Truce over…" She sniffed the air, and her eyes nearly rolled back into her head with pleasure. "Homemade spaghetti. God."

Jenner didn't look entirely convinced. "You're sure?"

No, she wasn't sure. Not about her anger, but about her ability to control her reactions to him. A single day wasn't enough time to develop much past lust. And yet she couldn't shake the feeling that Jenner could be far more important to her, was already far more important, than a simple object of desire. She had felt his heart pounding in her own veins, had heard his blood calling to hers.

Then take it, whispered that awful, seductive voice. *Take his blood and join with us...*

Inwardly, she recoiled. On the outside, she smiled as reassuringly as she could manage. "You stopped me from chewing up the upholstery in your truck. That alone earns you a do-over. Okay?"

He smiled back, but it quickly faded. His eyes were deadly serious. "I'm not good for much, and I'll definitely piss you off again," he said. "But you can trust me to protect you, Mia. If nothing else, I can give you my word on that. Gaines is dangerous, I won't lie."

Slowly, she nodded. "I know," she said.

"And I'm even more dangerous." She saw it then. He let her see it, the raw power, the hunger and instinct swirling in the depths of eyes that glowed like embers. But instead of feeling fear, the way she had when she'd seen what lurked inside of Jeff, Mia felt something completely unexpected: raw desire.

"You're safe with me," Jenner said, even as the blaze of his eyes faded to what passed for normal once again. "Okay?"

"Okay," she said. But as he slipped out of the truck with the same animal grace he did even the most mundane things with, Mia was anything but okay. It had nothing to do with Jeff Gaines, and everything to do with the surly, difficult, and entirely honorable man who'd sworn to protect her.

She wanted him. Badly.

And she had begun to fear that her desire might make her the most dangerous creature of all.

Chapter 9

She was all Jeff could think of, when he could think at all. But those moments seemed to be getting fewer and farther between, interspersed with lengthy periods of grey where he had some vague sense of moving from place to place, going through the motions of living while grappling with a terrible, fathomless hunger that increasingly threatened to consume him.

In his more lucid moments, Jeff sometimes thought he'd been a fool to take the deal the shadow had offered him. But it was far too late to go back now. All he could do was hope that the Shadowkin held up their end... and that Mia's blood truly was the key to everything he'd ever wanted. It was a shame he'd have to kill her to get it. But at this point, his trail had a high enough body count that it would hardly be his worst transgression. And he could no longer afford to indulge his conscience, if there was anything left of it.

Jeff Gaines lay curled on a dirty little cot, sweating and shivering with fever. All he could think of was getting Mia back. That, and destroying the wolves who'd dared lay a finger on her, who had taken away what was his. It was supposed to be over by now. All he'd been through, all he had yet to go through, and the key to it all was gone.

He'd ruined it all. The way he could always be counted on to ruin whatever he touched.

Stupid, the old familiar voice whispered in his head. *Worthless. Pathetic. Is it really any surprise?*

Jeff closed his eyes and willed that voice away. His father, the miserable old bastard, had been dead five years now. His voice, however, the voice of all Jeff's deepest fears and disappointments, had remained, unwanted but unyielding. The good news was that it now tended only to manifest when he was at his lowest points, the moments when he was hanging on to all his hard won control by what seemed like a gossamer thread.

The bad news was that this was one of the most important weeks of his life, and his father's disapproving baritone was trumpeting away in all its full-throated glory. If he couldn't get a handle on himself, and soon, this did not bode well. Not at all.

"You all right, Jeff?" Pete Burns, a burly ex-con whose interesting array of violent freelance work had drawn Jeff's attention over a year ago, cracked open the bedroom door and eyed him warily.

"Sick," Jeff growled. "Probably something I ate. Need to sleep a little so it can pass."

The mention of illness was all it took to send Pete running. "You got it," he said, and vanished, pulling the door shut behind him and filling Jeff with a relief he knew couldn't last. Burns and the four others he'd helped recruit were all bunking at the cabin now, restless and waiting for their orders. They had been promised supernatural strength, incredible power…and Jeff knew that if he didn't start delivering, there would be trouble. They were no match for his strength, of course. Not yet. But if he killed them, there was an ever increasing chance that he would leave evidence. That he would forget something important. Hell, who was he kidding? Lately, it wasn't just a chance, it was a likelihood. He didn't need the police after him. There had been too many slips in the last few years, and the cops might put two and two together.

Even before he'd found a woman stupid enough to turn him into one of the beasts he'd been fascinated with since his youth, there had been an animal inside of him, always fighting to get out. The shadows had known, though. On his many lonely childhood treks into the woods, they had become his constant companions, first playful and cajoling at first, then more demanding as he got older. They'd told him where to find the Silverback bitch, how to ingratiate himself. Just as they'd told him when it was time to go.

When he'd wormed his way into the Silverback, where his money and his background had made him instantly acceptable, he'd had no idea just how far removed from his fantasies these modern werewolves were. So cautious. So concerned about being discovered, when it was humanity who should still be fearing *them*. The Shadowkin had been right, about everything. He would help bring a return to the darkness, a return to the chaos the wolves had once thrived on. And in return, his own tortured soul would be set free, transformed yet again and reborn in a shower of blood.

That was, if he could hold it together long enough to get Mia back from these pathetic Blackpaw. The Silverback were beginning to arrive, too, though he was less worried about them. Tomas was weak, an ineffectual leader who had neutered his own power. Jeff was standing here because of it. He'd made a mistake in the way he'd left, had only barely restrained himself from tearing out the older wolf's throat in front of his fawning sycophants, knowing he would be merely exiled. But if Tomas tried to deal with him one on one, the Silverback Alpha would get a very nasty surprise.

Silverback. The memory of their faces, of the friendships he'd had to play at with them, had his claws biting into his palms as Jeff curled more tightly into himself. The Silverback were, by and large, soft and lazy. Entitled, by virtue of their pedigrees. Having grown up in the human equivalent of that world, he knew and understood the type. Not these Blackpaw, though. Of all the stupid places he could have stumbled into, this was one of the worst. He hadn't paid enough attention to territorial boundaries, to the homes of the other wolf packs, during his short time as a Silverback. He'd been thinking secluded…not *this*.

The door to the bedroom slammed open so hard that it bounced against the wall, and a man with a lean, hungry look about him rushed in, his thin face flushed from exertion and excitement.

"I know where she is!"

Jeff didn't think. He moved on pure instinct, raw emotion. In a swift series of movements he had landed in front of the newcomer, grabbed him by the front of the shirt, and lifted him off his feet to glare directly into his face, all before the man could do more than blink.

"Where?" Jeff snarled. "Where is she?"

Sy Wicks dangled helplessly from his fingertips, staring wide-eyed. It occurred to Jeff a little too late that such a display might be counterproductive. But then again, a little fear, in his experience, tended to go a long way.

"Caught sight of her in a truck downtown…big guy brought her, dangerous looking. A g-guard. They had dinner, then left. I followed them. She's…she's at his house. Outside of town, in the woods. She must be staying there."

Sy's voice was rushed, gasping. When he was finished, he simply hung there, looking pleadingly at Jeff. Slowly, and after taking a moment to suppress the urge to hurl the man across the room, Jeff lowered Sy's feet back to the floor and let go. No violence. Not yet. And not until he had the proper outlet for his rage.

He couldn't afford any more mistakes.

"One guard," Jeff said, a terrible smile slowly spreading across his face. Sy took a step back, while Pete watched warily from his position on the couch. Jeff didn't care. One guard? Pathetic. Taking Mia back would be easy. And it had to be her. He'd known from the moment he saw her, felt the magic shimmering around her. She was too stupid to realize the power she had, but that stupidity was to his benefit. Mia would have her useful moment, whether or not she ever realized the true extent of what she was. The possibilities inherent in what he had made her, if only for a short time. Jeff felt an unexpected pang as he imagined her face, beautiful, irresistibly genuine, her interest in him real in a way he'd only rarely experienced. Unnerved, he pushed it aside. Caring about a woman whose only true use was as a tool was more than ill-advised.

It was sloppy.

He could not abide sloppy work. If his cold bastard of a father had given him nothing else, he'd given him an appreciation for meticulousness. Of course, the old man hadn't done any of that hard work himself. He'd inherited the family fortune, and then set about letting the world at large know that nothing, and no one, would ever be up to his high standards.

The thought of his father set off another shooting pain in his head. Jeff winced, and had to fight not to stagger as he moved farther into the common area of the little camp. He needed to be alone again, in the dark. To hear the soothing voices of the shadows…his kind.

"That's great news, but it's not worth anything before sunset. Until then, I need to rest," Jeff said. "It's been a long couple of days, and I'm not…feeling myself. When I get up, we'll talk strategy."

He didn't miss the look Sy and Pete shared. He knew that look. It was one he'd seen on the faces of many through his life, friends, teachers, his own parents, before he'd learned to hide what was festering beneath. But it would all be fixed soon, cured.

Finally, he was making his own destiny.

Chapter 10

"Ha! Take that, you lying bastard!"

Mia grinned, pressed a button, and watched as her character, a badass elven warrior chick who carried a sword as tall as she was, spun gracefully and made a traitorous enemy explode onscreen. The euphoria, however, was short-lived. For as delighted as she'd been to discover that Jenner had stashed a copy of *Reckoning of Kings* behind his sports and racing games, nothing could distract her from her present situation for long. She was in an unfamiliar house, facing an uncertain future…and playing a video game.

It was something to do, but it didn't feel all that productive, exploding bad guys notwithstanding. Of course, she didn't exactly know what she should be doing, since her self-proclaimed protector was AWOL. *Again.*

Mia shut off the game and the television, then wandered to the front windows to look out, wondering what Jenner did in his garage that was so incredibly interesting. It certainly kept him occupied. He'd been out there all morning.

He'd been as good as his word about keeping her safe. A quick phone call to Bane from the restaurant had spared her having to try and link to Jeff again last night. Considering what had happened in the truck, Jenner figured that was enough for one night, and he'd been right, even though she hadn't wanted to admit it. It had sounded like the Silverback arriving were causing Bane enough headaches anyway.

So she'd had a pleasant evening instead of a terrifying one. But Jenner had been as good as his word on another important count too—he hadn't tried to touch her again.

And the more he kept his hands to himself, the more she wished he wouldn't. No amount of slaying virtual bad guys seemed to make that any better.

Mia paced the room and fiddled with her phone, which remained obstinately silent. The few friends she'd allowed into her life thought she was away on a romantic weekend, and she was in-between design jobs so there was no one to pester her on that count, either. Her sick call-in for work would wait for morning to make it (hopefully) more convincing. After a moment of consideration, Mia frowned at the little device and then turned off her cell completely. She'd pick up any messages later. Not that there would be any.

She tossed the phone on the counter, tipped her head back with a resigned groan, and gave in. Mia grabbed her jacket and headed outside shrugging into it as she went. Shortly thereafter she was blinking in the early afternoon sunshine. It felt so good to be out in it that she found herself silently grateful that she'd been bitten by a werewolf and *not* a vampire. She loved the moonlight, but there was nothing for a tired soul like sunshine.

The wind was crisp and smelled fantastic, and Mia was struck again by the beauty of Jenner's land as she walked. She had no memory of driving up to it Friday night, and in any case, it had been dark. But she'd gotten a good look at it when they'd returned from dinner last night, and now Mia stepped out into the yard far enough to drink in the sight of the large two-story log home, chalet style with a peaked roof and a large front porch. The lawn that rolled up to it, though no longer vibrant at this time of year, was obviously well-kept, and there were a couple of large pots of copper-colored mums at the foot of the porch steps that had made her smile on the way out yesterday, and did again now. Jenner fussing over flowers was tough to picture, but there were enough plantings out front to suggest it was something he did.

He had made a home, Mia thought with a pang of longing that for once had nothing to do with sex. It was something she'd been searching for ever since heading out on her own. And not just any home. She'd daydreamed about places so very like this that the reality of it gave her chills.

With a sigh, Mia headed around the house toward the detached garage, a big, three stall structure that was painted a deep forest green. It was as immaculate as the rest of Jenner's place on the outside, and she imagined it was the same inside. In fact, now that she thought about it, the whole house was surprisingly uncluttered for a bachelor pad.

Mia grinned at the thought that she was dealing with a werewolf who was not only a gardener, but also a neat freak. If the latter were actually true, he might throw her out before the full moon. She wasn't a slob, but she tended to make herself comfortable.

She entered through a small door on the side and was immediately greeted by the sound of Guns N' Roses echoing loudly throughout the space. Mia stepped inside, shut the door, and looked around her. It was, as she expected, immaculate. The floors were coated with a special paint to protect them. Tools were hung neatly from pegboard, work tables were ruthlessly organized. Even the messy things he had out and was working on managed to look like there was some sort of order to them. It amazed her that a big, tough-looking guy like Jenner could be so meticulous about his stuff. But then, he seemed to take care of the things that were important to him.

Mia took a few steps in, her eyes riveted on the scene in the center of the garage. There was a beautiful old muscle car, black with dual white stripes that went from hood to trunk. The hood was open, and Jenner was leaning over messing with something beneath it. The sight of his butt encased in jeans that were just snug enough to give her a good view had Mia's mouth watering immediately.

Wanting him might be one of the world's worst ideas. But even the most practical part of her couldn't deny that Jenner was just so…*hot*.

She had a sudden urge to sneak up behind him and wrap her arms around him. Fortunately, she had enough willpower not to. Barely.

Instead, she sauntered over to where he was obliviously tinkering away and leaned down to have a look at what he was up to. His eyes were totally focused on what he was doing, which seemed to involve screwing a piece of metal to another piece of metal. She wasn't mechanically inclined…it all looked the same to her. The car, though, was a beauty.

"Hey," she said. "What'cha doing?"

Jenner's eyes flicked to her, he dropped his wrench somewhere inside the hood, and then cursed at it before returning his attention to her and straightening.

"Um. Hey," he said. Mia smiled, both because he looked ridiculously cute covered in grease and because he seemed nervous that she'd showed up in a place he probably considered his man sanctuary. She'd discovered a few things about him since last night. Or more specifically, since she'd tried to grow fur and fangs in his truck. For all of Jenner's gruffness, there was a sweetness about him that lurked just beneath the surface. With a little prodding, he'd even managed to hold up his end of a conversation all the way through dinner, telling her about the town, introducing her to some of the other diners as if they were friends of his.

She still knew very little about Jenner himself. But this seemed like a good time to start finding out.

"Your car?" Mia asked. "It's a lot prettier than the truck."

Jenner grinned. "The truck is a workhorse. This is a thing of beauty."

Mia walked slowly around it, taking in the black leather interior, the gleaming chrome. "It really is. Chevelle?"

His eyes lit with pleasure. "Yeah. '70 SS 396. You know cars?"

His boyish excitement made her wish, very much that she did. "No," she admitted. "I read the bumper. But that doesn't mean I can't appreciate a hot car."

"Obviously a woman of discerning tastes, then," Jenner replied. His smile softened as he looked at her, and Mia could feel those invisible threads between them pulling at her, pulling her toward him. The silence wasn't uncomfortable, but there was a tension in it. Just like there was every time they were anywhere near each other. It was the first time on record that she'd smelled motor oil and actually gotten turned on.

"What's up?" he asked. "Can I do something for you?"

Oh, you have no idea, Mia thought.

"I just wondered what you were doing out here," Mia said with a shrug. "Your house is great, but I'm getting a little stir crazy. Played *Reckoning of Kings* on your Playstation for about an hour, but I've won it like three times at home, so…the challenge isn't really there anymore."

Jenner raised his eyebrows. "I still have that? I thought I'd tossed it."

Mia nodded and leaned her hip against the car. She didn't miss the way Jenner's eyes traveled the length of her. She loved the way he made her feel when he did that. How often had a man really made her feel beautiful?

"Huh. Well, I'm glad *someone* enjoyed playing it. Sure as hell wasn't me." Jenner reached into the engine compartment, fished around, and came out with the wrench he'd dropped. Then he carried it over to replace it on the pegboard, and wiped his hands on a grungy towel that looked like it would never come clean no matter how many times it was washed.

He returned, motioned for Mia to back up a little, and closed the hood.

"You call your family? In case you've got the kind of family that worries."

Mia shrugged uncomfortably. "My grandmother raised me. But she's gone now. I've got no one else."

She didn't mean for it to sound pathetic, just matter-of-fact. When Mia had left, so had Ada, packing up the little house and vanishing into what seemed like thin air. Her obligation, which was all the woman had ever thought of her granddaughter as, Mia knew, was done. Maybe Ada was still alive, maybe she wasn't. But she was gone, and Mia had no interest in finding her again. That truth no longer hurt the way it once had, but the words sounded pitiable to her own ears. Still, there was no reason to hide this. She was surprised when Jenner simply shrugged.

"Sorry to hear that, but it might make this easier. I've got only my father, at least nominally, but I've never told him what I am. Works out better for both of us."

"You lost your mother, then. I'm sorry," Mia said, and immediately wished she hadn't. Jenner's eyes darkened, and he looked away.

"Don't be. I don't know if she's dead or alive, and I don't much care. She took off when I was pretty young. My father's all right, but he found somebody else eventually, had a few more kids. I was always kind of the odd man out." He smiled, but Mia saw the sadness in it.

"Turning into a werewolf just gave me a more interesting reason to be a loner. It's not angry or anything. They just don't quite know what to do with me. Never have." He shrugged again, seemed to realize he had spoken several complete sentences about himself, and closed the subject with a wicked grin that made Mia feel like melting into a puddle at his feet.

"At least here no one's going to mistake me for a potential house pet."

Mia laughed, though the little Jenner had revealed about himself played over and over again in her mind. No mother and what sounded like an indifferent father… but Jenner seemed to have made the best of it. It said a lot about his strength.

Wonderful…another thing to be attracted to. Flustered, and irritated with herself for her inability to get past this stupid infatuation, Mia sought to switch topics. "So why did you think you had tossed *Reckoning of Kings?* It's only, like, four months old."

"Oh," he said, and this time his smile was more self-effacing than wicked. "Well, you probably noticed it doesn't really match the kind of stuff I usually go for. I wanted something new and that was the only thing that looked interesting. Turns out that if the game doesn't involve car chases, guns, or zombies, I suck at it. Lesson learned. How the hell have you beaten that game three times?"

Mia grinned. "A lethal combination of mad skills and no life. If you're bored later, I can show you how not to die at whatever part you're stuck at, I guess."

"Pass. I'll stick to zombies." He paused, considering her with those intense eyes of his. "You know, I wouldn't have pegged you as a web-designing gamer girl," Jenner said. "Maybe just because I've never met one of you before. Are you all this good-looking?"

The flattery, which Jenner immediately looked embarrassed for voicing, released what felt like a fusillade of butterflies in her stomach. That he seemed surprised he'd said it made it even nicer. She knew it was shallow to want him to find her attractive…but what was she supposed to do? Hope he was drawn in by her witty banter and superior gaming skills? Actually, she did hope that…she just wanted it supplemented with animal lust.

"We are," she said seriously. "We're just hard to catch outside of darkened rooms with glowing screens."

He watched her, looking as though he'd found some sort of new and fascinating creature. Mia felt herself flush. She'd gone through plenty of years of being the quirky geek girl back in school, attractive enough to be a curiosity, with interests unusual enough to be considered unworthy of dating. Her odd upbringing and constant fear of being found out as truly different had only compounded the problem. Finding a few like-minded friends in college, plus a lot of just growing into herself, had made a huge difference in her life. But plenty of self-consciousness had lingered, especially when it came to men.

Rattled, Mia sought to steer the conversation back into more comfortable territory. Maybe he thought she was cool, she had no idea. But that might not hold if he ever saw the pictures of her at DragonCon dressed as an elf.

"So you're a mechanic?" she asked. Tools like his, in this number and apparent quality, probably weren't just for a hobby. And he had mentioned "the shop" a few times last night in passing, though he'd never really clarified what that was. It made a lot more sense now... though she had to admit, his profession was as much a surprise to her as hers had been to him. He hadn't struck her at all as a motorhead, and she'd known a few. Though he certainly looked at ease leaning over that gorgeous car.

Her question seemed to snap Jenner out of it. "Yeah.

Yes. I am." He looked down at his grease-stained hands, then back up at her. The innocence in his expression was utterly disarming. "Is it that obvious?"

Mia laughed, and he joined her. Even after the laughter died, the warm feeling it had created lingered.

"I own the garage and body shop in town," Jenner explained.

Mia regarded him with new interest. "I don't know what I expected, but that wasn't it."

"Oh? Why not?"

She saw the hint of wariness in his expression, wondered if he would think she was looking down her nose at him. She sought to clear that up as quickly as she could.

"You have your video games arranged alphabetically," she explained. "And your wood floors are spotless. I don't usually associate that with a guy who likes getting his hands dirty under the hood of a car, but maybe that's just me."

Jenner relaxed immediately. "Trust me, there's plenty to be meticulous about under the hood of a car. And before I came to the Hollow, doing this for a living was the last thing on my radar. Come on. Let's go on in, and I'll tell you about it if you're that curious."

Mia nodded, and watched as he put a couple of things away and turned off the lights. The Chevelle gleamed softly in the semi-darkness. "It really is pretty," she said a little wistfully. "Does it run?"

"Sort of. And thanks," Jenner said, walking toward

her. "I've been restoring it for a few years now. A little here, a little there. It's almost done now."

"I want a ride in it when it's done," Mia said. "Whatever else happens, I demand a ride in the car. It's too cool."

"We'll see what we can do about that," Jenner said. His smile faded a little, and Mia wondered why. But he was quickly at her side, leading her out of the garage and back into the light. He was quiet as he locked the door, and Mia thought he might have used up his daily talking allowance; he did seem to have one, and it wasn't very large. So she was surprised when Jenner continued their conversation without a word from her.

"So let me see, the mechanic thing. Well, I always liked taking things apart and putting them back together, I guess. Loved the shop class in high school, and I was interested enough to take some auto classes at the tech center in high school. But it was a hobby at best. I figured I should go get the business degree my father was so big on. Actually, if I wanted the degree paid for, I didn't have much choice. And since I'd been such a pain in the ass as a teenager, I figured I owed him one."

"So where'd you get the degree?"

"Penn State," Jenner said as they headed up onto the porch. "Settled on a dual Economics/Business major. Landed a big deal of a job shortly thereafter, which made my bank account happy and me miserable. Sometimes I took little road trips on the weekends to make myself feel better. This turned out to be the eventual destination."

Mia tried to picture big, rough-around-the-edges Nick Jenner in a suit and tie and smiled. No, somehow it didn't fit him.

"Should I ask how you settled on Ferry's Hollow? I mean, it's pretty, but it's a little…remote."

Jenner gave her a lopsided grin. "It was more like the car decided to settle here. An old Camaro I was working on at the time, very cool and not at all reliable. Even then I was more into tinkering than just buying something all shiny and perfect from the get-go. It landed me here one day, in the Hollow, broken down again and at a garage run by the oldest guy I'd ever seen. He worked at his own speed, which could generously be called glacial."

Mia angled her head, skeptical, passing Jenner as he opened the door for her. "Hmm. He took so long you decided to just live here?"

There was a twinkle in his eye when he glanced at her. "Well. Not exactly."

Mia made a face. "A girl?"

"Nope. A guy."

Mia chuckled, enjoying Jenner's playful mood. He'd seemed so serious since she met him; it was nice to see this side of him.

"Do tell," she said.

"It was the mechanic. Guy who owned the garage. Jim Gibbons was his name. Crusty as hell and man was he slow, but he turned out to be an excellent teacher once I wore him down by hanging around so much and pestering about the car." Jenner smiled at the memory.

He headed for the fridge and grabbed a soda for himself. Mia was surprised when he pressed her favored kind into her hand, too. He'd been paying attention.

"Thanks," she said, feeling like a lovestruck teenager. Jenner nodded, and continued.

"Jim knew I belonged here before I did. And I never had to ask him for a job. He offered it, once he watched my impromptu week's vacation get longer. I learned just about everything I know from him. And I never stopped enjoying the work, so I kept on doing it. Now the place is mine."

Mia enjoyed hearing the story, but she knew there were pieces missing...in particular, whoever the woman was who'd initiated him. Jenner's version sounded far too neat. There had been a woman, she was sure of it. Jenner had fallen hard for one of the Blackpaw women. And that had been the one who'd messed him up so much that he didn't want to try again. The idea provoked a surprising hot surge of jealousy that Mia had to quickly tamp down as her skin began to prickle uncomfortably.

"Is he still here?" Mia asked, more to distract herself from the questions she really wanted to ask than anything. Though it would be interesting to meet the man who'd obviously had such an influence on Jenner.

"He and his wife packed up an RV a few years ago and headed out West," Jenner replied, then took a sip of his soda. "He sold me the business, and I expanded it. It's kind of a work in progress. For instance, we now do some restoration work, which is probably my favorite part. Something I really think we could grow, despite being in a small town. We're good, and word gets around. I have this one project…" Again, he stopped himself just as Mia was getting comfortable in the conversation. He didn't want to get too close, that was obvious. But she couldn't say he hadn't been honest about that.

"Never mind. Boring stuff," he said with a dismissive wave. "But there you have it. The story of how I went from a stiff in a suit to werewolf mechanic."

"And Lunari," Mia said. She saw the instant wariness on his face, but it didn't stop her. She wanted, *needed*, to understand this part of his life. "What, exactly, does a Lunari do? It's obviously an important position. You said you hunt?"

Jenner shifted uncomfortably. "I protect the pack. I hunt creatures who hunt us. Pretty simple."

Mia hesitated. "And what if these…whatever you hunt…have something to do with Jeff? My being here might be more of a threat to your pack than anything. I don't want anyone hurt on my account."

Jenner looked sharply at her. "Why would you think your being here would hurt anyone? We're more than capable of defending ourselves against the Shadowkin."

The word, finally spoken, filled Mia with a strange combination of relief and dread. He even knew the proper name for them—Shadowkin. Which meant it was likely he would know what she was, too. It was on the tip of her tongue to tell him…all of it. The desire to share that part of herself with him went against every instinct. But her need for him went even deeper than that.

The realization, and the shock it gave her, was all that kept her silent. For the first time in years, she was letting herself need someone. A someone who had already been very clear that he meant to walk away.

Knowing what she'd done, what she'd let herself do, took her breath away. She had to make it stop. She didn't know how to make it stop.

Jenner's expression indicated he hadn't meant to tell her as much as he had, and Mia tried to refocus on the conversation. Her feelings were her own problem. Still, her voice sounded strange to her own ears.

"Shadowkin. Supernatural creatures that hunt supernatural creatures, I guess. Makes sense."

"You don't sound too surprised," Jenner said slowly. "Mia, if there's anything more to tell me about what happened with you and Jeff, now would be the time."

She opened her mouth, expecting the usual denial to come out. Instead, she found herself giving him pieces of the truth.

"He had some kind of strange-looking knife," Mia admitted. "And he was ranting about blood, and doorways. Maybe he's crazy." She dropped her eyes, sure she would begin to see revulsion in his. "Or maybe it has something to do with your Shadowkin. Can they… get at people? Make them do things?"

When she chanced a look at his face, Jenner's expression was grim, but there was none of the disgust she'd expected. Darkness called to darkness…it was what she'd always been told. That her blood, full of dark magic, would repel every good thing. Part of her knew it was her grandmother's prejudice talking, lingering even now. But another part of her had always believed it.

And yet here was Jenner, big and strong and unquestionably good, and his only disgust was for Jeff Gaines and the Shadowkin. Relief flooded her. He had no idea what a chance she'd just taken on him. And he could have no idea what it meant that he was proving so much of what she'd feared wrong.

"The Shadowkin can definitely get at people," Jenner said flatly. "If they're weak…or just hungry for power. Some even invite them in." He looked away, his shoulders rigid. "Thanks for telling me that. Getting Gaines is even more important now. There are ways the Shadowkin can manifest fully in our world…it happened once, hundreds of years ago, and it was a disaster." He sighed and shook his head. "What a damn mess."

"It is," Mia agreed softly, staying still even though she wanted to wrap her arms around him and soothe away his thunderous frown. Foolish thoughts but impossible to stop. "I'm…I'm sorry for bringing this down on all of you."

"You didn't. Don't ever think that," Jenner said quickly. "Different things get us all here. It'll work out. You didn't make the psycho who's chasing you around. Just like you didn't ask to have somebody way back in your family who made a bad relationship decision."

Mia blinked. "What?"

Jenner just shook his head. "You'd have to have a

little dark fae blood in you for Gaines to be this determined. That's what opens the floodgates." His look
was all concern. He had no idea the wounds his words
reopened inside.

"Dark fae blood," Mia said softly. "And that's...
bad?"

"I've never seen an Unseelie," Jenner replied. "They
may be gone from this world, I don't know. But from the
stories, even I'd head in the other direction if I saw one
coming. It's a different kind of power than anything my
kind knows. Even the Shadowkin covet it." He finally
seemed to notice that his words had upset her. Mia was
silent, but she felt drained, cold. Here she was again,
being thought of as something dangerous, something
tainted. And Jenner didn't even know that he'd just told
her he'd run from her without a moment's hesitation if
he knew just how strong her blood was.

"It's not your fault, Mia," Jenner said with a frown.
Mia found that she took a little solace in the soothing
rumble of his voice. No, this wasn't her fault. Or his.
It simply *was*. The thought was wearying, but familiar. She pushed it away. This was nothing unexpected,
nothing new.

The only new thing was the sharp bite of the pain
he'd caused her, which had long been dull.

"What the Shadowkin sense in you is probably so
far back you'd never have any idea it was there. Don't
worry, okay? When you're fully a wolf, fully a part of
a pack, that should cancel out whatever the Shadowkin
sense in you. Wolf blood is strong as hell." He looked

away. "Just another reason we need to get Gaines and make sure you're safe for good."

Mia managed a smile and a nod. Inside, she was numb. So that was her only hope…to sleep with a stranger so that the strength of her wolf blood would make the Shadowkin leave her alone.

But the chances of it canceling her power out…she thought those were slim at best. She would always be part Unseelie. A thing Jenner considered a monster.

But not now. Right now, he only saw Mia, she thought. An unlucky woman who was doing the best she could with a bad situation. And he was right about that.

There was that slow burning fire in his eyes again when he looked at her, and she tried to imprint it on her memory so that she could take it out later and treasure it once all this was over. He might never be hers, but she already knew she would never be able to forget him.

"Look, I'm going to go grab a shower. We've got to be at Bane's this evening, and I want some time to fire up that game before we go," he said. "I won't believe you're a master until I see it."

Amused despite herself, Mia chuckled, though nothing could fully obscure the sick, nervous feeling she got every time she thought of going to Bane's, meeting a bunch of werewolves from a pack Jenner didn't seem to like much, and trying to get back in touch with Jeff. She fought it back. The worst was over. They would know what ran in her veins, and they weren't going to throw her out for it. Just how much magic she possessed was now a meaningless technicality. She should feel relieved, Mia told herself.

Not like she wanted to sit down and cry.

"You've got it," she said, hoping her cheerful tone wasn't overdone.

Jenner gave her a brief smile before disappearing into his room, and she saw that they were okay, for now.

It was going to have to be enough, Mia decided.

Because when it came to Jenner, it looked like now was all they had.

Chapter 11

Jeff? Are you listening?

Her voice. Jeff winced in pain, turning his head to rest it against the cool comfort of the wall. At first, he thought he was imagining her. But his senses filled with her scent, swirling around him until he felt surrounded by her.

"Mia," he murmured aloud. So beautiful. But he'd lost her. And now, she hid from him. He had provoked her fear and loathing…he hadn't meant to hurt her, didn't she see? He had no choices anymore.

Jeff…where are you? I can't see you. It's so dark…

Of course it was dark, he could have told her. It was always dark inside of him. The darkness colored everything he saw now.

I didn't want to hurt you, Mia, he thought, knowing

she could hear him. *Don't hate me...please...your blood is the only way out, and the shadows are all around me, filling me...*

Of course I don't hate you, she said, her voice soothing. *Just tell me where you are. I'll come to you. I'll help you stop this, help you get better. Whatever they've offered you, it's not worth losing yourself like this.*

It was too easy. Too tempting. He knew she was lying about helping him, no matter how much he wanted to believe it. It was those Blackpaw she was with, helping her mess with his head. Teaching her to hate what she didn't understand. Wolves were as bad as humans that way. They'd let themselves become too human.

No, he replied sadly. *I have to finish what I started. That's how it has to be. I love you, Mia. I'll find you. It will be quick, painless. I promise...*

Please, tell me where you are, Mia pleaded, her voice echoing loudly in his head, so soft and warm, a comfort in the dark cold of his mind. He was starting to come apart again. He knew it. But if he could just hang on a night, perhaps two, it would all be better.

I need to find you. I miss you. I want you to get better. Why are you doing this?

Her words shot straight through what was left of his heart. Jeff gasped, in pain, in wonder. He wanted it to be true, so badly. There was no way he could take the chance now, of course. He could not change course. The shadows would kill him. Still, had any woman ever said such a thing to him?

I miss you, too, Mia. I'm sorry it has to be this way.

But look, see what's coming...how could anyone re-sist this?

He opened his mind, and let her see his beautiful dream. They would soon share it.

Together.

Mia gasped as she surfaced from the nightmarish visions she'd fallen into.

It took precious seconds to center herself, to re-member where she was. But when she did, the relief was overwhelming. This was Bane's house. Jenner had brought her here. He'd promised to keep her safe...but she hadn't understood just what Bane would ask of her, or how it would feel.

As though he could sense her thoughts, Jenner quickly put his hands on her, and Mia gulped in fresh air, hoping it would quell her rolling stomach before she retched. Her nose was still full of the scents of blood, and smoke, and burning. And every time she closed her eyes, all she saw was a whirling dance of shadows with gleaming eyes. But Jenner was here, watching over her. Just as he'd promised earlier, when they'd laughed over a silly video game and all of this had seemed surpris-ingly far away. Jenner's presence was as strong as ever, and Mia used that to pull herself back.

As the blackness receded from her vision and she came around, she realized Jenner's hands had been joined by another's.

Jenner was on one side. And Kenyon, who had been

allowed to stay in the room at his Alpha's insistence, was on the other.

Mia sat up straighter in the large recliner she'd been settled in, pulling away from both of them. She shook from a cold that seemed to have permeated down to her very bones. It felt as though she would never be warm again.

"What happened?" Tomas, the Alpha of the Silverback, had shot to his feet from the small stool he'd positioned near her. Being the center of attention was unfamiliar, and incredibly unnerving. It was worse, however, when a powerful man she'd never met in her life had decided to try and run the show.

Mia wasn't yet sure what to think of Tomas. The compact, bullish man was in his fifties, with a ring of brown hair on his head and a ruddy complexion. He seemed to think a lot more of himself than any of the Blackpaw thought of him, but he knew his power, and he didn't seem to mind throwing his weight around. She wasn't sure he was bad-tempered, but he was certainly intimidating.

Bane, who she had decided gave new meaning to the phrase "grace under fire," took up a position right beside Tomas. She was glad not to have only those dark, glittering brown eyes to focus on.

"What did you see, Mia?" he asked. "Tell us everything."

She did, in a shaking voice that grew stronger as she related the experience. The chills ebbed, but slowly, and although Jenner and Kenyon had retreated just a few paces away, she could tell that either of them would have been happy to warm her. The problem was, while she appreciated Kenyon's efforts at playing the potential suitor, all she wanted was Jenner. And since even a fool could see it was going to create problems if she reached out only to him, she decided to suffer the misery by herself. Still shivering a little, Mia spoke about Jeff's message to her.

"I've never seen anything like it," Mia said. "It was already dark where I was, but these *things* were darker. Red eyes, like the last time we linked up this way. And I could tell they were hungry…waiting for something. Jeff is insane, and that's scary enough, but these were much worse. I don't know if they're figments of his imagination, or if they're…more. But he was very excited to show them to me."

She broke out in fresh gooseflesh at the thought of it. "They were pulling me down, under. It felt like I was drowning."

"Son of a bitch," Tomas snapped. His vehemence seemed to surprise everyone.

"What?" Mia asked.

"Jeff was always much too interested in the darker places. I think it's pretty obvious that whether these… shadows…are figments of his imagination or not, we have a problem on our hands. If it hasn't already, it's almost certainly going to draw—" All of a sudden, he seemed to remember that Mia was sitting there listening. His eyes snapped to her before returning to Bane.

"I'd prefer to talk about this privately. This is business for pack leadership, no one else."

Mia glowered. "Since I'm the one whose brain is connected to his, I'd say it concerns me even more than it does you. I'm staying."

She saw Tomas bristle, and could swear his lip started to curl. But then, she shouldn't be surprised. He'd done the same thing when he'd first laid eyes on her. Mia couldn't quite figure where the animosity came from, except that it seemed very obvious, from the little he'd said before starting, that he placed a lot of value on werewolf lineage.

Lineage which neither she, nor most of the Blackpaw, had.

"I'm staying," Mia repeated, more calmly now. "I'll be a wolf soon enough, from what they tell me."

Tomas's smile was knifelike. "No. You haven't even been through a change yet, have you? You don't know much about our world yet, either. You'll have to entrust this to those of us who know how to deal with these things."

Mia saw Jenner's eyes begin to glow, and even Kenyon looked displeased. If Tomas was deliberately trying to incite a fight by being an arrogant asshole, he was doing a fine job of it.

"I agree with Mia, Tomas," Jenner growled. "She should stay. Jeff Gaines wants her. Only her. He tried to open her up with a ritual knife once already."

The other wolves looked startled. Jenner nodded.

"Yeah, that's the kind of pertinent information you

get when you move forward on the assumption that the victim is not an idiot. She needs to know what's going on. All of it. Because she's the one who's ultimately going to draw him here."

Mia looked at him gratefully. She wasn't interested in sitting here and getting steamrolled much longer. It was nice to have some backup, because it was obvious Tomas had no interest in listening to her.

"I already know what the Shadowkin are," she explained. "And why they want me. Jenner told me when he started to piece together what Jeff was trying to do. I know he thinks he can use me to pull them here, physically. I'll do whatever I can to stop him—it's my life—but I insist on being kept in the loop. I can handle it."

Tomas slid his gaze to Jenner, letting all of his displeasure show. "Nick Jenner. Still fixing cars and chasing shadows, huh? I hear that mechanic gave you his shop and skipped town after you killed his daughter. I'm going to guess it wasn't your charm that convinced him." He turned to Bane, jerking his head back at Jenner. "We haven't kept a Lunari in over a hundred years. The brute strength required for the position came with too little sense most of the time. You might want to think about how wise it is to share power with a man who'd tell a human he's just met about the Shadowkin." He eyed Mia with a look she didn't like at all. "Well, mostly human. Though dark fae blood isn't something I'd go bragging about."

Mia sucked in a breath. She saw Bane, his eyes flashing, give Jenner a nearly imperceptible head shake. Jenner, rather than punching Tomas in the face—which Mia thought he would have deserved—came to stand right behind her. He rested his hands lightly on her shoulders, a subtle sign of support…or was it possession?

It was designed to irritate Tomas, she supposed, and from the way his nostrils flared, it did the trick.

Happy to participate, Mia slid a hand up to cover one of Jenner's.

"Mia didn't ask for any of this, and she's worth as much as any Silverback. More. I stand by my decision," Jenner growled. "You're on very thin ice, Tomas. This is not your territory. And here, whether you like it or not, I'm your equal."

Jenner's words went a long way toward making up for the blow he'd unwittingly dealt her earlier. And she felt a faint glimmer of hope, foolish though it might be, that he'd say the same even if he knew all of it. How she could hear the songs that blood carried, how she could draw power from the night and hold it in her hands. How she'd be able to do a lot more, if she wasn't always trying to tuck it all away.

She'd felt a lot of things, but never dangerous. She just worried that if she was exposed, those around her would never see her as anything but. And after what Jenner had said about the Unseelie today, she was never going to risk finding out.

Tomas opened his mouth to reply, and Mia caught the ominous flash of sharp, white teeth before Bane interrupted the brewing fight.

"Blackpaw ways are different than Silverback ways," Bane said sharply. "Don't insult my Lunari again, or I'll have you run out of here with your tails between your legs, the lot of you. I trust Jenner with my life, not that it's any concern of the Silverbacks'. You said you came to help. So help."

There was a soft but very audible growl as Tomas collected himself, and Mia wondered whether he'd be able to hold it together. Finally, though, he took a deep breath, straightened and spoke in a surprisingly even tone. Only his eyes showed his still-roiling anger.

"I never thought Jeff was a good fit for the pack," Tomas began. "He was moody, impulsive. He told Sara Dumont he loved her, and a couple weeks after she initiated him, he broke it off as though it had meant nothing. Manipulative. And even when he challenged me for Alpha, I thought there was more to it. He must have known he couldn't win, but he always seemed to have ulterior motives for things."

"So he was disliked?" Mia asked, surprised. "He was pretty charming up until just recently. At least with me."

Tomas lifted an eyebrow, but he didn't seem angry.

"No, actually. Despite everything, it was hard not to like him, at least when he was in a good mood. He *could* be charming. And there was something about him that made people...myself included...feel a little sorry for him. He came from money, but I don't think his upbringing was very happy."

"I don't think so, either. Is that why you let him go?" Mia asked quietly.

Tomas sighed heavily, then nodded. "I made a mistake. His problems were obviously deeper than I suspected. I thought him more troubled and pitiful than really dangerous. I was wrong. But I'll make right what I can."

Kenyon nodded, chiming in. "We will. We'll do right by you where he didn't, Mia."

Hearing that was no comfort, not when Jenner's hands still rested on her shoulders. She didn't want anything from the Silverback. But she felt more and more how out of her element she was. Normal rules didn't apply here. And she wasn't sure, no matter what Jenner said, that her own wants and needs would matter to these creatures.

She leaned back again, glad for the comfort of Jenner's touch while she could have it. Connecting with Jeff had been like winding through a house of horrors. His madness, his barely restrained violence, and worst of all, the depths of his obsession with finding her seemed to get worse each time. How had a creature like this, so twisted, managed to wear the mask of a normal human being for so long? she wondered. It was hard to remember the man she'd come to this place with, charming, witty, solicitous of her. All she'd wanted to see was the mask, and that he'd wanted her, needed her. That was her fault.

It was a mistake she didn't intend to make again.

Strange, that being here should make her realize that her own wants and needs had merit, too.

She looked at Bane, a steady, silent presence watching her from across the room.

"He can't hurt me when we connect this way, right? You're sure?"

Bane nodded slowly. "I'm sure. But that doesn't make the experience pleasant."

"It doesn't matter if it's unpleasant, as long as it's useful. Did you see or hear anything more? Some clue as to where he was?" Tomas interjected his questions, impatient for information.

Mia shook her head. She wished she had more for everyone to go on.

"I can't seem to *see* anything when I'm with him this way. There's only darkness, and voices," Mia explained. And the shrieking of his blood, the dark magic pulsing all around him in waves. Magic she knew she could harness, though nothing good would come of using what surrounded Jeff.

She hadn't even been tempted, Mia realized with a start. She'd been able to look at it impassively, immune to the lure of the violence of that sort of power. It was the first time she'd gotten that close to such a thing… and the temptation she'd always been told she would feel had never materialized.

Was it the wolf blood in her? Or was it just…her?

Tomas gave a dissatisfied grunt, but Jenner's voice, surprisingly patient, drew her attention to his face as he crouched down beside her chair. In that instant, he was the man who had led her out of the woods again, strong and competent, in control but not without compassion.

And just like that, she was completely focused on him, as though they were the only two people in the room.

"Seeing isn't as important as you think," he said. "I know it isn't fun, but think back over what happened. Did you hear anything? Smell anything? Sometimes that tells us more than our eyes would. It's part of having the wolf in your nature, and you do now, new though it is. Think, Mia. I'll bet there was something. Close your eyes and think back."

Mia sighed, but finally gave a short nod. She let her eyes slip shut, despite her misgivings about it.

With effort, she shook off the thoughts that made her skin crawl and sifted through what had happened with a more analytical eye. And Jenner was right, she realized. There were a few small details like what he'd said. But she didn't see how they would help anyone.

Mia opened her eyes and looked into Jenner's steady gold ones. That, and a new awareness of her own strength, gave her the courage to speak up without fear of embarrassment.

"I could hear him pacing on some kind of creaky wood floor," Mia said. "And wherever he is, it smelled like it had been closed up for a while. A little musty. It was chilly. I could smell the woods."

Jenner shifted his attention to Bane. "Hunting cabin," he said. "Bet you anything."

Bane blew out a breath. "Shit," he said. "He could be anywhere out in the woods. This is going to be like trying to find a needle in a haystack. Still, it's a start."

It didn't make her feel much better, looking at Bane's

handsome face wearing such a disappointed expression. Kenyon's words, however, made her feel decidedly worse.

"It won't matter," he said. "It's pretty obvious he's going to make a move on her first. We're just going to have to be ready for it." He slid a fulminating look at Jenner. "I still think she should be here, right in town. How can we protect her when she's only got one guard? She's a sitting duck out there with you!"

Jenner opened his mouth, but Mia cut him off smoothly. She'd had just about enough of being spoken about as though she wasn't there, good intentions or no.

"The *she* in question feels safe where she is," Mia said. "And what exactly are you saying? That you *want* to use me as bait?"

Kenyon's ready smile was gone. He looked older, and decidedly more intimidating when his dimples weren't in evidence.

"I'm saying you're bait whether you want to be or not, Mia. That's not meant as an insult, it's just the truth. He's fixated on you. He thinks he needs you to clear the way for the Shadowkin. That's going to be the thing that draws him out, and the thing that lets us take him down." He shook his head and looked at Jenner. "A ritual knife? Are you sure?"

"Long curved blade, engraved white handle," Mia said, answering for herself again. "I wouldn't have known what to call it, but Jenner knew right away. I've got Unseelie blood. He needs it. It's not that hard to understand."

She hadn't meant to say it that way, but it was hard to regret it when she heard Jenner's appreciative snort and saw Bane's smirk. Kenyon was nice, but Tomas's commentary on her heritage had been about enough for one night.

Kenyon, to his credit, managed a smile. "No, it isn't. And you're dealing with it better than I think any of us could have expected. Sorry."

Mia nodded, glad that at least one day the Silverback would have an Alpha who seemed to have both manners and a heart.

"This is all just a damned legend," Tomas interjected. "Unseelie were nasty creatures, if you believe the stories. Mischievous, self-interested, prone to grudge-holding. Powerful. But I've never seen one. No one has. And you're trying to tell me that they're going to use some girl with a little tainted blood to open a rift they can get through? Bull."

Mia's mouth went as dry as the desert at once. She tried to swallow, and found it difficult. She hadn't heard the words spoken since her grandmother had died. *Tainted blood. I can sense the darkness in you, girl.*

But for the first time, she fought back.

"My blood isn't tainted." Her voice was unsteady, but clear as a bell. "Not any more than yours is."

Tomas's eyes narrowed. "You have a lot to learn, if that's what you think."

The feel of Jenner's hand on her arm again surprised her. But she welcomed the solid warmth of it, and the support it represented.

"She's no different than any of us," he said. "And she's safe with me."

His words, simple, reassuring, were enough in that moment to soothe her. Tomas, however, exchanged an unpleasant look with Kenyon.

"Obviously, you're doing fine. But I think it might be a good idea to get her used to us before she joins us."

The words hit her like a steamroller.

"I'm sorry," Mia said. "What?"

Tomas's forehead creased. "You weren't told?"

Suddenly, it was all too much. Mia briefly considered running, but she'd done too much of that in her life already. This was something she would have to deal with, and it was long past time to lay down her own rules.

"I was told I would have a choice. And frankly, I'm tired of being treated like my feelings don't matter. In the last two days, I've been told that I'm going to turn into a werewolf in less than a week, I can't go back to my normal life, and that I have to…" Ugh, she couldn't say it. "Have to compromise myself so that I don't go insane. Oh, and there's also the fact that my now-ex *is* insane and hunting me because he thinks he can use my blood to open a magical portal. If there are any other decisions to be made, I'm making them for myself."

For the first time, she saw a glimmer of that compassion Kenyon had insisted Tomas had—the thing that had spared Jeff in the first place.

"I'm sorry, Mia. These feral situations are never easy, which is why it's good they don't happen very often. But since Gaines was one of mine, it falls to me to take in his victims. In this case, you. The old laws, which we live by, say as much. If it's any consolation, it works the same for males and females…this isn't about sex, but about responsibility. We take care of our own."

Maybe he was being sincere. But to Mia, he just sounded smug.

Kenyon's voice drew her attention, soft and warm. He'd lost his grim expression, and now looked at her with hope in his pretty blue eyes. *No wonder*, Mia thought. *No wonder he's been so strange with Jenner. He doesn't just like me. He's trying to stake a claim on me.*

Then she realized that with Jenner out of the way, he could well be the man she chose. He wasn't an unappealing option—just not the one she wanted. And maybe that was a warning sign, because so far, the men she did want in her life had ranged from indifferent and unsuitable to downright appalling. It was something to think about.

One thing, however, required no thought at all.

"I was told I could make my own decision, and that's what I intend to do," Mia said, her voice stronger now. "I won't be forced into something I don't want. Pack doesn't matter to me, and I'm certainly not going to be boxed in that way. This is the only choice I get in all of this, and it will be completely my own." She cast a pointed glare at all of the gathered men. She doubted the other werewolf females had to put up with crap like this. Of course, they'd either been born into the life or had made the choice themselves. But she refused to be a prize to be fought over.

Tomas and Kenyon looked thunderstruck.

"This isn't—" Tomas began.

"She's right," Bane interrupted, his voice gruff. "This isn't for us to say. None of us, Pack Law be damned."

Tomas looked disgusted, but he finally gave a grudging nod before turning his dark and gleaming gaze back on Mia. "Well. I won't fight you on it. It's your life. But you might want to give some thought to which pack can provide you with the kind of life you want. And you might also want to think about the fact that Lunari— shadow hunters—don't take mates. Especially not when they've had to kill one already."

"That's way the hell out of line, Tomas," Bane snapped. Mia appreciated the defense, but when she snuck a glance at Jenner, he looked away, his expression stony, and stalked from the room, slamming the door behind him. He'd told her he was off limits for initiation, for anything but protection. And she could see he'd meant it. But Tomas's nasty barbs were painting a more detailed, and disturbing picture, of just why.

Jenner was so self-contained, she wondered whether she'd ever know the truth of it…or if it would matter if she did.

"I plan to weigh all my options," Mia said calmly, meeting Tomas's gaze without flinching. "I'm just telling you that I will be looking at *all* the options. Not just one."

"Fair enough." That was Kenyon, and for once his

unwavering support of her was a relief. She allowed him to help her from the chair.

When she stood, she slid her hand from the warm reassuring pressure of Kenyon's and said her goodbyes. They might not be finished for the evening, but she was. It wasn't that she wanted to be with Jenner, per se, though his sudden exit had her worried about him. It was more that she needed some time to think, to be by herself. And to recover from her current state of overbearing-werewolf overload.

"Maybe we'll find him tonight, and this will all be over," Bane said, his dark eyes sincere.

"I hope so. And good luck," Mia said. "It was nice meeting you, Tomas."

The older Alpha inclined his head, and Mia headed for the door. Before she could leave, though, Kenyon caught up with her, his blue eyes giving off a faint glow.

"Hey, look…I get that I'm not choice number one here, but would you let me take you to lunch tomorrow?"

Mia hesitated, but between the earnest expression on Kenyon's handsome face and the fact that Jenner had been very clear about his lack of availability, she knew the only problem here was her own ridiculous infatuation. She'd finally done something positive tonight and taken control of part of her destiny.

It was time to start thinking—realistically—about how she would shape it.

"Sure," she said. "I'd love to."

His grin was so big she actually felt guilty. He was perfect in every way but one: He wasn't Jenner. And that was something she was just going to have to get used to, no matter who she chose.

With a wistful smile, Mia said good-night.

Chapter 12

She awakened in the wee hours of the morning and lay staring at the ceiling. Strange dreams full of racing shadows and eerie light had plagued her in sleep. Not really nightmares, but definitely unsettling. Mia had finally surfaced, opening her eyes in the darkness full of an indescribable yearning. Rather than being sleepy, energy coursed through her, and she was more alert now than she had been all day.

She thought of running beneath the moon...and of Jenner.

Neither fixation was terribly productive, Mia thought with a glance at the little clock on the nightstand, which read 1:00 a.m. Her stomach rumbled pitifully, until finally, with a sigh, Mia slid from the bed and headed into the quiet house, clad in her thin cotton sleep shorts and a tank. There were no rules against late night snacks, she supposed. Cooler air swirled around her legs as she moved, a pleasant sensation that prickled across her nerve endings and made her think again of her dreams.

Mia paused in front of the wall of windows, looking out into the night. She watched the trees sway gently in the night breeze, and longing again suffused her. She wanted to be out there, in the woods. Forgetting about the snack, she wrapped her arms around her midsection and stared into the night, occasionally seeing small shadows dart between the trees. Night creatures.

Like she would be. Coming here had allowed things she thought she'd buried long ago to come rushing to the surface. The woods had always been her place, coaxing magic from her until it became as natural as breathing. She had vague memories of running through the trees, light like fireflies shimmering all around her. It wasn't just blood that had a song. It was everything, the world, the night, the creatures.

It was no shock to her when her own reflection, glowing softly, appeared in the glass. Warmth coursed through her, pure and true. This is what she should have remembered, instead of years of cruel little barbs. Something, whether it was the woods or the wolf blood or a combination of everything that made up the Hollow, had made her magic begin to flow again from all the places she'd tried to hide it. It didn't feel wrong and dark. It felt like it had when she was a child—like a part of her, and the most natural thing in the world.

Tentatively, then more confidently, she embraced

it, and the woman in the glass glowed more brightly, a will-o'-the-wisp in the dark.

For all the stories about how frightening the Unseelie could be, Mia wondered how they really had been, whether they were extinct or simply gone from this world, like her grandmother. Ada had clung to the tattered threads of her family's fae lineage like a talisman, priding herself on a few drops of Seelie blood, dreaming of the Summer Court.

Her father had been a half-blood Unseelie, handsome and dark. But pictures were all she had to remember him by. Him and the beautiful, fair-haired woman who had been her mother. She doubted they'd thought her an abomination.

Maybe it was time to stop thinking of herself as one.

A simple thought, but one that arrowed through her like lightning. The wolves here embraced what they were. Most weren't the dark things of legend. And just because her blood could be used for evil didn't mean she was, or that her people had been.

She's no different than we are, Jenner had said. But would he feel the same if he saw her this way? Would any of them? Revealing herself would be a huge risk, Mia thought. But for the first time, she was seriously considering taking it. Especially because she knew instinctively that however much a werewolf she might become, the magic she already carried would always be with her.

Whichever pack she joined would have to accept that. Or…well, she'd just find her own way, like she always had. At least she'd be sane. She blew out a breath, frustrated by her own thoughts. There would be a time to deal with opening up about her abilities.

Now wasn't it.

A flicker of something larger, very near to the window, caught Mia's eye and drew her quickly out of her melancholy thoughts. She stepped closer, frowning, a glowing ghost in the glass. Had she seen a deer? she wondered. It could have been. The forest stilled while she scanned for the oddly shaped shadow through the window. Her vision sharpened as she looked. But the wonder of being able to see the trees as well as if it were daylight took a backseat to a growing sense of unease. The hair at the back of her neck prickled. She went perfectly still as something moved again beyond the glass, and this time she could see very well that it was no deer.

It was a wolf.

As she watched it, she became aware of a low rumbling noise vibrating somewhere nearby. Growling. Suddenly, she realized it was coming from her own throat. And rather than being a human sound, this was all animal.

Though it was soft, the large wolf just beyond the glass seemed to hear it. It picked up its head from where it had been sniffing the ground and turned toward her. For just an instant, their eyes met. Mia growled louder, an instinctive reaction, a warning. Bright yellow eyes flashed in the dark. Sharp white teeth were bared.

She knew those eyes. It would be hard to forget them.

They stood there facing each other for a moment that

seemed to spin out, suspended. That she felt fear was no surprise. But this time, there was something stronger that did surprise her: anger. Mia curled her lip in response to the wolf that she knew was Jeff Gaines, furious that he'd managed to find her, that he'd come hunting for her here…that he wouldn't just let her alone.

Heat raced over her skin, the way it had in the truck earlier when she'd let her anger at Jenner get the better of her. She felt the sharp pains begin, like thousands of knives pushing into her skin, but she accepted it. He needed to know he couldn't take her without a fight. That she wouldn't run this time. She hooked her fingers into claws, felt her nails lengthening, beginning to change.

Jeff's voice pushed into her head, a violation, an intrusion.

Mia. I told you I'd come for you.

She drew in a series of shallow breaths as her heartbeat accelerated. Responding to him without moving her lips seemed as natural as breathing.

You can't have me. I'll kill you first.

His mouth opened and his tongue lolled out, mocking her.

You said you missed me. Come out, Mia. I can see what you are, even if they can't. Come out and play with me. Let me love you. Let me bleed you.

I hate you. I hate you for this, she thought, with all the ferocity that was building inside of her. The pain intensified, threatening to bring her to her knees, but she kept her footing, kept her eyes locked with Jeff's. *Do you hear me? I hate you! You can't have me!*

The lolling tongue vanished. The voice she heard in her head now was full of a surprising amount of pain. *No...don't say things like that...I love you, don't you see?*

"I hate you!" She snarled it in a voice she barely recognized as her own. Power whipped out of her in a flash, light with a faintly violet cast that shot through the wolf that was Jeff. He stumbled backward as it passed through him, then turned and fled into the darkness past where her eyes could see. A mournful howl echoed in her ears, in her head.

She couldn't let him go. She wanted to finish it.

Before she could think better of it—before she could think at all—Mia had flung open the doors to the back patio and rushed into the night, chasing after Jeff. She could still feel his presence, could smell a scent that was sweat and man, and wolf, and madness. Faster than she ever had, she ran into the woods, her feet barely touching the bed of pine needles, rocks and sticks beneath her.

You won't escape me, she thought, the light that coursed through her changing to dark, red hot anger pulsing through her. *I'll find you...and when I do, you'll be sorry for choosing me.*

She could hear him, his rough breath panting not far ahead, his paws crunching through the underbrush. She'd hurt him, somehow, and she was gaining. Long, deadly claws hooked from her fingers. Her teeth were dagger sharp in her mouth, and it felt good, it felt *right*.

Every nerve ending sizzled with awareness. The pain just beneath her skin faded to a pleasant burn. The change was close enough to touch. And if she could hunt him as a wolf, a wolf with the abilities she already had, he would never escape her...

She caught a fleeting glimpse of him through a break in the trees, picking up speed again. In anger, in despair, she screamed, another bolt of violet light flashing from her fingertips as she hurled it toward him. She heard his piteous cry as it hit his retreating backside, as her power burned into him.

Remember just what it is you're hunting, you bastard, she thought, pushing it at him, hoping he could hear it in his mind as he ran.

Then she was alone, and the reality of what she'd been doing, the sheer foolishness of it, crashed down on Mia hard. She staggered as instinct fled and her wits returned. It was only then that she could sense other things moving about her in the woods. Darker, sinister things made only of shadow, waiting to see just how low her defenses were before they closed in.

A sharp bark drew her attention. Mia turned, barely staying on her feet, and caught a fleeting glimpse of a huge gray wolf with intense golden eyes rushing toward her. All she had to do was blink, however, and it was just Jenner, in a pair of jeans and nothing else. The worry written all over his face pushed back the cold that had come with her awareness of the Shadowkin watching.

"Mia!"

Then he was there, in front of her, catching her in his arms and pulling her into a rough embrace she'd been dreaming of since she'd met him.

"Damn it, Mia, what were you thinking? Are you all right? Jesus. Look at me!"

It wasn't until that moment that she realized how much her little supernatural burst had taken out of her. She'd held the wolf at bay, this time by herself. But she'd also used it, along with a bit of other magic she hadn't even known she was capable of.

Mia licked her lips. "Gone," she managed to say, when Jenner pulled her away from him, looked her over, and then crushed her in his arms again. "It was Jeff. But he ran away. He ran away from me." She smiled over it, despite everything. All those years of fear and doubt, and she'd controlled what she had. It had cost her, but she'd learned something valuable, too.

Jenner seemed a lot less excited about it.

"Let's get you back home. It's not safe out here."

He plucked her off the ground as though she weighed no more than a feather, cradling her in his arms the way he had at their first meeting in the woods. Mia buried her head against his bare chest as he took off at a run, carrying her back to the house at a speed no human could have managed. His bare chest was warm, and held her so tightly it was almost impossible to move.

Yet it didn't make her feel trapped. It made her feel safe.

Mia didn't fight it, and let herself go limp. Her ear pressed against his chest, and she soothed herself with the steady rhythm of his heart. It was no shock to her now when her own heart sought to match that beat, slowing, calming her as it steadied from its frantic pounding. The wind rushed by them as he ran, and Mia closed her eyes, losing herself in it. It seemed only moments before the door was opening and they were back in Jenner's house. Warm. Safe.

Alone with the only man she wanted.

Strangely, Jenner's voice sounded much less steady than she expected when he finally spoke, his deep voice rumbling through his chest.

"What the hell were you thinking? You weren't alone out there, not even after he ran. Damn it, Mia, couldn't you sense them, even a little?"

"I could…after," she murmured, then moistened lips that seemed to have gone as dry as the desert before continuing. "Sorry. I came out because I couldn't sleep. Jeff was there, outside. In the dark. I thought I would be afraid, and I was, but I was…so angry. Just so incredibly angry."

Jenner swore softly, and then was silent for a moment. Mia imagined he was calling out the cavalry. She was glad, though she expected Jeff was long gone by now. Somehow, she had gotten through to him. But she wasn't fool enough to think it would last. The madness had been pouring off of him, smelling like sickness. Like death.

She felt Jenner carrying her to the couch, where he sat with her still curled in his lap. His arms stayed tightly around her, and she was glad of it. Right now, she didn't want him to ever let her go.

"Why did he take off? Did he attack you?" Jenner asked.

"No. He just ran away," she said.

"He's a coward at heart," Jenner replied flatly. "I'm not surprised."

Mia began to shiver as the exhaustion of her body really took hold. "This whole thing is insane."

Jenner grunted. "What's insane is that the Silverback ever let him run free in the first place. Even if he's good at making people feel sorry for him, which I guess he must be, there's no excuse for setting something like him loose. Tomas should have known better."

"Yes, well. I didn't get the impression he likes having his decisions questioned. Or being told no."

Jenner snorted. "Tomas is a snob. His pack is full of hereditary werewolf families who think they're special because of their lineage. They don't really have to deal with Shadowkin because they live in a normal human city, most of them in cookie-cutter McMansions, with no open forest in sight. I don't know how they stand it. They don't know how we stand it here. To each his own."

Mia remembered the way Jenner had stormed out. She'd found him waiting for her outside, but he'd barely spoken before now. She hesitated to bring it back up, but it was either now or never.

"Jenner?"

"Hmm?"

"Did you really lose a mate to the Shadowkin?"

He was silent for so long she thought he wasn't going to answer, and guilt flooded her. She shouldn't have asked. It was really none of her business. But she couldn't seem to control her need to find out every little thing about him…even the painful, hidden parts.

Finally, though, he spoke. "I hadn't asked Tess to be my mate yet. Not officially, and we hadn't bonded that way. But it was coming. We were living together. She was…" He trailed off. "Vibrant. She had this lust for life that was just infectious. Wanted to know everything, experience everything. But she had a darker side. She could be very moody, dissatisfied with life in the Hollow, the limitations of pack life. She wanted out and couldn't figure a way. I tried to keep her content and happy. We all did. But it wasn't enough. She was easy prey for the Shadowkin. When she started to change, spending whole nights away, I knew something was very wrong. Still, I didn't want to think it could be that. I thought it was another man, for a while." His laugh was hollow. "No such luck."

The pain in his voice sliced through Mia. How he could be too little for anyone was beyond her. But she could tell that Tess's judgment still affected how he saw himself.

"Were you Lunari then?"

"Oh, hell no. I was still getting settled, and Bane was in the process of taking over from the last Alpha. I just wanted to mess with cars, settle down, have a passel of kids. You know. The good stuff. I'm pretty simple, Mia."

She tipped her head back to look up at him. "Yes and no. But I like that about you."

His faint smile tugged at every heartstring she had.

"When the attacks on the pack started, picking people off one by one, some part of me knew it was her. Wasn't until she got one of the young ones, kid named Danny Sawyer who was just fourteen, that I knew I had to find out for sure. I'm the one who found her drinking one of the pack women dry. We saved the woman. But we couldn't save Tess. She'd started to become one of them. They'd preyed on every weakness she had and turned her against us. Even me. She wanted to join them, to turn completely and slip into their world instead of staying in ours. With her parents. With me."

Mia could see that even now it still caused him so much pain.

"So you were the one who ended it," she said quietly.

"I…had to be. Even at the end, I hoped I could make the real Tess come back, but…she never did. And the things she had done…such awful things. Her parents couldn't handle being here anymore after that. I'd been closer to her father than my own, but I was one of the things he needed to get away from. I understood. And he gave me the gift of the shop. But it was no consolation. They moved out West, joined up with a different pack. Nobody blamed them."

"She's why you became the Lunari," Mia said.

"I hate those things in a way you can't even imagine," Jenner said, his voice going rough, dangerous. "Seeing someone you know completely drained of blood, and knowing one of those *things* is going to live even longer because of it, is one of the worst feelings a wolf can have. Preventing that keeps me going, I guess."

"I'm sorry," Mia said, and meant it. That was a terrible thing to have to go through. No wonder he was messed up about relationships. Who would want to open up again after that? But the strength it must have taken to be able to deal with Tess at the end left her a little in awe of him, too.

"Don't be," Jenner said. "It was a long time ago. Back then, I only saw what I wanted to see. I should have known what she was becoming. There's too much goddamn dark magic in the world, Mia, believe me. All I want is to be a wolf, and to be left the hell alone by everything else."

There was a sharp knock at the door, and Jenner gave her a quick squeeze before settling her on her own on the plush couch cushions. Mia could only hope he didn't see how pale she'd gone in the dark.

"Hang on. That'll be Meri."

Jenner headed for the front door. From her vantage point, Mia couldn't see who it was, but when she heard a female voice, she was glad that not everything among pack mates was silent and telepathic. But then, werewolves were still people too. Sometimes, she knew, you just wanted to see and hear someone to make sure they were okay.

She heard a quick exchange, and caught the gist. A

hunting party had been dispatched immediately when Jenner had called for help, but no one thought they would find much now...though there was always hope.

The aftereffects of her first bout of animal instinct had worn off, it seemed. Sitting here alone made her feel very vulnerable and exposed. She pulled her knees into her chest and wrapped her arms around her legs, shrinking herself like a child might. It was a very nice surprise when Jenner not only headed right back to the couch, but also pulled her right back into his arms. It should have been awkward, at the very least. But Mia sagged gratefully against him. She still needed that extra bit of comfort. And Jenner, despite the gruff and slightly intimidating exterior, knew it and responded accordingly. His skin in the sensitive curve where broad shoulder meets neck was like hot silk when she rested her cheek against it. She wanted to nuzzle it, breathe in his scent. To enjoy what she could of him before she had to leave him behind, because there was no way she could keep all of herself from a man like this. He would hate what she was. Or at the very least, he would reject her because of it. He didn't want magic beyond what the wolf already possessed.

Neither had she, for a long time. But tonight had begun to change her mind. She had defended herself with it, easily controlling the flow of power from her fingertips. She felt sure she could do it again. The new werewolf aspect of herself had seemed only to enhance her natural magic.

A strange thing. But not as unwelcome as she'd originally found it.

Lost in thought, Mia was startled when Jenner's voice rumbled beside her ear once again.

"How are you doing?" he asked softly. "Feeling steadier now?"

Mia nodded. "A little," she said. "I won't pretend I didn't freak myself out, but I'll manage."

"It's not always freaky. But you seem determined to work up to this the hard way."

When she pulled back to glower at him, Mia was surprised to find Jenner's gold eyes glittering with humor. He was teasing her, and enjoying the reaction, from the look of him.

"This is quite a time to find your sense of humor," she said flatly. His grin widened.

"Yeah, well, ask around. My sense of humor usually gets talked about with the word *sick* in front of it. Sorry."

She smiled a little as she put her head back against his shoulder. "No you're not."

"No," he agreed. "I'm not. But I really am teasing. Mostly. I'd imagine you woke up feeling like someone dumped a tanker of caffeine into your system."

"I did," she admitted, surprised. "Why is that?"

"It's the pull of the moon," Jenner said, and the words, spoken in that husky voice of his, gave Mia a shiver from head to toe that had nothing to do with cold.

"It's like this for you, too?" Mia asked. "Every night?"

"No," he replied. "Not every night, and you just learn

to work around becoming a more nocturnal person in some ways. But this time of the month, when the moon's nearly full, yeah, I have trouble settling down. You'd be amazed at the chores I've finished at 2:00 a.m. Just the nature of the beast."

"I'm glad you weren't asleep," Mia said quietly.

"Yeah," he replied. "Me, too."

They sat in companionable silence for several minutes. Mia comforted herself listening to the steady beat of Jenner's heart. Wanting him this way was madness. Pining over what could never be was futile. And yet here she was, curled up in his lap, torturing herself as he began, tentatively, to stroke her back.

He wasn't just watching over her, he was actively taking care of her. And Mia knew Jenner only took particular care with the things that mattered to him.

Mia could only hope he didn't come to regret that later…and that neither would she.

Chapter 13

Jenner knew he was playing with fire, holding her like this. He just couldn't seem to stop himself.

He hadn't allowed himself to respond this way to a woman since Tess. This was different, though. Mia was nothing like the woman he'd once loved and lost. Well, almost nothing. Despite Mia's innocence, there was still some kind of mystery about her. Not a deadly one. But something...*more*, nonetheless. Maybe it was that hint of fae blood that had drawn Gaines to her, but he didn't think so. It was just *Mia*. To his chagrin, every second he spent with her only drew him more strongly to her.

He wasn't stupid. He knew what it could mean if he let it. There was a reason werewolf courtships were short and their matings permanent. For his kind, when a thing was right, it just *was*.

And Mia felt it, too, or she wouldn't be curled up in his lap, leaning into his touch like a kitten.

Damn it, he'd meant it when he'd told her he couldn't be the one to bring her into the pack. He wouldn't risk himself again that way. But hell if he could keep his hands off of her. Especially when he thought of what might have happened earlier.

"Jenner?"

Her voice was warm and smooth, rich like cream. He looked down at her, so full of longing and frustration that he knew she must sense it. Seeing the look in her eyes confirmed it, and Jenner took some solace in the fact that it wasn't only he who'd been struggling.

Her eyes never leaving his, Mia tentatively lifted her hands to place them on either side of his face. She wasn't timid. Quiet sometimes, but not timid. Not at her heart. Tonight she'd shocked the hell out of the Silverback Alpha…and gotten exactly what she wanted. He got the feeling, more and more, that one underestimated Mia D'Alessandro at one's peril. It was one of the many things he found so appealing about her.

"Mia," he said softly, making that one word a desire-filled plea.

Then they reached for one another at the same time.

At first contact, Jenner felt his blood surge in his veins. Her lips were just as soft as he remembered, made for pleasure. She sank into the kiss with a soft gasp as his world became nothing more than exploring her with his mouth, tongue, hands. Her hands skimmed down the sides of his face, over rough night stubble, and then cruised over his shoulders, down the skin of his chest. Jenner could feel her heart change rhythm under his hands as he cupped one perfect breast with his palm, thumbing the taut nipple until she moaned into his mouth. Passion arced between them, electric in its intensity.

Jenner groaned in return, tangling his fingers in her hair. Mia made a sound, some soft, pleading sound of submission as she pressed herself against him. It drove him right to the brink of his sanity, of his precious control. And he was so dangerously close to letting go. There had been other women since Tess. But he'd never let himself truly want. Not until now.

She gave a soft cry as he broke the kiss. Mia's eyes were full of fire, glowing softly as she looked at him, and Jenner could see he wasn't the only one close to losing control. He could see the beast in those eyes… and something more. Something wild and shimmering and irresistibly beautiful. Something singularly Mia. He wanted to turn away from it…but so much of him wanted to simply fall into her.

"Mia," he breathed. "I can't…we can't…"

"I know," she said. "But I need you to touch me, Jenner. Even if it's only tonight. Just be with me. Be with me."

His answer was a series of hot and breathless kisses as he gave into temptation at last.

Moving with a grace and speed she hadn't thought herself capable of, Mia shifted position with a single fluid movement and straddled Jenner. His guttural groan, the way his hands clamped on her hips, told her she had won. Every nerve ending was alight with need. Her body felt like it was close to combustion. The feel of him, brutally aroused between her legs and thrust against the thin cotton of her pajama shorts, sent her to the edge of a blinding orgasm before she had time to think.

The magic with her awakened again, sending power and need flickering through her like fire in her veins. She heard her own secret song, heard his pulsing beneath his skin, twining with hers until they made a singular melody that was all their own. Thought fled in the face of instincts that were as old as time. When Jenner hissed in a breath as she arched into him, Mia let her head fall back, exposing her throat to him.

Be with me, she thought. *Take me.*

And though she knew it was impossible, she could have sworn she heard Jenner's voice inside her head.

As you wish.

She found herself flipped in an instant, flat on her back on the big, comfortable couch. And the feel of Jenner pressed against her, letting her have some of his weight, was something akin to heaven itself. His hands, so big and sure, slid up and under her tank top. Mia helped him remove it, eager to have nothing between them. It was quickly discarded, and Mia gave a hoarse cry of pleasure when they were skin to skin.

If she'd had any doubts that Jenner was as pulled to her as she was to him, they vanished in the face of his desire. His hands were all over her as they tangled together on the couch. His mouth was hot, hard, demanding. Mia arched into him, urging him on wordlessly as he filled his hands with her breasts, squeezed. Then she gasped as his hand slipped beneath the waistband of her pants. His name filled her head and her heart.

"Nick," she murmured, forgetting herself as he sought out the slick and swollen folds concealing the bud of her sex, then began to stroke her. For once, the use of his given name didn't seem to give Jenner any pause at all.

"Mmm," he agreed, almost a purr. Mia rose against his hand as he played her, his breathing as harsh as hers. She could feel his eyes on her, watching as he drove her toward her climax. Mia's eyes slipped closed. She could see nothing, only feel. And there was so much to feel.

"Look at me," he growled. "I want you to look at me."

Her eyes opened and locked with his, and then Mia was hit with a wave of pleasure that tore right through her. She cried out, arching upward and stiffening as she rode the waves of her orgasm. Jenner continued stroking, wringing every drop of pleasure from her until she should have had nothing left. And still she wanted more.

"Make love to me," she breathed, writhing against him, sliding her hand down to wrap her fingers around the hard and silken shaft that throbbed at her touch. Jenner's heart was pounding against her chest, that his breathing was as ragged as she'd ever heard it. He'd buried his face in her neck, and when Mia gave his back a testing stroke, he shuddered in response. It was only then that she realized just how close he was to losing all control.

"Need to…need to get—"

She had wondered how werewolves managed to have sex lives without turning every partner into one of them. The answer, Mia suddenly realized, was laughably simple, apart from being a good idea anyway. And she was ready to sprint wherever she was directed to get Jenner the box he needed.

"Where?" she asked breathlessly. "Nick," she purred, and she could actually *feel* his pleasure coursing through her as his given name fell from her lips again.

"Hang on," he breathed. "Just…hell…"

He vanished so quickly she barely felt him go, and she was gripped by a sudden, terrible fear that he wouldn't come back. But it was only moments and he returned. She heard the tearing of foil as he fumbled back onto the couch, uncharacteristically graceless in his need. Mia slid her arms around him, and he went still, breathing harshly.

"I just don't want to screw this up," he said.

"You won't," Mia reassured him. "You're not."

She helped him on with the condom, enjoying the way his breath shook as he exhaled. Then they were entwined again, moving together. He couldn't seem to get enough of her, and Mia twisted and turned so that he could touch more of her, all of her. She slid his pajama pants the rest of the way off, while he took care of her shorts. Jenner took her to the floor, sinking into the plush area rug and positioning himself over her.

He touched his forehead to hers, and then kissed her, a long, slow, decadent kiss that sent pleasure from her head to her toes. Mia moaned and stretched beneath him, and that's when he plunged. Mia sucked in a breath as Jenner buried himself in her. He stilled.

"God," he groaned. "So tight. Mia…"

She lifted her hips once, twice against him, and then Jenner began to move inside her with a primal rhythm all his own. Mia matched it, feeling the pressure building inside of her all over again. He filled her completely, and every stroke carried her closer to some decadent place where there was nothing but sensation, nothing but this kind of full-body bliss.

She watched his face as her breath caught with every stroke. He was beautiful, she thought. And tonight, he was hers.

He moved faster within her, and Mia felt the pleasure coiling, tightening. And yet she had the sense that there was more, lingering just out of reach. So much more Jenner could give her, if he were willing. She felt his heart thundering against her chest, keeping perfect time with her own.

Jenner linked his fingers with hers, moving them over her head so that she was captured completely. His mouth scorched her face, her breasts. Mia moaned low in the back of her throat, blind to all but the pleasure that was rushing at her.

The orgasm blew through her like a summer storm. She cried out, arching into Jenner as he found his own release, shouting as he came. Her entire body quivered as the aftershocks shimmered through her one by one. They rode the waves together, until they ebbed into delicate ripples of pleasure. Mia's entire body felt as though it were covered in stardust.

She curled against Jenner, her breathing slowly normalizing, wondering what they had created together. Even after he withdrew, she could feel him in her blood. Something had shifted fundamentally in her world when they'd joined. She just couldn't focus well enough to consider what, or what that was going to mean. All she could think of was that no matter how incredible their lovemaking had been, they had teetered on the precipice of even more.

She barely felt it as he lifted her, carrying her to his room where he lowered her to the bed. Jenner didn't want to let her go, any more than she wanted to be let go, Mia realized. Something else to think about…later. He vanished for a few long seconds, and then climbed in to join her. Mia slid easily into his arms, snuggling into the curve of his body.

Jenner's soft rumble made her smile.

"If we were going to flout Pack Law," he said, "we sure did it right."

He sounded as satisfied as she felt. Mia felt herself beginning to drift to sleep, cruising on the euphoria that came after an amazing session of lovemaking. Jenner said no more, seeming content to hold her.

Somewhere, in the dim recesses of her consciousness, she felt herself reaching for him, into him, re-creating that magic song they'd created together. With her guard down, Mia let it ripple through her, taking it into herself, taking *him* in, until she was aware of nothing but being enveloped by Jenner. In her mind, they danced together in a ring of faerie lights beneath the glowing moon. Eyes, kind and somehow familiar, watched them approvingly from the gently swaying trees.

Faewolf, they breathed, their voices as one. *Daughter of the magic moon.*

In innocent sleep, all Mia could think of was that she'd finally come home.

"Nick," she murmured, the soft sound reaching his ears as he shivered and pulled her closer, trying even in sleep to protect her from something that seemed to come from everywhere and nowhere, pulsing all around them.

In his dreams he watched Mia dance, laughing, into a strange and unfamiliar night. Her eyes were as bright as the moon…and then they were Tess's lifeless eyes, mocking him even in death for having loved her. Having trusted her.

Reminding him never to open his heart again.

Chapter 14

After a surprisingly deep sleep, Mia awakened to a silent house.

Even without checking, she knew Jenner was gone. She didn't know when he'd left, but she felt his absence as keenly as if she'd watched him walk out the door. It was strange, but Mia guessed it was no stranger than her last few days.

And if nothing else, the quiet gave her an opportunity to brood uninterrupted. She'd wanted to see him this morning, to wake up with his arms around her. What had happened between them last night had been about more than just sex—she'd felt that on a level so deep she couldn't question it. He had to have felt it, too.

But maybe he hadn't. Or worse, maybe he had and that was why he was gone.

She showered and got ready for the day, then wandered out of the room and down the stairs, thinking vaguely about finding something to eat. Around her, there wasn't a sound. She hadn't quite realized what a vital presence Jenner was until now. She wanted him here.

But then, she'd wanted a lot of things she couldn't have.

Mia replayed the events of last night over again in her mind, moving without really seeing anything around her. Had she missed something? Had something gone wrong? Or was he just being Nick Jenner, wandering the Hollow and brooding because he'd touched her when he'd sworn he wouldn't?

She wished she knew.

The sight of one long, lanky female sprawled on the couch stopped Mia dead in her tracks, right in the middle of the stairs. The woman didn't appear to notice her staring down, though. One leg was draped over the arm of the couch and was bobbing up and down rhythmically. Mia found if she focused, she could faintly hear music. The foot attached to the leg was bare, its toenails painted deep and shimmering purple. The other leg was bent.

Whoever this was, she didn't seem very worried about not belonging there.

"Um, hello?" Mia said as she descended the rest of the stairs, making the body of the woman disappear from view.

The leg stiffened for an instant, then disappeared

back over the arm of the couch. There was a moment of scrambling, and a head popped up to look over the back at her.

"Hey," the stranger said as she finished pulling a pair of ear buds out of her ears.

"Hey," Mia replied, eyebrows lifting. This, at least, was a distraction. Whoever this was, she was incredibly cute, in a gothic pixie sort of way. A choppy black bob set off a delicate, pointed little face dominated by a big, luminous pair of heavily lashed eyes such a dark blue they looked almost like polished onyx. As Mia stood staring at her, completely nonplused, the pixie's rose-bud lips parted and gave way to a big, irreverent grin.

"Bet you're wondering what I'm doing on the couch," she said cheerily.

"Yeah," Mia said slowly. "I guess you could say that. I'm Mia."

"Aislynn. Aislynn O'Doyle." She got lightly to her feet and came around the couch. The outfit marked her as being a few years younger than Mia herself, skinny black jeans, a T-shirt emblazoned with the name of a band Mia had heard of but didn't really listen to, and a ragged, oversized flannel shirt with the sleeves rolled. She was lithe, petite, and yet still exuded a tremendous amount of contained energy.

Mia wasn't sure whether to shake hands or flee.

"Sorry, should have been paying better attention, but I've been zoning out with my iPod. Jenner told me no video games while you were sleeping, all he has to read is auto magazines, and his junk food situation is pathetic, so I'm glad you're up. I was close to throwing myself out of a window."

Mia couldn't help the laugh that bubbled up in her throat. "I'm glad we avoided that, then. Look, I hope you don't mind my asking, but...who *are* you? And where's Jenner?"

Aislynn wrinkled her small, pointy little nose. The effect was one of charming disgust.

"I'm one of the pack's hunters. And I'm the *youngest* right now, since they don't usually take new hunters on until a prospect is out of college. I graduated in May. Hence, I get a disproportionate amount of crap from the older hunters, and I also get picked on when someone wants to stop babysitting and go play." She winced. "Sorry. Not that you're a baby. Figure of speech."

Fascinated by the steady stream of chatter, so different from Jenner's "pulling teeth" style of conversation, Mia hardly noticed the accidental insult.

"Don't worry about it," she said. "I'm not your average initiate. I get it."

That seemed to strike Aislynn funny. "Initiate, huh? I like it. Makes it sound so much more formal than the reality." She waved her hand, fingernails shimmering in the same shade of purple as her toes, a multitude of silver rings glinting in the light. "Anyway, Jenner got called out to have a look at some stuff in the woods early this morning. And I got tagged to chill here with you."

Mia tried not to show it as she breathed a sigh of relief. It was the one reason for Jenner's being gone that made sense, and she was glad to hear that he hadn't just bolted because of sleeping with her.

Not that she was any clearer on what he *did* think about that, but it could have been worse. Now that the only thing she'd been able to think about all morning was resolved, curiosity quickly replaced obsessing.

"Thanks for playing babysitter, then," Mia said with a smile.

"No problem," Aislynn said easily, shifting her weight from one foot to the other with fluid grace. She seemed to have too much natural energy to stand still. "I wasn't actually sure I'd get to meet you this morning. I figured Jenner would be back by now, but nothing about all this is really normal." She paused, eyes widening. "I mean, not that you're abnormal. Just the whole feral psycho thing."

"Got it," Mia replied, trying to stifle a laugh. It wasn't until right that moment that she realized just how much she'd missed female companionship.

Aislynn looked around and bounced lightly on the balls of her feet. "Want to go get lunch? I'm starving. I don't know what Jenner eats, but I have a hard time believing he exists on stale pretzels and beer."

"I think he used up all his breakfast stuff a couple of—wait, lunch?"

Aislynn tipped her chin down and arched one dark brow. "Yes, sleeping beauty. You slept in. I guess I'll pretend I have manners and not start teasing you about why. Yet. I usually wait at least an hour before I get really obnoxious."

Panic had set in too quickly for Mia to find that funny. All she could think of was that she'd slept until lunch. Which was about the time she'd agreed to go to lunch with a guy who was definitely *not* the one she'd spent the night with.

There was a quick knock at the door. Mia closed her eyes and groaned.

Aislynn looked toward the door and tilted her nose up into the air with a considering look on her face. Whatever she smelled, she seemed to enjoy it.

"Hmm. You don't like that?"

Mia inhaled and immediately scented him—warm, vital, and very male, an appealing blend of spices. She wondered whether an escape through a bathroom window was plausible.

"He smells good," Mia admitted.

"Looks good, too," Aislynn agreed with a smirk. "A little clean-cut for me, but then again, it could be hiding a wild side." She looked more closely at Mia, and even though they shared no telepathic connection, the feminine one was enough. "Uh-oh. Lunch date?"

"Yeah."

"He know about you and Jenner?"

Mia fought the urge to massage away the headache that was rapidly brewing at her temples. "There was no *me and Jenner* when I said I'd go. I'm still not exactly sure about that. But this isn't—"

Aislynn held up a hand. "Say no more. I'm your babysitter, remember? Where you go, I go. Even if it causes an awkward non-date during which I try really hard to make the cute Silverback blush."

Mia's looked at Aislynn in mute gratitude. This was what it meant to be part of a pack, she realized. It was having a big family to look out for you, watch your back. Even run interference with unwanted lunch dates.

Jenner had been right…the Hollow wasn't Philly, but it had plenty going for it. Maybe more than she'd realized.

"Thank you," Mia said. "I mean, I don't even know you…"

Aislynn waved her off. "My pleasure." Then she winked. "Seriously."

Chapter 15

Somehow, against all the odds, Mia was having some of the most fun she'd had in recent memory.

Aislynn O'Doyle, she had decided, was going to be a friend no matter what happened. Mia had already laughed so hard her stomach hurt, and they had plenty in common. They sat across from one another now in a booth, where Aislynn sat flipping through the songs available on the mini jukebox attached to the wall. Every booth had one, all connected to the large juke at the far end of the diner where the songs they selected would play.

For several minutes now, Aislynn had been debating over how best to torture the other diners. She was between an inexplicably popular teenaged boy who sounded disturbingly like an untalented girl, and a teen-aged television star who actually was an untalented girl.

"I'm plugging my ears," Kenyon protested, laughing. "I don't want to know what you pick, and I'm afraid my ears will start bleeding if I hear it."

Mia looked at Kenyon, who was sitting beside her. He had dimples, she noted, because of course he did. And nothing he'd done had changed Mia's impression of him. He was polite, charming, and so boyish he some-times seemed even younger than he was. He was also handsome enough that Mia had seen every woman in the place, from teenagers to old women, ogling him. Kenyon was just so ridiculously...*cute*.

She was also completely positive he wasn't for her. But at this point, she had to give him credit for persis-tence.

He turned to her, blue eyes crinkled up at the corners. And he'd gotten awfully close to her, she realized, by sliding slowly over when she wasn't paying attention. She could almost see the little hearts in his baby blues.

Uh-oh.

"So I was thinking," he said. "Why don't you come out with me tonight? We could grab some dinner, maybe catch a movie. The little theater here is actually pretty nice."

Mia smiled and tried to think of a nice way to let him down. Even if Jenner backed off again, Kenyon wasn't the kind of guy who would be all right with a single night. He deserved someone who...well, actually, someone who looked at him the way Aislynn was, if he'd just stop to notice.

"Actually, Kenyon…"

She heard the bell above the door ring, and a wave of joy crashed through her that took her completely by surprise. All Mia knew was that one moment, she felt normal, and the next, every nerve ending was singing with pleasure at some new sensation in the air. Something lovely and familiar and absolutely adored…

She looked up and saw Jenner, looking far too big and dangerous to be allowed in a silly kitsch diner, walking through the door. He zeroed in on her immediately, and the moment their eyes locked, Mia felt everything else fade away. She let out a breath she hadn't even been aware she was holding. Every instinct she had insisted she get up, go to him, drawn forward as though Jenner had an actual magnetic pull.

Her reaction to him had been intense enough before. Sleeping with him, it seemed, had multiplied that by a thousand.

Her heart beat once, twice, and she could hear the echo of his own in her head. She had the oddest thing happen then: her mind filled with the faint sound of a deep voice saying her name with a tenderness that made her ache inside. Then it was over, gone like the brush of butterfly wings. She wondered if she'd imagined it. But she hadn't imagined Jenner.

And she wasn't imagining the murderous look on his face when he saw who was sitting beside her. There was a soft but unmistakable sound beside her: growling. With a great deal of effort, Mia turned her attention away from Jenner to look incredulously at Kenyon.

"No," she said, hearing the pleading note in her own voice. "Please no. Not in the diner."

The only person who seemed to be amused was Aislynn. She was watching the scene unfold with a great deal of interest, and didn't look particularly concerned. That, despite the fact that Mia had a terrible feeling that Jenner and Kenyon were going to start pummeling one another any second.

Jenner strode to their booth, looking absolutely delicious in ripped jeans that hung low on his hips, scuffed boots, a black T-shirt, and a rumpled jacket. His lip twitched as though it wanted to curl, and his eyes seemed to burn. As angry as he was, though, the instant he turned those eyes on her, Mia thought she might melt into a puddle right there.

"Hate to interrupt," he growled in a tone that said the opposite, "but you're going to have to cut your lunch with these two short."

"Now?" Mia asked, trying to get her thoughts together. "Why?"

"I'll explain it when we get out of here."

"If this is about Gaines, then it concerns me, too," Kenyon said, every trace of sweetness gone from his voice. "I think I'll come with you."

"The hell you will," Jenner replied, and now his lip did curl. "Since all this concerns is me, Mia, and a healthy dose of 'you're not invited.'"

Kenyon stood up quickly, drawing the attention of

quite a few diners. Mia cringed inwardly. People tended to notice when there was a fight brewing, and the testosterone in here had just jumped to critical levels.

She stood up, too, though more slowly, and tried not to look as desperate as she felt. Men did not fight over her. Ever. And she now understood that having it happen was not nearly as cool as it sounded.

"You're not shoving me out of the way," Kenyon growled at Jenner. All traces of that boyishness Mia had seen in him were gone, and she could clearly see the wolf lurking beneath the surface. He might be a lover, but there was no question he was also a fighter.

She laid a hand on Kenyon's arm, feeling the tension that coiled through him like steel cables. But the gentle pressure of her hand got his attention.

"I'm going with him," she said. "And you're staying here. There's no reason for you and Aislynn to leave just because of me."

His face fell, and Mia felt terrible. She could see Jenner eyeing her hand with a particularly ugly look, but as long as he didn't decide to gnaw Kenyon's arm off, she would ignore it.

Kenyon didn't say another word to her, just gave a short nod and stepped out of the booth to let her pass. To Jenner, however, she heard him mutter, "I have a few things to say to you. Later."

She caught the smug look Jenner gave him, and felt her own temper spark. Just because Jenner had gotten his way was no reason to taunt the losing party. She turned and said goodbye to Aislynn, who promised she would see her later on in the day. Then she left without another word to Jenner, not trusting herself not to shout at him. He followed close behind her, and she could feel the warmth of his presence as though the sun were beating on her back.

She loved it, and she hated it. Because while every bit of her thrilled at just having him near her again, the logical part of her was terrified that this was all leading up to some huge disappointment. Almost from the start, Jenner had told her that he wasn't interested in any sort of relationship. But if he wasn't, then why did he look at her the way he did? And why had he touched her the way he had, as though she were something precious to him? Last night had been everything she'd wanted... but then, not quite everything. She wanted him to be with her, only her. She wanted him to ask her to stay.

And Mia had no idea if that was ever going to happen.

She made it only a few steps outside before whirling on him.

"Well?" she demanded.

"Well what?" he asked in a surly grunt. He still looked decidedly pissed off, his hands shoved deep into his pockets and his large frame slightly hunched.

"You storm in, act like a complete Neanderthal, demand I leave with you for some unspecified reason, and then storm out again. Sound weird to you?"

Jenner shrugged. "Doesn't sound very unusual to me."

Mia exhaled loudly. "No, it probably wouldn't to

you. In the world outside the Hollow, however, where people aren't used to you acting like a bully, that sort of thing is considered rude."

Jenner lifted one dark brow. "Good thing I live in the Hollow, then."

Mia stared at him, lifted her hands, and growled in frustration. "For the love of—*why* are you so awful to Kenyon?"

"Because he wants you."

The answer, honest and to the point, surprised Mia into stunned silence.

"And I want you, too, Mia," Jenner finished. "With wolves, that kind of thing means Chase and I aren't going to be friends. It also means I'm not going to just smile and deal with it when you decide to have lunch with him while I'm gone."

"You...want me." She said the words slowly, trying to be sure she'd heard them correctly. His actions had shown it, of course...but the admission was more than she'd expected.

Jenner glowered at her. "Pretty sure we were both there last night."

Mia gave an exasperated laugh and pushed an errant lock of hair out of her face. "I...okay, for one thing, you did see there were three of us in there, right?"

Jenner's stony expression didn't change. "Uh-huh. Aislynn can get her earful later."

Mia rolled her eyes. "She volunteered to run interference, Nick," she said, hoping the intimacy of his first name would remind him of just how much they'd shared last night. His gaze softened, ever so slightly. When he stayed silent, Mia pressed on, flustered by his reaction. Territorial werewolves were a new experience for her.

So was *being* the territory.

"I guess I'm not sure what I'm supposed to say to you. I want you, too? It's not very romantic."

"Neither am I, Mia. I'm warning you about that right up front."

"Okay," she said slowly. "I can handle that, if that's what you're asking."

"It isn't," he said, his voice a rough growl. Mia settled her hands on her hips, completely exasperated.

"Then what *are* you asking?"

Finally, the bluster fell away, and Mia could finally see what was beneath. He was just as nervous and uncertain as she was. Somehow, it made her feel better, knowing that this was new for both of them.

"I thought you might want to go for a ride," he said.

It was only then that Mia noticed the car parked beside the curb, hulking like a muscular metal beast and gleaming in the sun.

"I thought it wasn't done."

"Close enough," Jenner said. He watched her unblinkingly with those intense eyes of his. "It's a beautiful day."

"It is," Mia agreed, feeling strangely off balance. Jenner seemed to be good at doing that to her. He was such a mix of wild and civilized. It fascinated her.

"So?" he asked, and there was a wealth of meaning in that one simple question.

But when it came to Jenner, everything seemed to boil down to a single, simple answer.

"Let's go," Mia replied, and walked toward the car.

Riding in a growling hulk of a muscle car turned out to be better than good. It was exactly what Mia had needed.

She was inches away from sticking her head out the window and going the full canine route as they flew down a hilly back road. The day was warmer than had been expected, almost like the end of summer. She'd caught Jenner's bemused expression when she'd pulled an elastic out of her purse, tied her hair back in a quick ponytail, and rolled down the window.

"It's a beautiful day" was all she said. "I'll deal with the tangles later."

"Good choice," Jenner replied, and she wondered if either of them were actually talking about her hair.

There was something freeing about the speed, and the painted glory of the trees as they rushed past. Mia felt the tightness she'd had in her chest all weekend ease. She wanted things to be simple. Nothing ever was. Except this.

Jenner's presence was solid and reassuring beside her, and when she snuck glances at him he looked as comfortable as she'd ever seen him maneuvering the muscle car around curves and beneath tunnels of trees. They headed farther out into the country, and Mia watched farms and homes fly past. The air smelled rich, like decayed leaves and wood smoke. Some of her favorite smells.

When Jenner slowed and turned into a long drive, Mia looked around curiously. There was a lovely, weathered farmhouse at the end of the drive, and squatting nearby was a barn and chicken coop. Cattle grazed placidly in the fields surrounding the house.

She turned her head to look at Jenner. "I don't care what you say. You're not going to convince me to chase chickens. Not yet, anyway."

His laugh, the deep, warm roll of it, pushed her further toward the edge of a precipice she'd been inching toward ever since she'd met him.

He parked the car on the grass beside the house, then killed the engine. They sat in silence for a long, surprisingly comfortable moment. Finally, Mia looked over at him, genuinely curious.

"Can I ask what brought this on?"

Jenner's gold eyes caught hers when he turned his head. The lazy half smile made her feel like melting into her seat. But there was something in his expression that puzzled her…almost a kind of resignation. Mia wondered what it was about. Whether it was about her.

"I got up early."

She arched an eyebrow. "Okay."

"I had a lot of time to think while I was tracking this morning. We found a body, by the way. Didn't belong to Gaines." He frowned and put up a hand before she could ask any questions. "I should have saved that. It's not what I brought you here for."

"But was it one of…yours?" She'd almost said "ours." It had been on the tip of her tongue.

He shook his head. "No. We think he might have been one of Gaines' men. Unfortunately, that's about as much as we can figure right now. He…wasn't in good shape."

"Oh." He was right…this wasn't a great lead-in.

Jenner laughed quietly, as though he knew what she was thinking. "I mentioned I wasn't great at talking, right? Walk with me," Jenner said. "It's beautiful out here, and there are some things I guess we need to talk about."

That, at least, was a relief to hear. "Yes," Mia agreed. "I guess there are."

Without another word, Jenner got out of the car. Mia got out, too, noting that Jenner had come around to take her hand and shut the door. It was a small thing, but he kept her hand in his as they headed off down a narrow path that veered away from the house and through a meadow that Mia imagined would be in all its glory come the spring. There was a pond in the distance, and she could hear a few ducks and geese.

Jenner walked quietly beside her for a few minutes, and Mia waited. Though she hadn't known him long, she understood how he was. Jenner was a living illustration of how still waters ran deep.

Finally, he spoke. "I didn't think I'd ever be all that interested in anyone again, Mia. But every time I'm near you I forget every damn rule I've made for myself. Last night…" He trailed off, then stopped, turning to face her.

"Last night meant something. I knew it would, I guess, which is why I was trying not to let it happen. But it did, and I can't take it back. I wouldn't want to."

A hard knot she hadn't even been aware existed finally began to loosen deep within Mia's chest.

"I can't stop thinking about you," Mia admitted. "It ought to feel crazy, but it doesn't. Look at what I'm dealing with, what I just went through. The last thing that should be on my mind is a guy, but it's all I can do not to throw myself at you every time you walk in the room. And last night…" She tried to find the words and failed miserably.

The deep rumble of Jenner's laugh rippled through her, telling her he understood.

"It's like that with wolves, when things are…right," Jenner said. "Even faster with us because you're bitten already. Nobody's really sure why werewolves have accelerated courtships, but it's expected within the pack." He watched her from beneath long, impossibly dark lashes. "I won't lie, Mia. This might turn out to be a big mess no matter how you or I feel about it. But there's no way in hell I'm letting Kenyon Chase or any other man anywhere near you for even one night."

"You're offering to initiate me," Mia said.

Jenner shifted and ran a hand through his hair, finally showing some of his agitation. He blew out a breath, then said, "Yeah. And after that, we can maybe, you know…see where it goes. There were some good reasons I told you I wasn't the right guy to choose for your initiation, or for anything. I don't know how much I've got to give. I can't promise you anything. But I can tell you that what you're feeling, what I'm feeling, means we'd be good together. And…I'd like to give it a shot. I know what you said about wanting to take off soon, but…I'd like it if you stayed a little while. Maybe give it a try with the Blackpaw. With me."

Mia looked at him standing there, looking every inch the fierce, protective werewolf he was, and felt her heart clench painfully, then release. He was taking a big chance, one she'd never expected him to take.

She wasn't the only one who was learning to take risks, she supposed.

And she knew that before long, she would have to take a few more. Jenner couldn't stay in the dark about her gifts. She needed to find a way to tell him. Soon.

"Will Bane accept this?" she asked, hating that it was even a question. But this wasn't her world, and she didn't want Jenner to suffer on her behalf.

Jenner nodded. "Yeah. He, ah…wasn't exactly surprised. There are going to be ruffled feathers, but you made your position on choosing pretty clear." She saw a hint of his smile. "He only asks that we wait a couple of days. Until the night before the full moon. He's worried that if we close you off to Gaines, he'll just go and find someone else. Unseelie blood is rare, but…"

Mia nodded, relieved. She had a little time to figure out how to tell Jenner everything she needed to… hopefully in a way that wouldn't ruin everything. Even though it was selfish, she wanted to enjoy him right now, in this moment. She'd never had anyone, not really. It couldn't be wrong to want to enjoy a few hours of it, no matter what came after.

"So," Jenner said softly. "What do you think?"

Mia saw the way his Adam's apple moved and knew just how twisted up he was over this. She wanted to wrap her arms around his neck and reassure him, to feel all that wonderful warmth and strength and know it was hers...even if it was just for now.

"Yes" was all she said.

She immediately found herself crushed against Jenner's chest, his mouth on hers. Her head was full of him, every inch of her skin feeling like it was shooting off sparks. She opened her mouth for him, moaning as his tongue swept inside. Jenner lifted her up, and she wrapped her legs around his waist. She could feel how hard he was for her, and she arched, gasping, into all of that delicious heat.

It was an unpleasant shock to feel herself lowered quickly back to the ground, though Jenner wrapped his arms around her and tucked her head beneath his chin. It was some small consolation that she could feel his heart pounding just as quickly as hers was.

"I promised myself we were going to take it slow this time," Jenner said, his deep voice husky.

Mia laughed. "Nothing about this is slow," she said.

"Okay. Mostly I promised myself I wouldn't tear your clothes off in the middle of this field if you said yes." He looked down at her. "Let me take you home, Mia."

She nodded, then she put her hand back in his and held on tight, hoping she wasn't taking this step only to be forced to let go.

Chapter 16

By the next night, Mia had almost forgotten about the watching eyes out in the darkness.

No matter how intense her connection to Jenner seemed, the fact remained that she was only just beginning to learn about his life. And to her delight, he'd begun to show it to her. She'd gotten to see the garage he owned, enjoying the way he prowled around the cars like a restless animal. It was his territory, and she found she liked watching him on it.

It surprised her that the gruff werewolf was still tentative with her in some ways, as though he was afraid she would somehow find him lacking. How could he possibly know just how little he had to be afraid of? There didn't seem to be anything wrong with the man.

Or at least, nothing wrong with him that she didn't find strangely sexy anyway.

So Mia watched, and enjoyed, and wished there were more she could show him of her own life. His quiet, slightly awed appreciation of the design work she showed him meant a lot to her. But it wasn't until she watched Jenner's interactions with the tight-knit pack of the town that she realized what she'd been missing. The thing she couldn't share with him because it didn't really exist.

A network of friends and family. A home.

She'd been lonelier than she'd known. Here, she was less hidden than she had been in the city…and infinitely happier. Aislynn had been by again to see her, and people had begun to wave at her as if they knew her. More, Jenner's house had already begun to feel more like home than any she'd ever been in. And his bed, as she'd been frequently reminded, was a place she might happily spend days on end as long as Jenner was with her.

She could belong here, Mia thought.

She could almost believe nothing could touch her.

Almost.

The moon hung fat and heavy in the sky when Mia's eyes flew open in the darkened bedroom. She frowned, unsure of what had wakened her. Jenner was still beside her, his warmth reassuring in the silence.

Then she heard the whispers.

Mia…Miiiiiiaaaaaaaa…

Something flickered past one of the windows, darker

than the night. Her breath stilled in her throat. They
were outside. Waiting.

She lifted a hand to wake Jenner up, but paused just
before touching him. Moonlight poured into the room,
flooding her system with the kind of energy she and
Jenner had talked about. It was the power of the moon,
calling to the wolf now running in her veins. In seconds,
she was wide awake. And with her alertness came an
anger so deep it stunned her.

This was *hers*. Nothing in her life had ever inspired
this sort of raw possession. She immediately found
herself struggling with the urge to dash outside, teeth
bared, and make a stand against the things that wanted
to take all of this away from her. To take *Jenner* away
from her.

She knew what he would do if she woke him. He
would do exactly what she was trying not to. And as
strong as he was, if these things had slithered this far
into protected territory to taunt her, they were feeling
confident about their chances.

Mia pulled her hand back, eyes caressing Jenner as
he slept. The pull at her heart was deep, real, and ac-
companied by an ache she'd never felt before. He looked
so innocent in sleep, less hardened, less wary. His lips
were slightly parted as he breathed deeply.

Mia sighed softly as another shadow made the moonlight flicker through the window, then another.

She knew what she was feeling, even though it was
new and unexpected and unfamiliar. Jenner said that
when things were right between wolves, they just…

happened. Fast. That was an understatement, but she knew with a bone-deep certainty that she would give everything she had to keep him safe.

Miiiiiiiaaaaaaa...

She turned her head to glare at the dancing patches of darkness that continued to drift gleefully through her line of sight. The Shadowkin were tired of waiting. And she was tired of being a victim. A vision flickered through her head of Jeff in his wolf form running away from her, howling. *I could do that again*, she thought. She wouldn't have to go outside. She and Jenner would be safe for the rest of the night, at least. He would never have to know.

Silently, Mia slid out of the bed. Jenner didn't move a muscle, a relief.

Her anger rose quickly, something she would have to channel if she didn't want another episode where she nearly succumbed to the wolf. But she was getting stronger. This time, Mia felt a great deal more confident that she could handle it. And sending a few Shadowkin shrieking back into the woods should help.

She padded down the stairs in her bare feet, looking at the huge window. She tried to stay as far back from it as she could. It was dark, but she was hardly the only thing that could see in it. Her confidence faltered, but only for an instant. Because they would sense her weakness.

And there were dozens of them.

The woods were full of them, human-shaped patches of a black far deeper than any night. They slipped in and out of the trees, some walking, some running, others seeming to float…and a few actually flying. There were glints of red, bright fiery sparks. Their eyes.

Mia drew in a single, shuddering breath.

All at once, they stopped and turned to look directly at her.

For what seemed like forever, nothing moved. They were simply…waiting. And that was when she felt it, the power gathering inside of her with a strength she'd never known. It coursed through her blood, singing its wild midnight song as her skin lit, then burned brighter. Pale tendrils of violet light drifted upward from her skin like smoke. And as the magic rose, so did her fury.

She would banish these things from her life, from this place, for good. She knew she could do it, if she could only reach a little more deeply into herself, if she got just a little closer.

Mia felt herself descending the stairs the rest of the way, though she was barely aware of it. She let herself be pulled toward the moonlight, the starry night—the sources of her magic. Then she could hear the whispers rising all around her, taunts of what the Shadowkin planned to do to the Blackpaw, of how pathetic she was to even try to stop it.

Her entire being thrummed with magic, so that she began to shake with it. Somewhere deep in her mind, warning bells began to go off. This was too much. She didn't know if she could control this, she'd let them use her emotion to goad her too far.

And it was too late, because she had no idea how to

make this stop without releasing what was building inside of her. But she had to get out of this house, or she was going to unleash hell in here, and she had no idea what would happen.

Mia barely managed to stagger to the door, flinging it wide and forcing her legs to move to where the Shadowkin twisted and moved, waiting. She could feel them surrounding her, pressing in.

So much power. Show us...

Dimly, she heard a shout behind her, then a snarl. Her heart sank, even as she let go. A violent flash of light shook the very ground as a wave of magic tore through the gathered Shadowkin. But instead of hurting them, she could feel their pleasure, like a sigh. They vanished, at once, riding the wave of dark energy away from her, out of the clearing.

Mia fell to her knees, utterly empty. Every ounce of strength she had was gone, drained from her...and given, albeit unwittingly, to the very things she'd been trying to banish. This was what they'd wanted, she realized dully. A wave of nausea shook her. Her hands hit the ground. Her vision began to waver, but not so much that she couldn't see Jenner's bare feet move slowly into view.

"Jenner," she said softly. "Help me."

But when she looked up, it was into a face that was filled with so much horror it might have been a stranger's.

"Mia?" It was a question loaded with meaning, and Mia suddenly knew that if she gave the wrong answer, he was prepared to go from her lover to Lunari. What did he think he'd seen? What did he think she was?

This was what that display from the Shadowkin had really been about, Mia realized too late. They hadn't just taken her strength tonight. They'd taken Jenner's trust. And she was too weak to defend herself against the accusation she now saw in his eyes.

"I was trying to make them go away," Mia said, her voice barely above a whisper. "I thought I could make them go away."

Then she closed her eyes, finally feeling Jenner's hands on her just before she lost consciousness. He was giving her the benefit of the doubt, she guessed…but there was no feeling of relief. She'd seen the betrayal stamped all over his handsome face.

He wouldn't take her life.

But it seemed that Jeff and the shadows that swirled around him had taken everything else.

Chapter 17

Jenner sat slumped at the bar, completely disinterested in the plate of eggs over easy and hash browns that Rowdy had slid under his nose maybe ten minutes before. Now it was cold, and he was even less interested. All he could hear around him was the low and comfortable chatter of his fellow wolves after a hunt. Everyone knew the woods had suddenly come alive with Shadowkin last night, vanishing even before they needed to be chased off.

He was the only one who knew why.

He glared at the well-oiled wood his plate rested on, knowing the others would sense his mood and leave him be. He'd hoped the running, the chase, would help clear his head some. It hadn't, though. Instead of focusing on the fading scent of Jeff Gaines, all Jenner had been able to see in his mind's eye was Mia, glowing like a candle and so full of power that it was impossible for her not to have known she had it. The memory of it played over and over in his head, violet light slicing through the air, her eyes on fire. She'd drawn them. They'd fed off of her, leaving her so weak that he doubted she was yet awake. Aislynn was watching the house…from a distance this time, on his orders.

For a terrifying few minutes last night as he'd watched Mia, he'd been sure he was going to end up with another woman's blood on his hands. That he'd look into her eyes and see a dark and twisted thing that had eaten her alive, and would have to act accordingly.

But drained though she'd been, she was still herself. Even if he was no longer sure just who that was.

She'd been beautiful. A little frightening. And full of the kind of magic he'd sworn he'd never go anywhere near again. She wasn't just a Shadowkin target—and no goddamned wonder they wanted her so much. If she wasn't a half blood, she was close.

She was a walking weapon of mass destruction. And she wouldn't need a single Shadowkin to destroy everything he loved.

Except she wouldn't. Mia wouldn't do something like that, and you know it.

He didn't, though. Not anymore. When a woman who'd professed to be human started throwing fire from her fingertips, all bets were off. Whether or not her intentions were malicious—and somehow, he couldn't bring himself to believe they had been—she'd only barely been in control.

And she'd been lying to him about herself this whole time.

Though he would only admit it to himself—that was probably what had cut him worst of all. He'd laid everything out for her. He'd told her things he didn't share with anyone. And she'd kept this, and everything that went with it, to herself until it had nearly blown up on all of them.

Maybe she just didn't trust him. Or maybe she had some other, darker reason. Either way, it came to the same.

With all the dark thoughts swirling in his head, he barely noticed the tall, lanky figure settling in beside him on an empty stool. Bane's voice, low and smooth, sliced neatly through his thoughts.

"What's with the brooding? Did she throw you out already?"

Jenner looked up to glare balefully at the Alpha, ready to engage him if a fight was what he was looking for. Bane only looked curious, however, so with a little bit of effort, Jenner let it pass without a fist to the nose. Still, though he'd been waiting to have a word with Bane, this wasn't how he would have preferred to start the conversation.

Actually, he didn't know how the hell to start the conversation.

"No," he finally allowed, the only answer he could think of. Bane snorted softly.

Jenner sucked in a deep breath, then let it go. "I think we've got a problem, Bane."

Bane's cautious smile quickly hardened and vanished. "Well, shit. What's up?"

"The woman is a stone-cold liar, for one thing."

Now the Alpha just looked confused. "Mia? Are we talking about the same person? I can usually sniff out liars, Jenner, and she—"

"—is obviously very good at it," Jenner interjected. "She hasn't been straight with us from the start, Bane."

"What the hell is that supposed to mean?" Bane asked. "Spit it out." Then his eyes shifted to a point over Jenner's shoulder and narrowed. "Or maybe I'll just ask her myself."

Jenner closed his eyes as her scent flooded him, provoking an almost dizzying sensation of hunger and need in him. He only wished he could convince his body it didn't still want her, but that was going to take time. And time alone was something it seemed he was about to come into again.

He turned and saw her standing in the doorway, silhouetted against the daylight. He would have known her without even looking at her, he was so attuned to her presence now. But he didn't anticipate the way her beauty just sliced right through him. Man, she had it down. The worry in her eyes, the nervous way she scanned the darkened room. Then her eyes caught his, just for an instant, and he swore he heard a faint echo of her voice in his head.

I'm sorry. Please, it's not what you think.

Surprised, angry, he shoved the intrusion away. Was getting into his thoughts just another trick she hadn't mentioned was in her arsenal?

"She looks worried," Bane said. "And upset."

"Yeah, she should be both," Jenner returned, cursing Aislynn, who had to have brought her here. He turned his head away to stand and push the stool in with an angry little shove.

He saw the doubt in Bane's expression, and it only fueled the fire of anger that had been on a slow burn all morning.

"You don't believe me?" he snapped.

"I want to know what she lied about before I decide what to do about it. Jesus, Jenner, what do you think she *did*? I can smell guilt a mile away. It's part of my job. There's a little of that on her, but most of it is plain old anxiety. That and a hell of a lot of sadness. You sure about this?"

Rather than answer, Jenner did what he'd always done in his position as Lunari. He went on the attack rather than wait for an ambush. In just a few steps, he was standing in front of her, staring down into a face that looked drawn and pale and, yes, sad and anxious. Still, even now, the loveliest face he had ever seen. Doubt, never a friend of his, tried to creep in, but he quashed it ruthlessly.

You don't even know her. The woman is Unseelie, for Christ's sake. You asked her point blank if she knew why Gaines was chasing her, and she lied. She could have killed someone last night with the firepower she

*was carrying inside herself. If she'd hidden all this,
what else was she hiding?*

"Can I talk to you?" she asked quietly.

"Sure," Jenner replied. The sound of it must have
been sharp, because he saw a hint of a flinch before
Mia squared her shoulders again. He tried to stop himself, but last night was still too close…his eyes roamed
her hungrily, drinking in the way her jeans and sweater
hugged her curves in all the right places. Curves he'd
memorized already with his hands, his mouth…

"Alone, I mean," Mia said, sliding an uneasy look
around the bar.

"What, is there not enough light for you? Afraid
you'll start to glow in the dark here, too?" he asked, the
words falling from his lips before he could think better
of them. And he'd spoken far too loudly. All conversation stopped, all heads turned toward them. He could
feel them watching, listening, waiting for any sign that
his tension meant it was time to attack.

But attack was the last thing on his mind when he
saw the hurt in Mia's dark eyes. And not just the hurt—
a weary resignation that told him she'd expected some
of this…and had maybe even been through it before.
One of many things she'd kept to herself, if so, Jenner
thought, steeling himself. But he couldn't stop the guilt
from coiling through him at her answer.

"No," she said. "I learned a long time ago how to
stop that."

He bared his teeth. "You could have stopped that last
night? So you did know what you were doing."

Mia sucked in a breath and shook her head. "No! I didn't want you to get hurt. I've never let go like that, I...I thought I could do it on my own."

She sounded so sincere. He wanted to believe her, with an intensity that actually hurt. But he'd trusted her, and she'd damn near blown up the woods.

"You made them stronger," Bane growled.

Mia's face fell. "I didn't know it would happen. I was only trying to help. I..." Her voice dropped. "I wanted to protect you."

He could only stare at her. *Protect* him? It wasn't what he'd expected to hear. But what he knew of Mia—what he thought he knew of her—it made a twisted sort of sense. Frustrated, angry, he could only growl. His emotions hadn't yet bothered to translate themselves into words. Mia stepped into the void between them.

"I've always had magic. I know I should have told you, but I was taught to hide it. I was raised thinking I was something awful and wrong. I know that doesn't excuse me, but it also doesn't change the fact that I'm exactly the same right now as I was before you saw me last night. Would knowing what I am have changed anything?"

Sympathy stirred, but he brushed it aside furiously.

"I don't know. You didn't give me a chance to make that decision. You lied to me. To all of us. You're telling me that what I saw last night was you trying to fight about fifty Shadowkin by yourself, using something you don't even know how to control that ended up backfiring. That tells me you're either lying again, or you've lost your damn mind."

Now he saw the flash in her eyes. Hurt, he supposed, and anger. Good. Maybe it would make it easier to break this off clean, before he got any closer to falling. She wasn't for him. He'd known it from the beginning. Why had he fought that? She was something he couldn't fathom…and his need for her, even now, was something he couldn't control.

"I'm not crazy," Mia said, her tone clipped. "Inexperienced, yes. You want the truth? My father was a half blood Unseelie. My mother had light fae blood, though it was more diluted. They were killed in a car crash when I was very young, and I was raised by my grandmother, who never let me forget that I should never have been born. Tainted, she called me. And for a long time, I believed it." Her eyes were so haunted, so wounded, that for a moment Jenner saw a reflection of himself. He didn't want it, that connection. Didn't want to understand, to sympathize when her omission could well have placed them all in grave danger.

Mia looked around, her tone softening slightly when she spoke. "Then I came here, and met all of you. You embrace what you are, even though there are people who think you're just as tainted as I was raised to believe I was. I started to think maybe…"

She trailed off, then gave her head a short, angry shake. To his horror, Jenner realized Mia was close to tears. "I'm sorry to have to do it this way. I was taught to hide my…my gift, I guess…from when I was very young, but…it doesn't always stay under wraps." Her laugh was bitter. "I wanted to do my part, to stop the things that hunt both of us. So I used what I had, and it was exactly what they wanted. I would never hurt anyone. I never *have* hurt anyone. Except you," she said more softly to Jenner. "I broke your trust, when I know that's the one thing you're probably not going to be able to forgive. I just…I just wanted you to see who I was, instead of what I was. I didn't want to lose you. Not to them. And not because of this."

She stepped back, and once again she was incandescent, glowing with a silvery light that made her beauty look moon-kissed. Jenner felt his breath die in his throat despite himself. This was still Mia, but more. She'd become the fantasy Mia he'd already imagined her as—Diana, Goddess of the Hunt. There were gasps all around him. Mia held out one hand toward him, palm cupped. Within was a pulsing ball of light.

He felt as though she were holding his heart instead. And if she closed her fist around it, it would break him in a way even Tess hadn't been able to.

How had he let it go this far?

Mia watched him closely. Even her voice, when she spoke, seemed shot through with magic. Whoever had taught her to hide this side of her had done it well. But again, when he began to wonder what such suppression had cost her and felt the tug of sympathy borne of his own long experience with his father, Jenner forced himself to push it away.

"You told Tomas I was just like everyone else," she

said. "And I am. I'm still me. This doesn't change me. I think—I know I can learn to use what I was born with in a way that *will* help. But I can't change this."

"Mia." Bane's voice was surprisingly gentle when he appeared at her shoulder, touching her with a soothing hand. "Stop. It's a surprise, but it's not the end of the world. We'll figure it out. You're still one of us now—"

"How can you say that?" Jenner snapped, stunned that Bane could be so recklessly casual about this. "She lied about this, God knows what else she's lied about! You don't know what she's going to turn into! What she could do!"

"Jenner," Bane said, more sharply. "This is not Tess. Mia is nothing like Tess. If you really can't see that, then you're not only a jackass, you're blind."

"Please," Mia said softly, taking a step toward Jenner. Only a single word. But she was asking for everything. And right now, he couldn't see anything but what had come before. He'd let his guard down once, and people had died. So had a piece of himself.

He couldn't risk that again.

"Whatever you think," she said quietly. "You've got the real me. The magic is just…extra."

"I figured out a long time ago that I can't believe something like that just because I want to," Jenner replied, every word twisting like a knife in his heart. "I can't risk it. I just…can't."

"Jesus, Jenner," Bane growled, pulling his attention back to the fact that they had an audience. "Mia, look, I'll take you back to my place. You haven't hurt a soul here. You've got the benefit of my doubt, even if you don't have his."

Mia nodded, but her eyes, so big and dark, were only for him. He could hear her in his head, as intimate as a caress.

"It meant so much to me."

"I can't," he said hoarsely, hating the fear in his voice. Knowing, even now, that it wasn't her he was afraid of.

"All right. I'll go get my things. But I want you to know..." She trailed off, then simply shook her head.

"Bane is right. I'm not Tess, Nick. I'm just Mia. And for the last time, whether you believe it or not, I'm sorry. I trusted you, too. I might have been afraid, I might have made a mistake. I just didn't think it ought to matter. I didn't want it to matter."

He didn't know what to say. He needed time, damn it. He needed to sit with this until he was doing more than just reacting, sitting here nearly mute because all he could do was feel. So much of him wanted to just grab her and hope that holding on was the right thing. But he had his own kind of shadows in his past.

"Come on," Bane said. "I'll drive you out to his place and we'll get your things. You can bunk with me until everything is sorted out."

"No. I'll drive," Jenner interjected, surprising both of them. He didn't know why he said it. But he didn't question the instinct. Damn it, why couldn't he ask what he needed to ask, say how he really felt? Why hadn't he taken her someplace else to begin with?

Hurt, confusion and anger all mingled into a toxic

stew. And still, he couldn't allow anyone else to watch over her. Not yet. Not until he'd said his piece, too. And the words wouldn't come until they were ready. Bane gave him a warning look.

"I need to do this," Jenner said. "I have some things to say. I need a few minutes."

"You don't have to," Bane told her.

"No," Mia said. "It's fine. I'm not afraid of him, no matter how he feels about me."

Then she turned on her heel and headed for the door, head high. Jenner watched her go, and for the first time in years wondered whether he was trying to protect his pack, or himself.

But from the way he felt right this moment, plenty of damage had already been done.

He sat quietly in the corner of the living space in his cabin, legs splayed out on front of him. The curtains were drawn, blocking the sun that shone outside. He wanted no more to do with sunlight after this, Jeff decided. Only night, and darkness.

At least it was quiet now. He'd sent Pete and Jay into one of the neighboring towns for supplies. Sy was slinking around in the woods, imagining himself as an all-powerful night creature and waiting for Jeff to meet him. Sy, he would need to drug soon, while the others were gone. Blood was needed to begin the ritual—a lot of it would be, by the time the night was through—and those with the fewest brains got to be first in line. The man was stupid enough for it to be easy, at least.

Oh well, Jeff thought. He'd be giving his life for the noble cause of bringing a new age of darkness to this world.

And Troy…well, he wasn't exactly sure where Troy had gone. He hadn't been in the cabin when they'd all gotten up yesterday. His things were all still in the room the men were sharing, including his wallet, a fact which had caused some amusement among the others as they'd divvied up the cash inside. They seemed to think he'd turned tail and run away. Jeff doubted it, but that was nothing the others needed to know.

If they understood, they would likely run too. They thought he meant to give them power. But really, what he'd needed was their muscle, their ability to go where he could not and pass for sane. Maybe they would be rewarded with a new life, or maybe they'd simply be chewed up and spit out, drained in the Shadowkin's impending feast. He didn't know, and he didn't care. His moments of lucidity were fewer and farther between now. He could hear echoes of Mia in his head all the time, talking, laughing, weeping. He dreamed of his mouth on hers, her blood on his hands. Was it real? Was anything, anymore?

At least none of the others seemed to have heard the soft and questioning whispers in the dead of night, echoing through the woods. But he did. He heard the shadows calling to one another, gathering.

Jeff knew he and his men were being watched, had been watched since their arrival. His dark friends were making sure he did what he was supposed to, that he stopped screwing up. As long as nothing else went wrong, he himself had been promised safety, immunity from what was to come. The fact that the Shadowkin had, in all likelihood, lured one of his men out to be feasted upon was a little irritating. Still, better Troy than him. The rest were expendable.

For now he rested, saved his strength. Went over the words he'd memorized by heart, ancient words, given by a dark figure with red eyes. And dreamed of shadow.

Chapter 18

Despite the fact that he'd said he wanted to talk to her, the car was silent on the ride back to Jenner's house. He seemed to be trying to come up with something—the anxiety was something Mia could actually identify as a scent now. Part of her wanted him to try…and the other part just wanted to grab her stuff and run.

She wouldn't, though. She'd seen it in his eyes when he'd started to understand, even if he didn't want to. He had so much to give, even if he was afraid to. Even if he ended up closing himself off to her. But she wasn't ready to walk away.

He'd taken a risk with her once, against everything he'd promised himself.

So now she'd take this one last chance on him, that he really was the man she'd fallen in love with.

Mia was so lost in her own thoughts that she only halfway noticed when the truck turned down the long country road off of which sat Jenner's house. The sun shone intermittently through the clouds that had gathered, dappling her lap with sunlight. He made the turn into the drive, tires crunching on gravel.

They were halfway to the house when Jenner's muttered expletive pulled her back into the moment with a rude jolt.

"Damn it," he growled. "Hang on."

Mia jerked her head up. Jenner was frowning into his side view mirror and accelerating toward the house. She turned to look behind them and saw a large black SUV tearing up the driveway. She felt her stomach do a roll, and her heart began to pump rapidly as her adrenaline kicked in.

"Is it Jeff?" she asked.

Jenner's jaw was set, and he looked furious. "Looks like it is," he said in a voice that was little more than a low growl. "And he's brought company."

She didn't have time to digest all the implications of that. She only had a split-second to register that Jeff and whatever thugs he'd found to help him were finally making their move, and that the odds weren't good, when Jenner wrenched the wheel to the right and headed into the grass. The truck bounced on the uneven ground, but Jenner managed it. He turned again, and the tires slid a bit, but they kept going. She saw what he was doing, trying to arc around and get back onto the driveway behind the SUV, pointed so they could get back on the main road and get out of here.

Unfortunately, whoever was driving the SUV was an adept driver as well. The bigger truck spun, and pointed itself in the same direction, driving beside and just slightly behind Mia and Jenner and lining up so they could pull along Jenner's side. The windows were tinted so black that Mia couldn't make out who was inside, but remembering what Aislynn had said, she concentrated and tried to pick up what information she could simply from scent.

Four men. One of them Jeff Gaines.

"Call for Bane!" Mia cried, watching helplessly as the SUV pulled alongside them. Jenner's old truck was simply no match for a newer vehicle with so much horsepower. "How far away is he? Call for *anyone*!"

His eyes went to her just for a moment, and the fear she saw in them chilled her to the bone. Jenner didn't seem to be afraid of anything. But if he was afraid of this, then she figured she should be absolutely terrified.

"I don't know," he said. "Shit, they're getting close, Mia. Just hang on! Hang on, baby, hang on—"

The SUV swerved, slamming into the driver's side. Everything seemed to go into slow motion. Jenner grunted at the impact, his whole body jerking over to one side. The truck skidded a little, then with excruciating slowness, rolled. Mia heard the groan of metal, saw the world outside turning upside down. There was a terrible crunch as the windshield broke, fracturing into intricate spiderwebs in some places and shattering in others. Glass sprayed into the cab, and she instinctively shut her eyes against it.

For a moment, there was dead silence, so strange in the aftermath of such terrible sounds that Mia knew she would never forget it. But almost as soon as she took note of it, the silence was broken by the sounds of car doors slamming, running feet…and voices.

"Get her out. Now. We don't have time for this."

Still stunned, Mia dangled from her seat belt and turned her head to the side. Immediately, she saw that the impact and roll-over had been a great deal more traumatic for Jenner, whose side had taken the hit. And he was also, Mia realized with sick horror, a much bigger person than she. He hadn't had much space between the roof and his head when the whole thing had gone over and compressed.

"Jenner," she said in a shaking whisper. Her hands didn't seem to want to work right, fluttering helplessly as she reached for him. "J-Jenner? Oh, God, please… please no, Jenner, say something…"

There was blood on his head, on his face. His eyes were half open, but saw nothing, and his head rested on the crushed roof beneath them, cocked at an odd angle. She grabbed for his hand, limp and unmoving, and squeezed. Panic and terror flooded her system.

"Jenner," she tried again, her voice a sob. "Wake up! Nick! Please!"

Someone wrenched her door open, and she felt unfamiliar hands on her, dragging her out. Mia panicked, struggling wildly. Her eyes never left Jenner's, which looked lifeless and empty. His beautiful golden eyes.

"No!" she shrieked. "No, what did you do? Call an ambulance—let me go—he's hurt! What did you *do?*"

But there was no one on his side, and whoever had her seemed to take her thrashing in stride. She was dragged from the wrecked truck, over shattered glass that she didn't feel slicing into her skin even though a glance at her arms told Mia that she had plenty of shards that would need to be removed.

"Get her arms and tie her," said a voice she recognized. Her arms were yanked behind her back roughly by whoever had pulled her out, and Mia began to thrash wildly, kicking her legs. It didn't seem to do any good, though, only annoying her rescuer.

"Damn it, stop moving or I'll *make* you stop."

When the hands encircling her arms squeezed so hard that it hurt, Mia stilled, looking up and seeing Jeff standing in front of her. He didn't look ruffled at all by what he had just caused, and his eyes, as they met hers, were flat and cold. He looked far worse off than the last time she'd seen him. His clothing was dirty, disheveled. His hair was standing up in strange places, and there was a wild flush high on his pale cheeks. This wasn't the man she remembered.

The old Jeff had been consumed by something much darker.

"Why?" she asked, pleading. "At least get him out of the truck. You've got me. You don't need to hurt him!" She knew that for whatever was left of her life, which was likely now to be short, she would be haunted by the sight of Jenner crumpled in that truck. By his eyes, devoid of light.

"It's very simple, Mia. He took what was mine," Jeff said. "If the Blackpaw had backed off, maybe he could have had a little more time, though trust me, he wouldn't have had much. So this is how it has to be."

Mia stared at him, horrified at the implications of what he was saying. "You're really going to kill them all? Why would you want to help those *things?* You were a good man, Jeff. Somewhere in there, you were, once. Whatever happened to you—"

That seemed to break through his icy calm. His face contorted, just for a moment, into the same hideous thing she'd seen the night of the attack. "Stop!" he snarled. "I'm not what you think! I'm better than that, stronger than that! I never did a damned thing right in my life. I was never good enough! But this time, I have you. And I'm finally going to get mine. Jenner is doing just what he needs to, which is dying." He shook his head, lip curled in disgust as his eyes drifted to the crumpled truck. "Stupid bastard. His kind was never going to win."

"They're your kind, too, Jeff," Mia said softly.

"No," Jeff replied. "They're not. They rejected me. Just like everyone else. They wanted me to be something I wasn't, and when I couldn't be, when I tried for better, they threw me away. But the shadows never have. They've always been there. No matter how bad it got." His sudden grin was cracked, hideous, and even his rough-looking henchmen looked at him nervously. They saw his madness, she knew. They were just hoping to milk him for whatever he'd promised before he went off the deep end completely. But she saw more… for just an instant, she saw the wounded child beneath all the layers of hate and disappointment and want. It filled her with sick, hopeless pity. Maybe, long ago, Jeff might have been reachable. But he was so far gone now. Too far.

Her eyes went to the truck. Nothing moved inside, and all the air felt like it was being slowly squeezed out of her lungs. "Please," she said. "Please don't do this." In desperation, she tried to summon the dark and beautiful music that flowed in her veins. But her terror seemed to have frozen it, leaving her with nothing more than a faint echo and the barest glow of power.

It was one of just a handful of times in her life she truly cursed the woman who'd raised her. So many secrets she still needed to unlock, so much potential. And no more time.

"Fight me, and I'll finish it now," Jeff said, eyeing her. He'd seen the shimmer, Mia realized. Terrified he would go for Jenner whatever she did next, she shut it down.

"There's a good girl. He's dead anyway, honey. But we'll let his buddies find the body. A shame. The Shadowkin would have enjoyed him."

She saw Jeff signal to whoever held her. She felt a sharp pain in her temple. And then there was nothing but darkness.

* * *

Jenner could hear her crying.

It was all that made him push through the pain, through the overwhelming urge to go back under, to sleep, maybe forever.

His eyes slitted open. There was a terrible pain in his head, and his body ached like he'd been run over a few times. As he came to fully, he realized that wasn't so far off the truth. Raw fury bloomed quickly, overtaking what pain he still felt. He'd been lucky: living through the crash meant his body was already hard at work healing itself. Still, he knew he wouldn't be one hundred percent for a while yet. Not as soon as he needed to be.

Mia was gone. Pulled away from him, destined to become another sacrificial lamb for the Shadowkin. But this time, their victim had done nothing more than have ancient, magic blood. He could still hear her screams echoing in his ears. She hadn't wanted this. How could he have ever entertained the idea that she might? She hadn't even been able to do anything to protect herself!

So much for his fears about her terrible power, Jenner thought, groaning a little as he tried to move. But even that had been just a shitty excuse to walk away. Because he'd realized something when she'd stood there, offering herself one last time, without strings, without anything but concern for *him*, his kind.

He'd fallen in love with her. And to the part of him that had been twisted and torn the night he'd had to take Tess's life, that had been unconscionable. Terrifying. So he'd shut down, turned away.

He'd been a fool. He was about to lose the woman he loved far more than he'd ever loved the smoke and mirrors that had hidden the true Tess from him. And this time, it really would be his fault.

Jeff Gaines. He would kill that bastard if it was the last thing he did.

Though his limbs felt weighted down with sandbags, his anger gave Jenner the strength to get moving. He carefully removed the seat belt, trying to be as gentle as he could not to injure anything else as he dropped. He took some of the hit with his shoulder, feeling shards of glass slice into his skin through his shirt. Slowly, he pushed himself across the roof of the car, over where Mia had been sitting, and out the door that had been wrenched open.

Jenner gritted his teeth as he righted himself, getting to his feet with considerable effort. He touched his head gingerly, worried about what he'd find. When he pulled the hand away, his fingers were covered in sticky blood, but there had been no open wound.

Hell, yes he'd been lucky.

Then he heard the sound again, the one that had awakened him. The distant sound of Mia weeping. Instantly alert, he looked around him, seeing only the ruts that his truck and Jeff's SUV had made in his lawn. No, she was gone.

"Mia," he murmured, beginning to lurch toward his house. Maybe it was an auditory hallucination, something left over from being hit so hard in the head. But then he heard his name mixed in amongst the gut-wrenching sobs. It was the saddest sound he had ever heard.

It was at that moment he realized what was going on, what all those brief instances of deeper connection between the two of them had really meant, though he'd tried hard to brush them off, first as imagination, then as some kind of unwanted magic.

It was also the moment he realized he didn't just love her, didn't just want her.

He had truly found his mate.

The realization of it, the simple truth of it, stopped Jenner in his unsteady tracks. Mia was his one, his other half. After years spent thinking that he'd already had his chance at a life mate and failed, he finally realized that it had never been Tess. That had been youthful infatuation mixed with the lovesick desperation that comes when your partner doesn't truly belong to you and never will. But all the stories he'd heard, everything he'd been told about the bond that formed between true mates now made sense. It was why he'd never quite worked around to sealing his bond with Tess. She hadn't been for him.

And the woman he was meant to be with was out there somewhere mourning him, because she thought he was dead. Jeff thought so, too, or he wouldn't have left. He could use that to his advantage, but he would have to be quick. Quicker, really, than his broken body would allow, but he was going to have to push it if he wanted to save the woman who had already saved him. Determined, he limped as fast as he could toward his home, and at the same time called out to all his brothers and sisters. He felt their answer, a howl of such force and fury that Jenner felt strength flooding back into him. His gait evened out, and the pain began to recede. He needed to heal now, for his pack. For Mia.

Mia's weeping had vanished from his mind, but he felt sure she was still out there, losing hope. He didn't know whether she could hear him the way he'd heard her, but if what he needed to make it happen was will-power, Jenner had it in spades. With all he had, Jenner sent a thought into the vast darkness that existed beyond the warm circle of his pack. He hoped it would find her. Even if the words didn't come through, maybe the sentiment would.

Mia. Hold on. I love you. And I'm coming.

Chapter 19

Mia huddled into a ball, making herself as small as she could. If only she could make herself so small they couldn't see her, she wished. If only they would forget about her. But it wasn't going to happen.

Her wounds had once again healed with stunning speed. Even the tiny pieces of glass embedded in her skin had been pushed out and fallen harmlessly to the ground as the flesh had knit back together. Though her body had ached terribly at first, the sensation had vanished while they were riding in the SUV, she with her hands bound laying down in the back, and the three men who had abducted her keeping an eye on her from the front and middle row.

She had been warned that to try and escape would mean a long and painful death once they were through with her…as opposed to the quicker version they'd been planning for her, she supposed. She had no reason not to believe them. After all, they had killed Jenner…and laughed about it.

A wave of nausea roiled her stomach at the memory, and Mia tried to block it out. She wished she could block everything out. Especially the sight of Jenner, covered in blood, suspended upside down in his truck. Outwardly, Mia showed no emotion, because she knew to do so was to invite attention from her abductors. Inside, however…inside was another story. She had only begun to mourn, and the pain was beyond anything she had ever imagined. "Maybe we should cut her," one of the men suggested, sliding Mia a look that chilled her. He thought of her as less than human, somehow. Just a tool. And if it was entertaining and useful to cut her, he'd be happy to do it.

"Not yet. Not until it's time. It's just a waste of blood, and besides, she's being a good girl now, aren't you, Mia?" Jeff growled, standing with his arms crossed over his chest. Mia could only see his profile, as he was turned to his side, but it was easy to see that his excitement was growing, and that his grip on reality was slipping. His eyes were wild when he glanced at her to give her what was probably meant to be a warm smile.

"But won't the Shadowkin get here more quickly if we spread some of her blood around? Just a little?"

Jeff bared his teeth at the man, who Mia thought she'd heard called Sy. Both Sy and the others of Jeff's thugs were big and intimidating, mainly because she could tell their loyalty to this cause, if not to Jeff, was unwavering. They wanted power. And their eyes were cold, dead when they looked at her.

"You idiot. They know we're here. I'm just waiting for them to tell me where to go. They're preparing a place…I know it."

Mia sat on the ground, leaning against the knobby bark of a tree. She watched as Jeff turned his attention to her and started over. Mia wanted to recoil, but managed to simply look passive. She was terrified. They'd left the truck at an abandoned gas station outside of town hours ago, and then trekked into the woods. She would have felt confident that the Blackpaw could sniff them out…but no one was coming. No one knew what had happened. And by the time they figured it out, it would be too late. Jeff had been very clear.

And despite his madness, she knew that when it came to his plans with the Shadowkin, he was telling the truth.

"Mia," Jeff said, stopping just a foot away from her and looking down at her with what might have passed for friendly interest, if she hadn't seen the cruel glint in his eye.

"Call the shadows."

Her breath stilled in her throat.

"I…I don't know…"

The smile turned into a sneer. "Yes you do. Yes you do, you bitch. They'll come a lot faster when they feel how powerful you are. Call them with that fae blood of yours. Call them!"

The open-handed slap rocked her head back, slamming it hard into the tree. Mia cried out, both from the pain and the miserable fear. She didn't want to be here, didn't want to do this. She wished she were still with Jenner, that he was alive and they were trying to talk things out. She wished everything was going to be all right, but it wasn't.

It was never going to be all right again.

Jeff's eyes burned like fire when he looked down at her, glowing in the half-light of the forest.

"Call them, you stupid little feral bitch. I don't have time for this. The wolf in your blood will pull them as strongly as the magic. You'll be irresistible."

His voice was barely human. Mia closed her eyes, partially in self-defense. If she looked at him too much longer, she was afraid she'd just…break. Slowly, she did as Bane had once instructed her. But this time, it was no man she sought.

Almost instantly, she felt herself surrounded by inky darkness. It was hard to hear anything in the sudden cacophonous burble of snarling and wailing and hungry moans, hard to understand a single coherent thought through the murky veil. Still, that vast and shadowy collective seemed to sense her all at once. Cold sweat broke out on her brow, nausea rolling through her stomach. But she had no choice.

"Who calls us?"

"I am Mia."

"You are faewolf. You are the key. The fool has finally done his job." The voice was deep, sonorous, and full of darkest pleasure. It was seductive, in its way. It would be easy to lose yourself to such a voice…but she had so much more to live for than whatever this thing could promise.

So she begged, though she knew it would be exactly what this creature would wish her to do.

"I don't want to die."

"Nor shall you. We will take your essence, give you ours. You will be perfect, changed. Our dark faewolf, free of your disgusting humanity."

"No, please…"

"Fret not. We will let you kill him. The fool. He may be your first. Useless, weak thing he is. Come to us. I will lead you."

After long and tortuous minutes, Mia opened her eyes. She felt as though she'd just gazed into an abyss. But she had done as she was told, because every second of her life had now become precious. What would Jeff do, she wondered, when the shadows turned on him? What would she do, when she could already feel how easily the Shadowkin could taint her, draining all the good away? Goddess above, what was she about to become?

She had a terrible feeling that death would be the better option…and not one she would be allowed to take after all. Not, at least, for long.

"Well?" snapped Jeff. "Did you speak to him? And don't lie to me, Mia. I'll know."

"He said he's preparing for the ritual," Mia said softly. "But he told me where to lead you from here.

And he said…" She hesitated, and Jeff pulled back his arm as though he were thinking of striking her again. Mia looked up dully, knowing there were likely to be more blows regardless.

"He said he's ready for you to join them."

Jeff lowered his arm, but his eyes were warning enough. "Damn right he is," he said. "Lead us, Mia. And if you try anything, there are plenty of ways I— and we—can hurt you that won't shed a drop of that precious blood."

He turned from her, heading back to discuss something with the others in hushed voices. Mia didn't care. In all her life, she had never felt despair like this.

Jenner, she thought, clinging to his memory like a talisman. And then, incredibly, she heard a faint echo of a reply. Probably it was imagined, Mia knew. But even so, hearing Jenner's voice, even so far away, gave her back the tiniest shred of something she thought was gone for good: hope.

Hang on, Mia. I'm coming. We're coming.

They ran in a mass, every member of the Blackpaw who could be spared. The wolves dashed through the trees in the fading light of day, the gold of the setting sun glinting intermittently off of fur that ranged from rich red to darkest black as it filtered through the forest's canopy.

Jenner ran in front with Bane, his heart pumping hard from the adrenaline. His head still ached, but he'd been given something for the pain. And it hardly mattered, whether he hurt or not. All that mattered was Mia.

It had taken too much time to find the damned SUV. Jenner knew they were all deep in the woods by now, though why he couldn't imagine. Fortunately, once they'd picked up the scent, following had become easy. Catching up, however...

He'd spent years fighting the Shadowkin that haunted the woods like malevolent ghosts, waiting to pick off the young, the sick, the weak who ventured too far alone. He'd seen what they could do to the minds of the vulnerable. And if he wasn't quick enough, he would finally have to fight them in a form no Shadowkin should be allowed to take in this world. A form he had no idea whether he and the others could defeat.

Jenner pushed it from his mind, focusing instead on what was ahead. He tried not to think about the pale wolf running on Bane's other side, nor the heavyset russet wolf beside him, leading their small contingent of Silverback. Kenyon Chase had been determined to come, truly worried about Mia's fate. Nor had Tomas hesitated, despite the look in his eyes when Mia's fae blood had been mentioned. He doubted Tomas would still be quite so eager to mate her with his second-in-command now, though Jenner knew that if Mia gave him any hope of reciprocation, Chase would fight to have her.

But that wasn't going to happen. Because even if he had to get on his damned knees and beg, he was going to win Mia back. He wasn't going to go through losing her once just to lose her again.

He could smell Mia now, the sweet scent of her growing stronger by the second. But the light was fading. And from what little he knew of such things, Jenner had gleaned that twilight was when it was best to call out to the Shadowkin and expect an answer. Not that he had ever tried, except to curse them on the rare occasion they'd managed to cause harm.

There were other scents in the air tonight. Madness and fire, sweat and anticipation. And now, faint but growing stronger, the unmistakable tang of blood.

Dread formed a knot deep in his belly. *Please let it not be Mia,* he thought. *That's all I ask. Please.*

Mia, he thought, reaching out with his mind, wishing she could hear him, feel him. Wishing he could know for certain she was all right.

He was stunned when he heard her, soft but unmistakably there. She sounded uncertain, frightened...but alive. In an instant, he was surrounded by her essence, so close and real she might have been beside him. He felt her warmth, her love...and her crushing sadness.

Jenner? Is...is that really you, or am I imagining it?

I'm coming for you. Soon. I'm coming for you. Can you hear me? Mia, I'm so sorry, baby. I was wrong. I love you. I love you...

But like a bad telephone connection, her voice was gone again, as was all sense of her, blocked off by the oozing blackness that seemed to blanket this entire area, thickening the farther into the woods they got.

All around them, the light faded to silvery purple, and things began to slip from behind and beneath trees, nothing but abstract figures created of darkness itself. Bane gave the signal to stop, and the pack stood in silence as the insubstantial wisps of pure black were drawn toward whatever lay in the distance. For the first time Jenner could remember, the shadows ignored the presence of the wolves in the forest. They had more important matters to attend to tonight.

Bane, a massive black wolf with gleaming yellow eyes, turned to look at Jenner.

We need someone to go on ahead, scope it out.

Jenner knew he was the one to go. He was the Lunari, the moon hunter, the shadow slayer. And despite the uncertainty ahead, he wouldn't have it any other way. *Get them surrounded. I'll let you know when.*

Kenyon seemed to know what was going on even though, as a Silverback, he wasn't privy to their conversation. In an instant, he was a man again, though his stance was very much that of an aggressive animal.

"You're not going in there without me," he growled.

Jenner had no intention of bringing a tagalong who had designs on his woman. He let his form shift, drawing himself up into his human shape, and glared at Kenyon.

"No way. One is enough. More, and they'll know we're there right away. They may anyway. No reason to sacrifice another wolf."

Kenyon bared his teeth. "Spare me the altruism. I

have just as much invested in this as you do, Jenner. She's not going to forget you rejected her."

Bane shifted form, standing between them. "We don't have time for this, you two. Jenner, take him with you. In this case, two *is* better than one. And it's his right as much as yours."

"That's right," Tomas said, looking more bullish than wolfish as he materialized beside Bane. "I can't say what the woman wants, and she seemed determined to flout Pack Law anyway, but you two need to go in. Kenyon is the best we have. She'd be lucky to have him…especially considering what she is."

Jenner growled. "I'm sure she'd be grateful you'd overlook her mongrel status, Tomas. But Mia's mine. I'm not giving her up."

He couldn't miss the flicker of relief over Tomas's features, though Kenyon bristled. "That's not your decision."

It was, for once, surprisingly painless to say exactly how he felt.

"Yes it is. I'm in love with her. I feel the bond with her. She's going to be my mate."

"Bullshit!" In an instant, Kenyon was a wolf again, lunging at Jenner. Jenner made the shift just in time to take the blow, and the two of them rolled together, biting, snapping, heedless of the noise they were making. A claw raked Jenner's face, drawing blood. He winced, then sank his teeth into Kenyon's scruff and shook his head, eliciting a yelp from his adversary.

The two of them went flying as Bane barreled into

them in wolf form, knocking the two of them apart. His hackles were raised almost straight up, and the fury in his eyes was unmistakable as he shifted back into a man. He held out an arm to warn Jenner back, while Tomas had to physically restrain a furious Kenyon.

"Get up, both of you," Bane snapped. "This is about more than who gets the damned girl! Jenner, you should know better than anyone. The Shadowkin barely exist on this plain. I don't know where they come from, and I don't care—they're dangerous enough as they are— but give them bodies, shape and form, and we're in some serious trouble. We need to make it stop. Now. So get your asses in gear and grow the hell up. If we get through this and get her out, fight over her then. I'm sure she'll be really impressed with the both of you." He curled his lip.

Jenner, still a wolf, glanced warily at Kenyon. He knew Bane was right. This would have to wait. But he wouldn't pretend he was going to step back. He got to his feet, and gave Bane a nod. Kenyon followed suit, prodded, Jenner noticed, by Tomas's foot in his backside.

"Then hurry," Tomas said. "We'll close in, and wait for your signal. Go."

Without another word, the two wolves raced into the night.

Chapter 20

Mia stumbled forward as Jeff gave her a little push into the clearing. Her eyes widened as she saw what they had brought her to. She stopped, tried to back up, but the men directly behind her prevented her from backing up more than a step.

"Uh-uh, sweetheart. This is the end of the line for you."

"Go on," Jeff crooned from behind her. He sounded absurdly thrilled, as though he was about to be given the greatest gift a man could have. "Nothing is going to hurt you…yet."

Mia swallowed hard. She didn't know if she could keep going. Not toward this.

A single figure stood before them, shirtless in the middle of a ring of fire. Though he looked, in great part, like a man, there was something slightly insubstantial about his shape and form, and if he turned the right way, Mia realized, she could see right through him. He was very tall, intimidatingly broad, with a cruel beauty about him. Tousled hair of snowy white was a stark contrast to dark, slashing brows. His face was that of a young warrior. But his eyes were ageless, and burning. There was blood spattered on his chest, but it didn't seem to be his. It likely belonged to the man on the ground in front of him.

"Ah. So that's where Troy went."

Jeff sounded strangely unconcerned as he moved up from the back and approached the circle.

The white-haired warrior spoke, and Mia immediately recognized the voice. He was the one who had led her here.

"A useful creature. His blood helped me light the fire of *Ab-ashoth*." His strange eyes drifted to Mia. "And here is the woman. Our faewolf." His voice grew almost tender. "We have waited long for you. The blood of your line grows faint, the Unseelie magic dim. They have retreated deep into the veil, far from the humans who have forgotten them. And yet here you are."

"I don't want this," Mia said, her voice little more than a whisper.

His smile was a thin blade. "You will."

Jeff turned to glare at her, obviously displeased that she was getting more attention than he was.

"You're a means to an end, Mia. Life's a bitch. Men, bring her."

Hands clamped on her upper arms as she was pushed forward toward the burning ring. She didn't struggle… it seemed pointless. And the closer she got, the more lethargic she felt. She grew lightheaded, sleepy. She looked around for something to focus on, to pull her out of this onrushing stupor, but all she found were the bright eyes of the Shadowkin warrior. Her knees began to buckle. Her head lolled on her neck.

"Quit dragging your feet, you stupid bitch," hissed a voice in her ear.

Mia.

Mia forced her head up, all her attention shifting to that voice, soft but so familiar, calling her again. The first time, she'd been certain it wasn't real. But…could it really be Jenner? Nearly sick with her sudden, irrational hope, Mia reached out for him with her thoughts. She heard the faintest start of a response before his voice vanished. The words she'd heard surged through her blood, and gave her something to hang on to.

We're coming.

She felt anything but strong as she was led to the ring of fire, seeing the dark things that had begun to drift from the woods and swirl lazily above the circle like carrion birds. There was power in the air, dark power. The night seemed to thrum with it like a live wire.

"Come to me. All of you," said the warrior. His voice brooked no refusal. She could feel the hesitation of the men at her sides, smell the sudden tang of fear on the air from the rest. *Oh, now you decide to be frightened?* she thought, suddenly angry. What had they expected?

That a creature who could promise eternal life, incredible power, would look tame?

Jeff looked at all of them sharply, his disdain obvious.

"Do as Murdock says. There's no turning back now. You know what'll happen if you do." He indicated the swirling black figures, now all around them, with a wave of his hand and a thin smile.

"Jeff," she said softly. "Do you really think they'll let you live? All they want is me."

It was a lost cause, maybe. But she had to try one more time to get through. Indeed, all she got from Murdock was a smug little smirk. And true to form, Jeff pushed away any appeal to reason.

"You would think that. You think your blood makes you better than me, better than everyone. Well, you're wrong. These are my friends. My only friends. They chose me, a very long time ago, when no one else would have. But don't feel bad. You'll get a moment in the sun. A very brief one."

"They're using you."

Jeff regarded her for a moment, and at first she thought she'd gotten through. He looked like himself again, polite, reasonable, a little sad. But when he spoke, she realized that whatever was inside of Jeff Gaines was irreparably broken.

"They...*love*...me," he whispered. "They need me. Murdock promised. Do you know what it's like, to never be loved? I do, Mia. But it's all right now. It's all right. I'll finally be in charge of something that matters. I'll finally have done it right. Everything is waiting for me. *Everything.*"

She pitied him as much as she could pity a monster like him, hearing the kernel of truth in his words. Maybe he had never felt love. But nothing was an excuse for becoming what he had, for sacrificing his sanity for power. His smile was insane.

"I wish I'd met you a long time ago," Mia said. "Maybe I could have helped."

"You're just jealous he didn't pick you," Jeff said flatly. "Come on, Mia. The fun's about to start."

"Yes," Murdock agreed. "Come, all of you, into the ring. The moon rises. It's time."

The man at Murdock's feet groaned and writhed, drawing Mia's attention. She saw with horror that dozens of tiny cuts had been made in his skin. Out of them ran thin rivulets of blood. The man himself appeared out of it. Drugged, maybe, or just coming to after being knocked out.

Jeff noticed the direction of her gaze and gave her a small smile.

"Don't worry about him. He's just another necessary sacrifice." He flicked his hand above his head and looked up. "She's yours. You can have the men, as well. As promised."

Several of the tattered and inky shadows separated from the circling horde and rushed at them. One of the men holding her shrieked, but the sound had only barely begun to leave his mouth when it was choked off. She was pushed away into the fire, but she didn't even feel the flames as she passed through it, stumbling as she turned to see what was happening. Mia watched in horror as Jeff's companions were enveloped in a shifting, swirling blanket of darkness. Two of them bolted, dashing for the trees. Two more of the shadows followed in hot pursuit.

And one more, the final one, was swooping toward Jeff. The fool held out his arms, as though he were about to receive an embrace.

"Come to me! I'm ready!" he cried.

"I wouldn't watch…we are very hungry tonight," Murdock's voice murmured in her ear. She felt his hand, ice cold, stroke the length of her arm. As Jeff's tortured scream rose into the night sky, his body beginning to convulse as more shadows descended upon him, cocooning his body in red-tinged darkness, Mia somehow found it within her to run.

She heard Murdock's surprised snarl as she broke away, springing back through the fire with a grace and speed she had felt the night she'd chased Jeff into the woods. Adrenaline surged, snapping her out of the horrible lethargy she'd been afflicted with. She barely felt her feet hitting the ground as she ran, and a terrible hope filled her. Maybe she could get away. Maybe the wolves were close enough to save her. Maybe…

A massive shadow swooped down from the sky, heading straight for her. Mia threw up her hands, poor protection at best, her body going rigid in anticipation of the strike. Incredibly, the shadow stopped short, drifting just out of reach. Now that it was closer, she could see the hint of red eyes, and they were narrowed, all its attention focused on the wolf. Her wolf.

"Jenner." She knew it was him, even though she'd only seen him in this form once before, and briefly. Her heart knew it was him. And the knowledge brought with it such relief that it nearly took her down. All that had happened, all she'd been through, faded away in the face of the only things she knew to be true: Jenner was alive. He was here.

Out of the corner of her eye, Mia saw another wolf, sleek and red, streak out of the forest like a phantom and round the edge of the circle. Looking to flank Murdock, Mia thought. But she had a terrible feeling that even lacking full substance in this world, Murdock would be no easy prey. The Shadowkin warrior looked furious.

"Wolf! Shadow hunter! You're too late!"

As the one shadow drifted back, Jenner coiled around her legs to face Murdock. He didn't look at her, didn't make a sound. But the warm security of his touch was more than enough reassurance for now. She was no longer on her own. Despite everything, Jenner had come for her. Mia wanted to throw her arms around him so badly it hurt.

"You," Murdock snarled. "You came for her abductor, yes? We've already taken care of him, I'm afraid. There's none left for you. I suggest you run back to your fellow wolves and tell them to hide. We'll enjoy the game. See how you like being hunted. At least it will be a challenge, unlike this one."

He jerked his head at where Jeff lay on the ground.

Mia sucked in a breath at the sight of him as the Shadowkin that had targeted him swooped into the air and headed back into the swarm of its brethren. Jeff was sheet-white, and appeared to have been completely drained of blood. Mia pressed a hand against her mouth as nausea rolled through her. A man she had just seen walking and talking was now a dried-up corpse. She managed to dredge up a small, very small, amount of pity. He'd been so broken.

Murdock held out his hand to her, even as the shadow he had sent to fetch her continued to hang back in the face of Jenner's furious growling.

"Come to me, Mia. Make this easy. He's going to die. They're all going to. You can live forever."

"I would rather die with them, then!" she cried, her fear replaced with a sudden fury.

Murdock's face contorted as he bared sharp, jagged teeth. "You should be honored! We share the Unseelie blood, you and I! I was favored by our queen once, long ago, before she cast me out! We are the same!"

"We are *nothing* alike!" she spat. Jenner's presence seemed to have returned her fully to herself, giving her a strength she wouldn't have felt otherwise. Her blood heated in her veins. She would have to be careful, Mia realized. So careful not to let it get the better of her. The moon was nearly full, and she sensed the increasingly frantic stirrings of the beast now within her. She couldn't let her anger goad her into making the change and turning feral forever. Not when Jenner had come back to her, and she had so much to live for…if she could just live through this.

Jenner took a step forward, then another, all the while growling viciously deep in his throat. It drove some of the shadows back toward the circle, and Mia realized she could hear them hissing.

"Last chance, Mia," Murdock said. "Come easily, or watch him be ripped apart."

"You underestimate him. All of them. And me," she replied, hoping she was right.

Murdock waved a hand, dismissive, his displeasure etched on his face. "Fine. Watch them die up close. It hardly matters."

He threw up his hands, shouting a word Mia didn't understand. The flames shot up around him, turning into a wall. Jenner gave a single, short bark.

There was a mournful howl, and then there seemed to be wolves everywhere, crashing through the trees, a sea of shining coats and teeth. Mia found herself surrounded in seconds by the pack, and was awed by them. Such strength, such beauty. And formidable, when seen all together. But all the hope she felt soar as they appeared was quickly dashed as the wolves tried to hurl themselves through the flames to attack. One by one, they hit the flames as though there were an invisible wall, slamming into an unseen barrier and falling to the ground.

Through the flickering flames, Mia could see Murdock rapidly chanting, his arms upraised over the body before him. The man staked to the ground writhed, and began to glow. His body was suffused with a pulsing red light that seemed to come from inside of him. And one by one, the shadows began to drop to the earth around him, forming a circle within a circle. Then the shadows began to change…shift…their shapes becoming something far more human.

Mia watched, transfixed. Jenner had vanished in the sea of wolves, probably joining those trying desperately to get in and stop what Murdock was doing. She hardly noticed, so fascinating and terrible was the transformation going on before her. Then she felt the chill. It wrapped itself around her, lifting her up until her feet were no longer touching the ground. She tried to scream, but it was choked off as she inhaled biting cold.

A terrible numbness invaded her. She couldn't move her arms, her legs. Everything suddenly seemed very far away. She drifted up, away from all the violence, all the pain and fear. A voice whispered in her mind. Murdock.

Sleep, pretty one. Let me drink from you. We are protected here, oh yes, in the ritual circle. Soon, we will walk among men again. The wolf is a fool…forget him. Forget all. Sleep…sleep while we rise…and you rise with us.

Mia struggled against it. But her eyes began to close. She felt herself settled gently on the ground within the circle, a wall of flame around her. The world began to go gray, and dark, and cold.

Jenner had left her side only briefly, but it was long enough. He watched with horror as Mia was enveloped by one of the shadowy abominations and lifted into the circle.

"No!" he wanted to shout. Instead, it came out as a heartbreaking howl. He raced at the flames, throwing himself at them again and again. He barely felt each impact. All he knew was that if he didn't get through, Mia would be dead, and the woods would be overrun by Shadowkin in a far more dangerous form than he had ever seen them assume. Gaines was gone, cast aside like a broken toy. The real enemy now had Mia in his arms.

Everything he'd protected would be lost. The woman he loved would be torn from him. Forever.

He shifted into human form almost without thinking. He wanted her to hear him.

"Mia!" he roared above the din of the wolves and the mad chanting from within the circle. He could see her on the ground, covered in swirling darkness, the white-haired warrior crouching over her. He raced to the flames, beat his fists against it. "Mia, no! Fight it! I love you!" His voice broke as anguish bubbled up through all of the fury. "Don't leave me!"

He could see the Shadowkin taking shape, gathering around Mia. A sacrificial lamb. And still Murdock chanted, all of them did, words older than humanity, older than this world. A bright beam of light shot upward from her, from the center of her chest. He saw her body jerk, saw her eyes open wide and sightless.

He roared Mia's name again, and saw her head jerk toward him, trying to free herself from the oppressive blanket of shadow even as Murdock passed through the light that poured from her, bathing in her magic.

Mia could hear him. Jenner knew she could. If he could just send her strength, help her to free herself…

And then, clear as day, he knew what to do.

Knowing the connection was there, and hoping it was strong enough for her to hear him now, Jenner reached out to Mia with his mind. And if he couldn't save her, he'd be damned if he didn't tell her what was in his heart.

Please. Please don't leave me, Mia. I shouldn't have fought it, and I shouldn't have been such an ass. I love you. Please fight, please try. You're the brightest part of my life. I don't want to let you go.

He pressed his hands against the barrier surrounding the flames, watching helplessly as all around him, his brothers and sisters tried everything they could to get in. At first, he heard nothing. But then, softly:

Jenner. Not a question, but a sigh of relief, full of warmth…just like Mia. *I'm trying. I can't. I love you, too…*

The flames melted away beneath his hands the instant she gave him the words, dissipating before him like so much smoke. Jenner didn't think, didn't have time. He raced through the breach, feeling the surge of power as he leaped into the circle the Shadowkin had cast. Murdock, now completely solid, spun to look at him as Jenner leaped again, shifting into his wolf form in midair.

There was a single, furious roar in the split second that Murdock realized what had happened.

"No!"

Jenner saw an instant of pure terror reflected in the Shadowkin's eyes before he was on him, teeth sinking into flesh, foul, thick blood pouring from the creature's throat as Murdock's new life left him as quickly as he'd gained it. The shadows still feeding on the bound victim scattered as the rest of the Blackpaw rushed in, tearing at the wisps of malignant darkness that were thick in the circle and drawing spatters of inky black blood.

Jenner had no time to savor Murdock's death. Jenner charged the few shadows that still enveloped Mia, lapping at the blood that ran freely from tiny bite wounds on her arms, her neck, trying desperately to coax enough magic from her to keep the doorway open. He leaped, bit in, and shook his head viciously as one insubstantial creature caught in his jaws screeched in pain and fright. It tore away from him, ruins of it trailing behind in tatters.

In seconds, the Shadowkin were gone, rushed back to whatever dark place they were confined to on some other plain. But even as he became a man again and scooped Mia's limp body into his arms and cradled her, even as he shouted for help, he realized that they had been just a little too late. Three men, their inner darkness still clinging to them like cloaks, sprang out of the circle, dashing away from the victim at a speed greater than any werewolf could muster. One turned to look directly at Jenner, locking eyes with him and giving him the faintest condescending smirk before join-ing the other two and dashing into the night.

Three had escaped, and were loose in the world for the first time in a thousand years. Jenner's heart sank, but he turned away from it. There were only three, and there was nothing he could do about it right now. All he cared about, as he gathered Mia close, was that she lived.

He looked up briefly, and his eyes met Kenyon Chase's. For a moment he thought the young wolf would challenge him now, try to take her from him. Jenner's thoughts were still half wild, primed from the fight. But instead of approaching, Kenyon looked from Mia to Jenner, then lowered his head in a sign of deference.

The surge of triumphant possession was as over-whelming as it was fleeting. Mia's skin was like ice, her lips faintly blue. But as he held her, he knew she wouldn't go down easily.

And he felt the beat of her heart, keeping time with his.

Chapter 21

Mia awakened to the most wonderful warmth imaginable.

She drifted slowly up from the depths of sleep, feeling nothing but the arms wrapped around her, thinking of nothing but how lovely they felt. This was where she wanted to be, always: with Jenner, enveloped by all the wonderful things that made up the man she loved.

Memory pricked at her bliss, at first gently, then more insistently. All the terror, and the loss…and the joy as she'd realized he was alive, and had come for her after all. But then had come the cold, and some sense that she and Jenner had exchanged words that were very important.

A voice rumbled softly by her ear.

"You shouldn't think so much as soon as you wake up. It'll give you a headache."

Mia opened her eyes, saw that she was curled in Jenner's bed. With him. The warm familiarity of her surroundings, the rightness of being in Jenner's arms, had Mia drawing in a shaking breath. She hadn't thought she would ever be here again.

She rolled over to look at him, saw his handsome face set in the lazy half smile she loved so well. His eyes, though, told the true story of what he was feeling as he looked at her. It was like looking into a tempest.

She was no better. Mia sniffed back the tears that wanted to come.

"Hey, don't do that," Jenner said gently, catching a stray tear with his thumb and stroking it down her cheek. "It's over. It's all over. You're with me now, and that's how it's staying."

Her lips quivered into a smile. "Even though I'm not what you wanted?"

There was so much remorse in his beautiful, golden eyes, she forgave him everything in an instant.

"You're everything I ever wanted. Everything. I'm so damned sorry, Mia. I was…I didn't know what to—"

She pressed her hand to his lips. "Shh," she said. "I know. It's okay. We're here now. That's all that matters."

"No one should ever have made you feel like you weren't good enough, me included. I'm going to make it up to you, if it's the last thing I do." His voice was gruff, and full of all the emotion she wanted him to feel for her.

"Well," she said, "you already saved me from a monster by jumping through a magical ring of fire."

His crooked grin was the most beautiful thing she'd ever seen. "Baby, stick with me. That's just the beginning."

She laughed, even through the tears that started despite her best efforts. How he had become so important to her so quickly, she didn't know. All Mia knew was that she never wanted to be without him.

"I was so scared," she said. "I thought you were gone. I saw you, and I thought—"

"Didn't happen. I'm pretty tough to kill," he soothed, brushing her hair back from her face. He didn't seem to want to stop touching her. Maybe he thought she'd just disappear if he stopped, Mia thought. She was certainly afraid Jenner was going to vanish and turn out to have been just a beautiful dream.

But no. He was real, solid. Here. And he was staying.

In quiet tones, he told her what had happened. How he had crawled from the truck and called to his pack, how they had lost precious time tracking her because Gaines had done such a good job covering his tracks. How Kenyon had stepped up and proved himself a fierce ally, despite his realization that Mia belonged with Jenner. And finally, how three of the Shadowkin had gotten their wish, and disappeared just as Murdock was taken down, his circle destroyed.

Mia listened to all of it with alternating hope and sadness.

"I know they weren't good people," Mia murmured.

"But I wish there hadn't been so much death last night. That poor man the Shadowkin were feeding on..."

Jenner shook his head. "It was too late. It's small consolation, Mia, but he was one of the ones who'd been running with Gaines while he was here, probably longer. He knew what he was risking. Bad enough that three of those creatures are loose out there now. Gaines did enough damage before he died. We'll have to alert the other packs to be on their guard. Shadowkin are a nuisance in their less corporeal form, but walking as men..." He trailed off. Mia didn't ask. She could guess.

Mia sighed, resting her head on the pillow and enjoying Jenner's touch. She had dozens more questions, but for most, the answers could wait a bit. All she really wanted was to enjoy the fact that she was alive, and here. Right now, those two things counted for a lot.

Still, there was something pertinent she felt she had to address.

"You mentioned Kenyon," she began cautiously, hoping the name didn't provoke a tirade. To her surprise, Jenner gave a rueful little grin.

"Yeah, I did. His pack thinks a lot of him, and I guess I finally see why. He fights like a hellhound. And despite everything, once he saw what happened with you and me, he backed right down. He even apologized later on." Jenner shook his head. "I have a bad feeling he'll be hard to keep hating, but I guess I'll try. Just on principle. Maybe he'll harden up a little now. Losing you to me could be good for him."

Mia looked at Jenner, surprised. "Kenyon becoming bitter and cynical would be a *good* thing?"

Jenner shrugged, then gave Mia one of his brilliant smiles. "Can't hurt."

Mia looked blandly at him. She was never going to understand men. But hearing about Kenyon was a relief. "He's like…a cute, fuzzy puppy. He'll find the right person someday, I'm sure," she said. "He has time."

Jenner grunted. "Puppy, my ass. But as long as he keeps his paws off of you, he can look wherever he wants."

Mia thought a moment, then looked up at Jenner. "What do you mean, when Kenyon saw what happened with you and me? What *did* happen?"

"You don't remember?"

Mia shook her head. "Only very vaguely. I thought, though…I thought we said…"

"We did," Jenner interrupted, cutting her off neatly. "And I'll say it again. Actually, I'll say it as many times as you want me to. I love you, Mia. I love you with everything I've got. And I never want to let you go. Losing you would have been like tearing my heart out and then having to go on living. I thought I'd been through that, but this would have been a thousand times worse." He touched his forehead to hers, a simple gesture that touched Mia with its sweetness.

"I love you. God, I love you, Mia. It scares the hell out of me, but I don't want it to stop. Whatever kind of magic you've got, I never want to be away from it.

From you. Please be mine. I'll spend my life trying to be worthy of you."

Instead of answering right away, Mia claimed Jenner's mouth in a long, lingering kiss that sizzled right through her. She savored the taste of him lazily, enjoying the brush of his tongue against hers, the way she could feel his temperature rise. When she pulled away, she could see she'd done a lot to turn Jenner's mind away from last night.

"I love you, too, Nick," she said softly. "But the only thing I'm scared of is losing you. I don't ever want to do that again."

His eyes glowed faintly. "You'll never have to. Make a life with me, Mia. Be my wife. My mate. I didn't realize how much I was missing until I had you. I was so busy fighting how I felt that I didn't realize what it all meant: falling so hard and fast, and then being able to sense you, even hear some of your thoughts though we weren't pack bonded. We're right for each other. True mates don't come along that often. And I'm such an ass that I almost missed it."

Mia felt her heart leap in her chest. She'd dreamed of this, the man who was perfect for her, offering her everything she ever wanted. There was only one possible answer.

"Yes," she breathed. Then she buried her face in his chest and squeezed him tight. "Yes!"

He laughed, and Mia realized he'd actually been nervous when it came out a little shaky.

"I'll...I'll get you a ring. Soon. But after everything

that's gone on, I wasn't going to go one more day without making you mine, Mia. I'm far from perfect, and I'll probably drive you crazy sometimes. But I will love you for the rest of my life, pretty glowing skin and all. And hopefully that'll make up for all the future things you'll want to kill me for."

"I'm not perfect, either, so same goes," Mia replied, lifting her head to look into his beautiful eyes. "But I don't expect perfect, Nick. I just want you. Fur and all."

"Speaking of," he said, his voice dropping to a growl. "It's the middle of the afternoon. I won't push if you're not ready, but tonight's the full moon, and there's sort of an outstanding problem with your lack of initiation…"

He trailed off, looking at her hopefully, and Mia laughed before slipping a leg over his hip. She found him already hard for her, and the lingering remnants of her fatigue vanished. Desire coiled through her, suffusing her with a warm glow.

"Hmm," she purred, touching her nose to his. "I hate to be the source of any outstanding problems. We'd better fix that as soon as possible."

His grin could only be described as wolfish. "My pleasure."

Then his hands were on her hips, and he was pulling her into him. Jenner gave a guttural groan of pleasure as Mia's breasts pressed against his bare skin. As quickly as they could, they removed what scant clothing they were wearing. She loved the way he felt, hard everywhere and so blissfully warm. Then his mouth came down on hers and she was drowning in pure sensation, his clever tongue lighting fires inside her that only he would be able to extinguish. His hands were on her, everywhere, as though he couldn't get enough of her.

She gasped at the first tender stroke of his fingertip against her swollen sex.

Jenner quickly coaxed her into a rhythm, Mia arching her hips against his rubbing, stroking fingers while he claimed her mouth in hot, open-mouthed kisses. Already, Mia could feel herself building toward climax. She tried to hold back, wanting this to last. Her head fell back and she gave a soft cry of pleasure.

"Yes," Jenner murmured, trailing hot kisses down her jawline, her neck as he pushed her further toward the edge. "Come for me now. I want you ready."

The low vibration of his voice against her skin was all it took. Mia dug her nails into his back as her body arched and stiffened against his, riding the shimmering waves of sparks that rocketed through her bloodstream. As they began to ebb, she opened her eyes to look into Jenner's, seeing hot desire and purely male satisfaction.

Incredibly, her own need for him caught fire again, this time even stronger than the last.

The wilder half of her, so new and unfamiliar, flooded her senses with the man who loomed over her, his body pressing against hers, his heart pounding against her chest. Mia stretched beneath him, breathing him in, feeling all of her nerve endings begin to sing at the slightest contact. He removed his hand from the place where she still ached and throbbed for him, and gave her more of his weight, letting her feel how hard he was for her.

Jenner rolled his hips against her, his eyes going hazy and slipping to half-mast. He exhaled her name breathlessly. It was only then she realized how much power she truly had over him. It was heady stuff, awakening instincts that she'd never known she had. The need to join with him, to feel him moving inside of her, was sudden and overwhelming. But just as urgent was the need to please him as he'd pleased her. To have him quivering beneath her hands, wanting her as much as she wanted him. With a soft growl, Mia slid her leg up Jenner's side, cradling him more snugly against her.

His eyes glowed like twin flames as he looked back at her. There was such raw possession in that gaze that Mia wondered how she could have missed it before. She'd been so worried…but the love had been there all the time, even before he'd been able to admit it.

Mia rose to her knees, Jenner rising up against her, sliding skin against skin. His hands, so large and yet so impossibly gentle, slid up her torso, cupped her breasts. He dipped his head, and proceeded to suckle at each taut nipple with his tongue, grazing them with his teeth in a way that had fresh moisture pooling between Mia's legs. Then his mouth dipped lower…lower…

She pushed herself back, grabbing his upper arm to pull him with her. Then he was against her again, hot, insistent, nothing between them but skin. Emboldened, her heat rising, Mia nipped at Jenner's lips when he kissed her. His response was a roughening of his touch, and his breathing grew increasingly ragged.

"I want you, Mia," he growled. "So bad. It's hard for me to hold back."

"Then don't," she breathed.

He pulled away just far enough for her to see his eyes, wolf bright. When he spoke, she could see his lengthened, sharpened canines. She knew why he was worried about letting go with her. But he didn't need to be.

"I don't want to scare you away from me," he said. "Ever."

"You never will." Mia slid her hands into his hair and dragged his mouth back to hers with new urgency. She felt Jenner relenting, felt the points of his fangs in each kiss, felt the tips of his nails begin to scrape more like claws against her skin. It fueled the wild thing inside of her, now struggling to get out. They rolled across the bed, each vying for supremacy. Strength unlike any she'd ever had flooded Mia's body, and she managed to flip Jenner so that he was beneath her. Triumphant, she scrambled on top of him, but no sooner had she slipped her fingers around his shaft with the intention of guiding it home than he'd pinned her beneath him, and with a single hard thrust, buried himself in her to the hilt.

Mia cried out, her body bowing. The pleasure was intense. He filled her completely, and every small movement was exquisite torment. And still, there was more. She could feel it, just out of reach. Through unfocused eyes, Mia saw Jenner's face change with concern.

"God, I'm sorry, Mia, I didn't hurt you, did I?"

She couldn't speak. She didn't especially trust herself to form coherent sentences at that moment. Instead, she moved her hips against him, beginning a slow and pulsing rhythm that had Jenner's eyes slipping shut with a look of utter bliss. He started to move inside of her, harder and harder until the bed shook with the force of it. Mia raised her knees and took him deeper, rushing to the edge of a shattering orgasm. As she tensed, her entire body coiling tight and begging for release, a flash of heat so intense it seemed as though it should have left her in ashes tore through her. Magic, bright and pure, flashed around them as her skin began to glow once more.

This time, when she cried out, it had nothing to do with pleasure.

Jenner snarled her name, but he didn't slow. He seemed caught up in some invisible current, and his hips moved faster, faster. The burst of hot pain ebbed quickly, replaced once more by exquisite and building pressure. Now liquid heat coiled up her legs, through her body, feeling like it was running through her veins. Jenner's mouth grazed hers, then moved to graze his sharp teeth down the side of her neck.

Mia didn't think, only acted on instincts that were now screaming at her to join with Jenner fully, to complete the ritual. The air around them shimmered, a beautiful haze. She felt her own claws, teeth, could sense all the wonder of that could come with being a child of the moon dangling just out of her reach.

"Please" was all she could get out as she clung to him. "Please."

He growled, this time a sound that wasn't at all human, and buried himself deep inside her. At the same moment, she felt his teeth break the tender flesh at the base of her neck, the same place that Jeff had bitten her. But this time, there was no fear, no pain.

Mia came in a white hot flash of blinding light, her body arcing off the bed and taking Jenner even deeper. The pleasure was intense, consuming her, burning away everything but the feel of him inside of her. As she flexed tight around him, Jenner threw his head back and gave a hoarse cry, his own climax tearing through him and washing like a wave through Mia. As he shuddered against her, all Mia could do was hang on. Her head was full of voices, rising and falling, a chant in a language she didn't understand. And then there was howling, a wild and mournful sound that reverberated through her very soul. And in the distance, the wild music of her other half, whirling upward into the night sky, spinning into the song that she had dreamed of. Her song. Nick's song.

Their song.

The sound faded away, her body slowly descended from its dizzying peak. But when she finally opened her eyes again, she still had Jenner. Her arms were around him, and he was real and warm and solid. And hers.

Looking dazed, Jenner eased onto his side, reaching down to grab the blanket folded at the end of the bed and then draping it over the two of them before pulling Mia's body back into his. Jenner brushed the hair away from her neck and gave the place he'd bitten her a soft kiss.

Mia snuggled back into him. She could still hear faint echoes of other voices, though with a little effort she found she could silence them if she liked. The voices of the pack, she supposed. *Her* pack.

"You're Blackpaw now," he said softly, and then lay back down, wrapping his arms around her. "And more important, you're mine. Forever. I love you, Mia."

"I love you, Nick."

They curled together, fitted perfectly, two halves of the same whole, and waited for the moon to rise.

They were one.

* * * * *

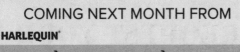

REQUEST YOUR FREE BOOKS!

2 FREE NOVELS FROM THE PARANORMAL ROMANCE COLLECTION PLUS 2 FREE GIFTS!

YES! Please send me 2 FREE novels from the Paranormal Romance Collection and my 2 FREE gifts (gifts are worth about $10). After receiving them, if I don't wish to receive any more books, I can return the shipping statement marked "cancel." If I don't cancel, I will receive 4 brand-new novels every month and be billed just $21.42 in the U.S. or $23.46 in Canada. That's a savings of at least 21% off the cover price of all 4 books. It's quite a bargain! Shipping and handling is just 50¢ per book in the U.S. and 75¢ per book in Canada.* I understand that accepting the 2 free books and gifts places me under no obligation to buy anything. I can always return a shipment and cancel at any time. Even if I never buy another book, the two free books and gifts are mine to keep forever.

237/337 HDN FVVV

Name	(PLEASE PRINT)
Address	Apt. #
City	State/Prov.	Zip/Postal Code

Signature (if under 18, a parent or guardian must sign)

Mail to the Harlequin® Reader Service:
IN U.S.A.: P.O. Box 1867, Buffalo, NY 14240-1867
IN CANADA: P.O. Box 609, Fort Erie, Ontario L2A 5X3

Want to try two free books from another line?
Call 1-800-873-8635 or visit www.ReaderService.com.

* Terms and prices subject to change without notice. Prices do not include applicable taxes. Sales tax applicable in N.Y. Canadian residents will be charged applicable taxes. Offer not valid in Quebec. This offer is limited to one order per household. Not valid for current subscribers to Paranormal Romance Collection or Harlequin® Nocturne™ books. All orders subject to credit approval. Credit or debit balances in a customer's account(s) may be offset by any other outstanding balance owed by or to the customer. Please allow 4 to 6 weeks for delivery. Offer available while quantities last.

Your Privacy—The Harlequin® Reader Service is committed to protecting your privacy. Our Privacy Policy is available online at www.ReaderService.com or upon request from the Harlequin Reader Service.

We make a portion of our mailing list available to reputable third parties that offer products we believe may interest you. If you prefer that we not exchange your name with third parties, or if you wish to clarify or modify your communication preferences, please visit us at www.ReaderService.com/consumerchoice or write to us at Harlequin Reader Service Preference Service, P.O. Box 9062, Buffalo, NY 14269. Include your complete name and address.

PARA1

When an explosion rocks Prince Ruben's castle,
he suspects beautiful Willow, a Sidhe princess,
of playing a role. To uncover the truth, he's
forced to journey to the land of Shadows where
nothing, including Willow, is as it seems....

Read a sneak-peek from

THE WOLF PRINCE

by Karen Whiddon

When their gazes met, every jangling noise inside Willow
went still. Who was he? What was he? Whatever he was, he
wasn't human. The darkness emanating from him drew her, as
surely as a moth to a flame. She wondered if this was because
of her secret Shadow heritage or if, as always, the part of her
that was Bright felt a compulsion to bring light to the faintest
bit of darkness.

Of course, since she had no magic, she never could. But
that didn't stop the longing.

As he began to move toward her, certain and sure and
clearly determined to reach her, she panicked. Glancing left,
then right, she quickly calculated an escape route and tried to
leap toward it. She didn't know if she was afraid because she'd
crashed his party, or because he was so damn beautiful. She
went with her gut reaction to flee. However, she'd completely
forgotten about her long skirt and high heels, and as a result,
she stumbled and nearly fell.

Miraculously, she caught herself. Casting a quick glance over her shoulder, she saw he was drawing impossibly closer. She weaved her way toward a balcony she noticed on the other side.

Finally there, she opened the French style door and slipped out into the cool darkness, lit by the brightness of the full moon. Safe, at least for now.

Gripping the iron railing, she wasn't surprised to note her hands were trembling.

Inhaling the sharp, fresh air, she wondered when she'd become such a coward. As she pondered this, behind her the door opened with a click. Even though she'd remained in the shadows, she knew he'd found her, even before he spoke.

"I'm not dangerous, you know." The husky-as-sin voice sounded exactly that. Dangerous as hell.

Find out just how dangerous Prince Ruben can be in THE WOLF PRINCE. Available April 2013 only from Harlequin® Nocturne™, wherever books are sold.